NATE'S NEW AGE

NATE'S NEW AGE

a novel

MICHAEL HANSON

atmosphere press

Nate's New Age
2021, Michael Hanson

atmospherepress.com

for Lou,
no minor character

I know my place, I just can't stay there.
—Graham Parker

Now for the other life. The one without mistakes.
—Lou Lipsitz

PART ONE

No Coffee For The Weary . . . The Logic Of
Lying To Mama . . . Real Badasses . . . The Woman
In The Wine Cellar . . . Is Rebecca Home? . . .
Bushmills Irish Whiskey Delicious Despite
IRA Terrorist Bombings . . . Escaping Sumpton . . .
Skydiving Into The Penthouse . . .
Kimberly's Wicked Finger . . . THE DEEP . . .
Trouble With Daddy . . .

'We started out thinking we'd just do some muscle-testing, see
what kind of answers we got. And oh, did I need it. I mean, I've
been dealing with all this *ennnormous* stuff, right? *Huuuge*. And at
this point I'm like, *Okay, Universe, how about some guidance here?*'
   Brenda's from Northern California, as you can see. I don't
speak the language myself, but it interests me, doesn't seem so
loony like it does to some. Which supports what my friend Alice
said once: 'You may not speak that language, Nate, but it speaks
to you.'
   I won't deny it.
   'But once we get started Shuly says to me—because she can

1

tell I'm just wide open—that she'd like to try something. It's something she's been gearing up for, she says. Something *big*. And she's been waiting for the right time to try it. So I'm like, you got it. I'm your girl.'

My coffee cup is empty, and before Brenda gets too deep into this I'd like to get a refill. She's a talker, takes a long time to tell a story. And every story she tells is life-changing, earthshattering. Brenda has an epiphany every fifteen minutes.

Hey, I'm only poking a little fun. Fact is she's a sweetheart, a genuine kindhearted soul for whom I wish only the best. But there are times when I'm not necessarily in the mood for one of her sagas that'll shake the heavens, and today is one of those times. Impatience is my prevailing dictator these days.

Make no mistake: I'm a mess at the moment. But hey—at least now I'm admitting it. Better late than never, or so it's said . . .

And what would be best, at this moment, is another cup of coffee. But Brenda's eyes are bearing down on me, these great brown eyes, and it's obvious she's locked into this thing already, no way for me to break away without being a rude bastard. So I just fiddle with the empty cup and strive for a face conveying interest.

'I'm curious what Shuly's got in mind, you know? I mean, we've done some wild things before, but I could tell that whatever this was was major, because she was being so *serious* about it. And when Shuly gets serious, I *know* something's up. Something *big*.'

She's beautiful to look at, Brenda. Okay, that doesn't hurt, that she's so easy on the eyes. I'll sit and listen to a beautiful woman talk about anything, way-out or otherwise. No sweat to me.

And if you want the truth of it, it's a turn-on when what she's saying is risky. Risky in the sense of its being meaningful to her, but sort of out there. Something she could be ridiculed for.

And that's the sort of stuff Brenda talks about every single time I see her.

The second I laid eyes on her I wanted to know. This was about six months ago, sitting in this same coffeeshop, brokenhearted over the breakup with Sadie. I'm a regular, every Friday morning while I wait on my laundry spinning in the machines next door. I like it here because it's where the Pretty People come to have a healthy breakfast (ten bucks for a bowl of granola and a cup of coffee), or linger over steeping herbal tea while perusing a yoga magazine. You know the sort of place I mean? Cushy couches, cozy chairs, little tables with fresh flowers vased in the center, and the whole vibe livened by big leafy plants in terracotta pots, bougainvillea climbing the walls like a pretty cancer. On the Friday in question this great-looking chick drifts in, clearly new around here—I'd never seen her before.

So I walk over and give her a good hard stare . . . kick the dust at our feet with the dirty pointed toe of my boot and cock the Stetson back off my brow, shift the toothpick to the other side of my mouth and say, *Howdy, stranger. You're not from around these parts, are you?*

If only.

Instead I remain planted and watch while she sits at a table by herself, starts dunking a scone into her coffee. She's got blonde hair in some kind of cool mod cut—who knows the names of hairstyles anymore?—with this severe part on one side sweeping across her eyes, her body something cut straight from my fantasies.

Now, Ansley Heights is a college town, so there's no shortage of attractive women. Fact is it's filled to overflowing with them, which is one of the perks of the place. Sure it's small, with a downtown that essentially boils down to five or six blocks square, but you can get damn-near any kind of food imaginable—Mediterranean, Thai, Indian, along with all the usuals—even a cool little art museum. Plus, a ten-minute drive in any direction puts you in country as pretty as any you'll find: corn fields, pastures a plenty with cows or horses or goats, dense stretches of woods that remind you what the place looked like before we carved a town out of it.

But the women are a serious draw—make no mistake.

I've brought along a book to read, but I don't dare look at it: I'm watching every move this woman makes, an assumed-dead hope quickening my pulse. At some point she stands and walks over to where some newspapers are bunched in a wicker basket. She's wearing a long flowy skirt brightly-colored, tucked into which is a skintight top, décolletage designed to draw the eyes right where mine land. She's a ballerina, must be, her moves mesmerizing, like wind blowing a bunch of trees.

Lithe: that's the word that comes to me.

The thing is she's older, and *stunning*, elegant. She exudes money, like she's married to a millionaire and hasn't worked a job since she was twenty-one. During the day she enjoys long leisurely breakfasts at joints just like this one, then strolls the breezy botanical gardens for a while before meeting a few friends for lunch on a sunny patio with umbrellaed tables. Goes to the gym to maintain that figure (he's rich! keep him happy!), maybe gets a massage afterwards, or a pedicure. What a life she has.

Me, I'm thinking I'd make a deal with the devil to see her naked and stretched out in my bed, begging for it.

I'm no stranger to risk, mind you. I'm a skydiving instructor at Psycho Sky Sports, got licensed as a Tandem Jump Instructor just over a year ago. To clients we call ourselves Jump Masters: first-timers are hooked to us in a harness. We do the 'work,' as it were; they just enjoy the ride.

I was a virgin myself, long ago: Jump Master John carried me on my maiden voyage when I was nineteen (an idea cooked-up by me and my new college roommate, Max, who chickened out at the last minute and watched the plane take off without him). John's chute didn't deploy, and he failed to conceal a few interminable seconds of supreme panic before the backup chute saved both of our asses. We fell a hell of a lot faster, though, because the backup's smaller, and when we landed I sprained my ankle and John squashed me and took the air from my body.

Later, both of us shaking like crazy and stunned into a remarkably brief but nonetheless miraculous sense of new wonder, John says, 'I guess we won't be selling any more skydive packages to *you*,' chuckling to make the most of our brush with the Big Guy. But less than a decade later the first-timers were flying with *me*.

What a difference a decade makes.

Max's response to the whole thing? 'You should've seen your *face*! I wish to hell I'd managed to get a picture of it.'

My mother never knew about my job. It's so long ago that I've forgotten, but I had to do something like seven or eight tandem jumps (after the first debacle, years prior) before I was allowed to jump by myself. And on that first solo flight John jumped along with me and filmed my fall with a camera attached to his helmet—it's something we offer, part of the package people get for a hundred bucks extra so they can do one 'crazy' thing in their entire life and have proof of it. Show the footage to their doubting friends.

And years after the fact they'll show it to *themselves*—curled up on the couch with a six-pack—to remember what they could've been.

Me, I used that footage—the first of a series of jumps I did five years later in training to get licensed—to blow my mother's mind. Here I'm afraid to fly on a commercial jet (don't ask), yet there I am on television diving out of a prop plane's open door. What a trip. She can't believe it, keeps saying 'Oh my *god*!' over and over, like maybe she's about to view footage of her son falling to his death. Never mind that he's right there next to her on the sofa, cackling like a kid. She watches the thing only once, can't even bear to see it a second time.

'I'm so glad you didn't tell me about this before you did it.'

She thinks that's it, in other words, a one-shot deal—which hadn't occurred to me. I replenish our wine glasses, consider the quandary. My feet straddle the moral fence and my eyes sink to see what awaits me on either side—a snake pit. What am I going to do: lie to my mother, or give her reason to worry for the rest of her life?

This coffeeshop can be brutal when it comes to great-looking women. I mean it—on a particularly crowded day, when the women are plentiful, a guy can get whiplash just trying to keep up. But this new one, she really had it going on. I could hardly keep my eyes off her.

Mind you, I'm not afraid of women, like some guys—they're just people. And being brokenhearted ups the ante with regard to risk-taking. Just a few months prior, I'd joined souls with Sadie during the most intensely satisfying sexual experience of my life. *The place of perfect love*, she'd called it afterwards, a line so shamelessly sappy you had to be there to buy it. And *there* is exactly where I was, buying it hook, line, and sinker. That is until her confused heart took its leave of me.

So what the hell. What's this chick going to do—*hurt* me?

I rise to get a third refill of coffee (thank God for coffee) but en route I damn the torpedoes and stop at her table. 'Excuse me,' says the Subtle Suitor, sort of bent toward her and noting with gratitude the empty table next to hers—no one to hear me shame myself. 'I hope you'll not take offense, but I'd hate myself forever if I didn't tell you how lovely you are. *Really*,' backing away now so she'll see I mean it, that I'm not going to stand there waiting on my reward (or lack thereof). Her face looks flabbergasted, and a delicate hand with long creamy fingers spreads itself over that exposed sweep of skin above her breasts as she says, 'Thank you so much.'

Success, of a sort. At least I know it was worth doing regardless of the reward I won't get. Made her feel good.

Trust me: one of the best strategies I know for coping with a sick heart is doing something audacious. Anything. And if it involves extending a kindness to someone else, all the better. Win-win.

At the table with the big self-serve coffee-urns, I have an accident with the cream and slop the stuff all over the place, my nervous hands rebelling. Behind me, a tall guy's being patient while I wipe up the mess I've made—I wonder if he saw my spectacle at that woman's table. I don't dare look in her direction as I head back to my seat, but watch peripherally when I sit down, my face cosmetically buried in the book of poems of which I've yet to read a single word.

These games.

My heart's rebelling right along with my hands, beating so fast I feel it in my throat.

> *The grief spreads into my sleep*
> *it climbs down the ladder from the roof*
> *and slips in the window and lies down*
> *beside me with its twig fingers.*

That's as far as I get before noticing a lot of movement happening her way, and a quick look confirms that she's gathering her things to go. I don't think she saw me sneak the peek, but I make extra effort to zero-in on the book when she walks by my table on her way out.

Achtung!

She's stopped and bending toward me.

'I was doing some stuff at the house this morning, and a voice—a *palpable* voice—said I should come here for breakfast. *Be there by ten*, the voice said.'

'Damn,' says I.

'Now I know why that voice told me to come here. I can't thank you enough for what you said. No one's said anything like that to me in forever.'

'Just calling it like I see it.'

8

'You've made my day.'

Then she's off. She busses her own table—a good sign—and heads for the door while I'm back at war. A *voice* told her to come here? Sure, she sounds a bit flaky, but that body, and the ache of my solitude, keeps me curious. What to do—chase her down?

The beauty I've yet to know as Brenda is headed out the door when I make my move, catching her just outside.

'Listen, I honestly had no intention of doing this, but would you be willing to have a cup of coffee with me sometime?'

She smiles: *'I see myself stretched out naked in your bed, begging for it . . . '*

Hey, a guy can dream.

Instead: 'You know, that'd be nice, actually. Could you do tomorrow?'

Do *tomorrow*? I suppose I might be able to squeeze her in . . .

All of us at Psycho dig the gig, but given the choice most of the guys prefer flying solo. Which is what makes me different (along with the carrot-top). Much as I dig the rush of plunging headfirst out of that plane alone—the buoyancy of my body leaning into the wind with the false feeling that I'm actually able to fly—the fact is I'm even more excited to share the experience with someone. Especially when that someone is a rare beauty with big brown eyes (big green eyes, big blue eyes, you get the idea). Like I'm the guy who'll save her.

A power trip? Well, I wouldn't call it that exactly. It's more about being *needed*, no longer the lonely little twerp who never did anything more with his life past the point of finding a pretty fun way to spend the rest of it.

Of course there are other perks: I may not make much money, but chained to a desk doing data-entry forty hours a week would destroy me. I don't begrudge those who live that life (*someone's* got to—or do they?), but I do begrudge those who think *I* ought to live it. And what are they doing with all that money they're slaving to make, anyway? Buying the latest iGadget, plusher furniture to get swallowed-up in, a third car for the two-party household—one day little Johnny's going to be old enough to drive so . . .

You can have it. Here's what I'll have:

Lucy The Lovely shows up for her first skydive just after I get licensed. At the time, I've been on the wagon for a couple of months (no small task, but I'm trying to pull myself out of an emotional tailspin that's nobody's fault but mine), so anything I can do to inject a shot of excitement into my day is welcomed, even if it's just some serious flirting with a client. It's two-thirty in the afternoon on a Saturday, and three years later I'm still the new guy at Psycho, lucky enough to have a looker like Lucy among his first clients. She's twenty-seven, a petite accountant with a tight little body you could bounce coins off of. Breasts that look like a handful even when pushed down by the jumpsuit we put her in.

My word for her is *racktastic*.

I'm helping her with all the straps of her harness and trying to quell thoughts of what it'd be like to tie her up, and she's staring at me with this intoxicating expression of scared determination, one I well know but never tire of seeing. The sight of her mouth alone makes mush of me.

She fires the usual ration of nervous questions regarding what I do, looking for reassurance—*were you scared the first time? are you still scared?* the like—when out of nowhere she says, 'Your hair is gorgeous.'

I thank her, sincerely: the mop of red hair that made youth a hazard of unearned abuse is a godsend now that I'm nearing thirty, distinguishing me from the herd. So the gratitude I give for the remark is genuine.

Twenty-four of us on the flight up, Lucy leans with her back against my chest, fussing with all the straps and hooks of her suit. Anxious energy. Then lays her head back on my shoulder (killing me softly) and takes a bunch of deep breaths, the fabric of the flightsuit stretching over those wise breasts. When we reach thirteen-five everyone prepares to exit; Lucy and I straddle a varnish-slick bench we slide forward on each time someone else takes off. We're hooked into one another, my legs on either side of her, and even with all the cumbersome equipment clogging our contact my body is about to burst. I'm so hot for her I can hardly focus, and according to my altimeter we're about to jump out of a plane.

As we move toward the door, a flat layer of grey cloud blocking our view of the ground, she says, 'Oh, this is *crazy*,' and I say, 'You're going to love it,' before we kneel at the edge and I grab the overhead bar.

Magic moment.

Lucy x's her arms across her chest as she's supposed to, and I pull her head back to my right shoulder and count to three before hurling our bodies out into Bliss.

Trust me—there's nothing like skydiving. Nothing. Only sex can top it.

Everything goes exactly as it should. My spread gets us righted and I pull the drogue so as to slow things down and get us balanced before instructing her to assume her own spread— my god, even the words work on me. Falling at a hundred-and-twenty miles per hour, my cheek pressed to hers, I talk Lucy through some steering to tap her own thrill-seeker. Left revolution half-way, followed by a half revolution to the right, then a full turn all the way around. By the time we finish the full turn, we drop through the dampness of the cloud layer and I deploy our chute just as we emerge beneath it, get us situated for the slow descent, the sweeping view now clear all around us.

While lacking the urgency of the freefall, the drift-down creates its own quiet intensity, especially for the first-timer. Relishing the tremendous relief of having survived the freefall and seen the chute succeed in saving us, she can then watch with wonder—the lay of the land from that insane vantage, suspended eight thousand feet above the surface of solid ground with only a fabric umbrella to fend off gravity.

'It's unbelievable!'

She says this over and over, like she still doesn't believe it.

'Not a bad view,' says the Cool Instructor.

I stifle an urge to show off, tell her what I think damn near every time I see the Earth from up here—that it looks like a Diebenkorn painting, all colored patches, cut diagonals. Which consistently leads to questions regarding the badass painter I love (including, almost always, the spelling of his name), followed by me daring them into a date to go to the art museum so I can show them. At least that's how it works *some* of the time, proof that life is nothing if not completely unpredictable.

And sometimes generous beyond measure.

On this occasion I keep my show-off trap shut, instead let Lucy hear how quiet it is, the strangeness of real silence, unknown to the ground-bound. The descent to our sand-filled drop zone will take about seven minutes, which is when my time with this particular beauty will get yanked out from under me. The story of my life.

So I steer us over a few thermals, pushing us up. Prolonging the fall.

All excited, Lucy starts gushing a bit, says the real reason she's come skydiving is to convince herself she has the courage to quit her job. 'I make a great salary, but already I feel trapped. My office is like a prison.'

Which is when I deliver the line that, believe it or not, paves the way to our sleeping together that very night.

'Well, take a look around,' I say. 'How do you like *my* office?'

'So what Shuly proposes we do is this: she wants to invite the Divine Feminine Energy to join us, to actually . . . come *into* me. Like I'm this . . . like this *vessel*, this open receptacle. And she thinks now's the perfect time, not only because of me and where I am, but also because the Energy's ready, too. *Cosmically*, you know? Because of all the insanity going on in the world. It's like so many people are fed up with things, so we're all trying to raise consciousness. Together. And the creative energies of the Universe—the *other* energies, the ones not caught-up in war, all the hatred and terrorism—they're ready to start making themselves known. Manifesting. Turn things around.'

Already you can see that the real Brenda is, let's say, a bit removed from the skirt-sheathed fantasy that first enticed me. I was on target about one thing, though: a Southerner she's not, only recently relocated to Ansley Heights from Arcata, California, because her mom lives here, and—in her eighties—beginning to have health issues. She also told me straight-up that she's not looking for a lover, so that's that. But damn Brenda's a looker, right? And since Sadie left me in the lurch I'd been saddled with a loneliness that was new to me, different: a yearning that felt bottomless, crippling. So the hell with it, thinks the Non-Suitor. Maybe there's something else to be gained here.

These are *swim* days: I'm trying to convince myself that sinking isn't an option. Not that it's an easy sell . . .

Turns out she's a reiki practitioner, so none of this cosmic-talk throws me. Well, maybe a little, but I'm used to it now because Sadie spoke some of that language, too. Plus, I feel like I know where Brenda's coming from, regardless whether I buy into it all. Despite having just been involved with (dumped by) a massage therapist/acupuncture practitioner, I can't claim to have heard of reiki, a kind of so-called 'energy work,' but by the end of our first coffeedate Brenda convinced me to have a session with her.

Hey—this gorgeous woman wants to put her hands on me, work with my 'energy?' What would *you* say?

The stuff she's telling me today, though, this business of inviting the 'Divine Feminine Energy' into a living room in California, is pretty out there, I'll admit. *Huuuge*, Brenda would say. Will they serve Her refreshments?

My twenty-ninth birthday—just under a month away—is bearing down like bad news. Damn. I want to believe my birth is worthy of being celebrated, but I'll confess to wondering sometimes. Self-pity? Guilty as charged. On top of which, this broken heart I'm hauling around is well aware that this year marks the fifth anniversary of my divorce—my therapist Lynn says I'm getting hit with 'emotional memory,' feelings that seem sourceless yet in fact are just the surfacing of old sadnesses. In a way, five years feels like yesterday. But in another way it's like the divorce happened a zillion years ago, in another life.

The first life, the one I made such a mess of.

I married Margaret (Meg) right at the end of our college senior year—we'd been dating since high school, and living together since sophomore year at University. Still residing in the hometown we'd yet to tire of (Sumpton, a port city near the coast that has an excellent little liberal arts college, Sumpton State), we moved into a duplex recently vacated by some woman Meg studied with. It was Meg's suggestion we get married, and since we'd been shacking up most of the three years prior I figured no sweat, why not? What a dummy—sweat is *exactly* what I should've done, because I can see clearly now that I wasn't even remotely ready, that the day I went through with it I'd begin building resentments toward Meg for 'forcing' me into matrimony.

As indeed I did. Hell, my parents' marriage was warning enough: I never knew them to be anything other than miserable with one another.

Don't get me started about my parents.

Meg planned to go to grad school, study to become a speech pathologist, but decided to take a year off, give herself a little break first so when she went back she'd be ready to buckle down and give it her all. I'd majored in English (minored in Art History), dug it because I got to read great novels, poetry.

The poets and painters—they're the real badasses.

But having no aptitude for writing, I was tired of the endless struggle and anxiety one measly paper entailed, to say nothing of being sick of regurgitating what my instructors wanted to hear, so decided an advanced degree wasn't in the cards.

That first year after graduation, we both worked fourteen- and fifteen-hour days for Jeffrey and Dennis, a couple of wealthy caterers we'd fallen in with through My Lovely Man Max, who'd shared an apartment with me and Meg senior year. Our bosses loved their picture of us—we were the happy young couple just out of college and ready for a future we'd mapped-out every move of with an efficiency that today causes me to cringe, given what I now know about plans and the fatuousness of making them.

J.D. (as I abridged them) were great, if eccentric, guys to work for, with a lot of money and a lot of clients who had even *more* money. So their operation, small though it may have been (seven or eight of us), was a lucrative one.

We'd spend all day in the shop (kitchen) cooking, ten in the morning until four or five, then head home only long enough to shower and go right back over, now well-groomed in black-and-white tuxedo clothes, penguin garb. We'd pack everything in the two vans and show up at So-And-So's mansion an hour later, lay out the fancified grub and serve up our best subservient smiles for the next five hours while the wealthy wined and dined. After which, we'd spend a couple of hours cleaning up and polishing silver platters, Tupperwaring leftovers and returning the house to order before heading back to the shop to drop everything off.

Exhausted (no lie—catering can be a slog), but also jacked-up and determined to have fun since we'd watched everyone *else* have it all night, we'd almost always go out for a drink (or four) at some late-night place; call it a night (tipsy) around three; and show up at the shop by ten the next morning to begin again the long grueling business of serving the rich so the Machine will stay on track.

Twenty years of schooling and they put me on the day shift. Hell, the *night* shift, too.

It's true the money was good, but we worked our asses off

for it. And it does something to your soul (mine at least) to be part of the service industry that caters to those who have more dough than you can even *imagine* having. While it's wrong to generalize, the fact is that some of these swine got their money by being calculating sonsabitches who couldn't care less who they screwed over to get it. So to stand dutifully before them every night in my bow tie, pleated shirt and tuxedo pants, mixing drinks while they babbled on to fellow richies with ne'er a nod to the lowly sap who's serving them, drove a part of me mad with envy and resentment.

But that's the world, a wise man once warned. Some get rich, some eat shit and die. And the rest of us? We're right in the middle, not sure whether to be pissed or grateful.

Their women cluck like starved pullets, wrote the poet, *dying for love*. The metaphor's not quite right for these moneyfied chicks, however, who were more akin to some exotic breed of cat. But many of them *were* dying for love, or at least I'd wager. Which would explain why one of them, a woman whose name I never knew, asked me at one Saturday night gig to accompany her to her husband's wine cellar under the guise of getting some special bottle of French red.

Their house was enormous, every room bigger than our whole duplex: you could leave one room and enter another and feel very far away from the place you'd just left. So going downstairs to this wine cellar gave me the sense of being on another *planet*, and once we got down there into the cool gloom, far from the maddening crowd, this beauty stuck a warm wet tongue down my unsuspecting throat with a feverish urgency I couldn't say no to, even had Meg been standing there beside me with a loaded shotgun (and what about her *husband*?). Not wearing underwear (never have) I couldn't conceal the bulge that captured her attention in no time, and to which she subsequently gave her all. This rich goddess went down on me with something like desperation behind it, one I didn't know a woman could possess (shows you how much I knew about women). When I tried to stand her up so I could give her what I thought she wanted (and knew *I* wanted), she stood quickly and looked right through me with these breathy eyes and said, 'Oh no. Noooooooo. Just give me that juice of yours so the night won't be a total waste.'

Think I'm kidding? I can't tell you how happy I am to report that's *exactly* what she said.

God help us.

She was wearing this loose-fitting dress, dark red, string-thin straps, and I was able to slide those off her shoulders and lap up a little of those astonishing breasts before she was back down there, going at me for all she was worth. Meg wasn't into fellatio, so this whole business sent a shiver through me that threatened to buckle my knees. Both of her hands were busy as well, working away every bit as much as her mouth. I'm telling you, this chick had talent. It goes without saying I didn't last long, which would've been embarrassing but for the hurried nature of the whole steamy business.

She didn't lose any of it. I was thrilled and horrified at the same time.

After that, it was all business. She stood and pulled a hand towel from the drawer of a little desk (making me wonder) while I'm sort of frozen standing tall beside her—well, tall enough. With her dress bunched around her waist and my god those tits looking more perfect than I could believe (implants?), she took that towel and wiped away my wetness like a doctor doing a job on me. I'm flinching like crazy, super-sensitive to touch now, so she says (with some impatience), 'Just hold on.' So I drop my head back, close my eyes and stare at my mind's blank ceiling for a bit.

'We're done,' she says when finished, pulling her dress back up and looping those shoulder-straps to effectively end what would've been my best fantasy ever . . . had it not actually happened. While I straighten myself up she grabs a canvas bag from the back of a chair and puts the hand towel in it, then takes two bottles of wine from the dozens in the rack without even bothering to look at them.

Special French red? Not unless the label's in Braille . . .

I manage to ask her name, but she just says—cold as ice—'It doesn't matter. This won't happen again.'

Back upstairs in the too-bright kitchen my coworker Edwin was spooning capers onto a big platter of salmon canapés, and when he sees me finally returning he says, 'Took her long enough. How much wine did they *have* down there?'

There's a famous story about Scott Fitzgerald and Hemingway discussing wealth. Scott supposedly observed, 'The rich are different from us,' to which Hemingway purportedly replied, 'Yes. They have more money.'

The Woman In The Wine Cellar proved Hemingway's point, as far as I was concerned. Besides, the truth I dare admit at this point is that these were the days when I saw people as being pretty much the same no matter how much (or little) money they had: something to be gotten *through*, not *into*.

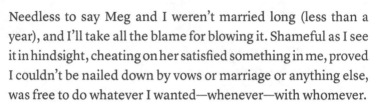

Needless to say Meg and I weren't married long (less than a year), and I'll take all the blame for blowing it. Shameful as I see it in hindsight, cheating on her satisfied something in me, proved I couldn't be nailed down by vows or marriage or anything else, was free to do whatever I wanted—whenever—with whomever.

On the outside I was a twenty-three-year-old college graduate who'd wedded his high-school sweetheart and now worked for a catering company in the hometown he couldn't seem to get shed of. But on the inside, the rebel every boy dreams of being was alive and well and ready to run wild whenever and wherever I'd let him.

Some rebel. I married a woman who wouldn't give me a blowjob.

That was a weird year, and getting married was just the start of it.

It was the year my dad died.

At this point—that hindsight business—I can see that my father's death rattled me to the roots, sent me off an imaginary deep end and categorically killed any chance of getting my shit together enough to become the decent man who'd work to make a sound marriage.

Good riddance, thinks the not-so-dutiful son. Deep down, though, some starving kid even I couldn't hear was wailing at what was gone for good.

Hospice called it 'complications resulting from cirrhosis of the liver,' which is only a polite way of saying he drank himself to death, pure and simple. Make no mistake: at twenty-three I saw my father as nothing more—or less—than a hateful son of a bitch I'd just as soon kick the shit out of as talk to. His cool and reticent demeanor might've kept the rest of the world thinking he must be a humble man, a good husband and father, but the ugly truth beneath the surface veneer was that the vodka to which he was so devoted had wreaked more havoc than could ever be catalogued.

The calm in the eye of the storm is what it was.

But his death threw me, blindsided me with a bunch of baggage I wasn't prepared to deal with, wasn't even aware I was carrying. (Therapy, years later, showed me this.) Again, I'm not shirking responsibility for my actions—no one blew my marriage but me. At this point I'm just trying to understand it all, put the pieces of the puzzle together in a way that might make some kind of sense. So I can *learn*.

Well, that's the idea, anyway.

Meg and I accompanied my mother to the funeral: even though she'd been emotionally and physically abused for the better part of two decades (the first time I saw him hit her was when I was ten), my mother was devastated by the loss, confusing me beyond measure and confirming my conviction that there's something downright twisted in our need for one another. Naively imagining my father's death might set-off some kind of internal alarm and fuel my mom's ostensible wake-up call with regard to her own habits, I watched her dive right back into the same addiction she'd seen destroy her husband. And, feeling like the ten-year-old I once was, I just stood by, powerless, paralyzed by the contradictory nature of her behaviors.

For the funeral I did the only thing I knew *to* do: I got blitzed beforehand, Meg just as powerless to stop me as I was to stop my mom.

Poor Meg. Poor all of us.

It's the damnedest thing about someone dying. When it happened with my dad, it's like he became more alive than he'd been when he was only a phone call away. Which is to say he was more in my business than he'd been in years, hounding me more than ever. I couldn't shake him.

Max is the one who reminded me about the package my dad had sent senior year, the year Max lived with me and Meg. I'd fallen hard for poetry in a class I was taking (20th Century Verse—Dr. Hilton), a course that introduced me to more great stuff than I could believe, like discovering a good-time drug that didn't give you hangovers. An American poet (Robinson Jeffers) was among the first to light a new fire in me, and it was his "Advice To Pilgrims" that struck such a chord I decided to damn the torpedoes and send it to my dad, who I thought might like it (never mind that he'd never read a poem in his life, to my knowledge). But there was something about this one, maybe the speaker's distrust of humanity (my dad seemed to hate everyone), or even Jeffers' didactic, know-it-all tone. Whatever it was didn't matter so much as the motive—essentially a son's half-baked notion of bridge-building, a rare occasion when I felt really good about a move I was making, especially whereas it regarded my parents. So I made a photocopy and put it in the mail, wrote that heroes like this cat were making college tolerable. Mind you, I could've just gone over there and handed it to him, home being a mere fifteen-minute drive, but I'd made a habit (starting freshman year) of at least *pretending* I'd gone away to college, and god knows neither of them ever bothered to call me, so in a way I might as well've gone away since I rarely saw or heard from either of them. I was still in my home town, sure, but it goes without saying I traveled in different circles than my folks, who—truth told—hardly ever left the house save to replenish their booze supply.

Now, I'd never sent the guy so much as a postcard, so sending that poem was an *event*, at least as far as I was concerned.

I ate complete silence for a month, not a peep, hence wrote it off as a wasted effort I still felt pretty good about making. Which is when his oversized envelope showed up in our mailbox. Max had just gotten home, brought the mail in, and cracked open a beer for each of us when I opened the big manila mailer, gawked in stunned disbelief as its contents revealed themselves to my shaking hands.

Photographs of slaughtered Jews.

One after another, most of them printed from magazines, some from newspapers, books. *Pages* of this stuff. Rack-ribbed men, women, and children, starved doing slave labor in concentration camps; hundreds of bodies heaped like debris in huge, gaping maws of earth; close-ups of corpses with their skulls smashed open by the butts of German rifles.

What the hell?

Clarity came by way of a few lines he'd scrawled on a big Post-It, saying he'd done a little research on Jeffers (thanks to the Almighty Internet, all it takes is a few keystrokes and someone can claim they're doing 'research') and discovered the poet's passionate, outspoken pacifism, the beginnings of which probably dated back to WWI. Truth is I knew damned little about this—all I really cared about was that he was one hell of a poet.

Writes the Patriarch: *You call this guy a hero? So I guess he'd just sit back and write poems while Hitler got away with genocide.*

Max saw it written all over my face, took the stuff from my

hands to see for himself. I was speechless, clueless, something so ugly welling up I couldn't imagine what to do with it.

'Wait—is this because of that poem you sent him?'

I just nod, ashamed, embarrassed, wishing I could disappear.

'For fuck's sake,' says Max, straight as ever. 'I see his point but . . . what a fucking *asshole*.' He tosses the stuff onto the sofa, hands me the beer. Then, as if remembering who it is he's talking about, adds, 'Sorry man, but your dad's a dick.'

Never thought I'd be married, much less divorced. And suddenly, at 23, I was both.

It's easy to be cynical about the whole thing—one look at the divorce rate tells the tale. And whoever said monogamy is the way to go, anyway, other than a bunch of asexual priests? Far as I can tell there's nothing even remotely natural about monogamy—only a few species of birds can even hack it.

Besides, my parents did nothing to disprove my hunch that it was a hopeless enterprise for anyone seeking Happiness. In other words, for a hell of a lot of us the first step toward being able to buy into marriage as a viable option is looking past our parents.

Nowadays I'd like to think that it isn't a death-sentence, even for a guy like me, but in the days of Meg it littered my world with landmines, one of which was planted right next door. Rebecca Benton lived in the apartment adjacent to Meg and me. She was twenty-two and had graduated just a couple of semesters behind us, supposedly preparing to leave for London where she'd live with her best friend, whom she'd met during a study abroad stint junior year. Neither of us knew Rebecca all that well (save that she staunchly refused to let anyone reduce her name to the diminutive 'Becky'), but every now and then one or the other of us (usually me) would go over for a chat and a glass of wine.

She was a flirter, and sexy as hell, in a tomboyish sort of way, her dark hair shorter than any guy I knew. I remember once she stopped by our place to get an opinion on a new dress. Holy shit. That's the night I realized the Tomboy could be a Bombshell, depending on what she wanted. Meg said she looked 'gorgeous,' and I said she looked 'really nice,' downplaying my true feeling for fear that Meg might hear the lust in it. Truth is she looked devastating.

The week we got back from my father's funeral, Rebecca had slid a condolence card under our door. Along with the usual ration of regrets, the card said she'd be leaving for London in a week, but that she hoped we'd know how much she enjoyed 'having such easy neighbors.' And that Thursday, when Meg helped a couple of coworkers cater a small dinner party, I ended up spending the evening at Rebecca's place.

Easy's a label I like.

Intending to lay low at home, I drink a few beers and reconsider, decide to shift gears by walking next door with a bottle of wine, just to see. Rebecca answers wearing cut-offs and what we carelessly call a wife-beater. No bra. Her nipples dark beneath the fabric, and big around as half-dollars.

She says some friends tried to talk her into going out but that she didn't feel like it. 'Thanks for giving me a good excuse not to.'

Her apartment's mostly cleared out but for a few odds and ends, among them a boom box sneering the Rolling Stones' *Some Girls*. I figure she'll excuse herself, slip on a shirt of some kind over the tank, but instead she goes straight to the kitchen to open the wine. She pours us each a glass in big oversized tumblers, and we sit on the carpeted floor of the empty living room, me forcing focus on her eyes for fear of drifting down to the other. No small task, that.

Saturday she'll drive to New Jersey to visit her family for a week, drop off her car for her younger brother to keep. Then the week following she'll fly out of Newark to relocate in London.

My contribution to the small talk is bemoaning the dull business of my dad's death (*sans* any hint of emotion, mind you), focused solely on the formalities of the funeral and whatnot. But I ditch it abruptly, throw caution to the wind and take the plunge.

'Jesus I'd kill to kiss you,' I spill out of nowhere, acting slightly drunker than I am.

'What are you waiting for?'

We're all tongues.

In the midst of it, I make an effort toward conscientiousness by asking if she's sure about this. She responds by pressing her lips to mine more forcefully than before, her roaming tongue caressing parts of my mouth I'd never noticed, then pulling back only long enough to strip off her own shirt, those erect nipples alive like a thing about to crawl off her . . .

'Baby,' she says, 'I'm going to Europe. You think I care how many bridges I burn on the way?'

She liked it sort of rough, and loud. God she was loud, and spewed a sexier, filthier gutter-talk than I could've fantasized. It was so hot I finished a hell of a lot faster than I would've liked, pulling out just in time to soil her stomach.

She doesn't miss a beat.

'Don't leave me hanging,' she pants, writhing around like a snake and pushing my head down to her working hips, like she's trying to grind a hole in the floor beneath her buttocks. I've had next to no experience down there (Meg not into it), but Rebecca basically does the work for me: I lather up my tongue and leave it out there while she works my head with her hands, her hips keeping up a steady pace until suddenly she's screaming, 'Oh baby make me come! Don't you dare stop! Oh baby!' so loud I can't believe it, pulling the hair on the back of my head such that I figure she'll have fistfuls of the stuff by the time she's finished.

But I like it. I'm feeling like a stud.

'Fuck *yes!*' she says when done, all out of breath, this crazy quivering thing happening in her thighs. I kneel up and try to fish-out a hair stuck on the back of my tongue—it's driving me crazy—and dress quickly, Rebecca using the tank to clean herself off. Leaving is admittedly awkward, but in truth I'm already wondering if we might be able to have at it one more time before she leaves for London. Maybe Friday night after Meg goes to bed?

None of this is discussed, though: we say goodnight with her still topless, she thanks me with a sly smile, and I walk next door and open up to the terrifying, heart-sinking sight of Meg sitting at the little round table in our kitchen.

'Jesus,' I say, sure my voice is shaking. 'You guys got done awfully early.'

She'll have nothing of it.

'I think she violated a noise ordinance,' she says, a line I later decide she must've devised while sitting there, waiting for us to finish. Waiting, stewing, heart breaking.

'So much for marriage,' says my soon-to-be-ex wife.

My Lovely Man Max says I crave disorder. 'Just like a poet,' he says.

Never mind that I don't write poetry.

'Yeah, but you *read* the stuff.'

Maybe Max never craved the chaos of a poet's life, but back in college he wasn't the straight-liner he is now.

We met sophomore year in an Art History course, one of those rare classes I relished, even hated to come to the end of, so many cool things did it turn me onto. Something like a history of the twentieth century told through art, or that was the idea. And one day when a couple of chicks were trashing Jackson Pollock, saying he couldn't paint, Max was the guy who raised his hand and openly challenged both of them to 'make one canvas that can compete with that crappy painter who changed the course of art forever.'

The classroom silence was deafening.

Our professor might've been cringing (dutifully, I supposed), but I can't deny being wooed by the guy's audacity. Needless to say neither of those girls ever made a painting, not that they showed the class, anyway. Me, I screwed my courage to the sticking place and approached Max after class when we were walking out of Park Hall, told him some of us appreciated his comment. 'I've got a low threshold for that shit,' he said, clearly unconcerned with the potential of offending me. 'Ignorant little coeds trashing Greatness one minute, doing beer bongs and blowing frat boys the next.'

I loved him instantly.

By second semester we'd decided to share an apartment off-campus, get out of the dorms, which for me had felt like living in a high school gym class. I liked the idea of rooming with Max, connecting myself to him. He was hipper than anyone I'd ever met, smarter than the average bear, and cool women were always coming around to see him—artists, musicians. Lots of cleavage and tattoos. He was in good shape, too, a runner, tall with curly blond hair and bright blue eyes. God knows I'm not into guys, but if I were Max would send me. He's just flat-out great to look at, the proverbial tall drink of water.

Truth is, Max had so much going for him he was the kind of cat I'd normally *hate*—unless of course he happened to be a friend of mine.

So we moved in. Before I knew it that bastard had me running with him three days a week. Mind you, the fact that he stayed in shape didn't make him some nerdy health-nut: after all, he's the guy who got me high for the first time. Two rips from a big blue bong and the next thing I know I'm stretched out on the floor listening to *The White Album*, what Max called The Beatles' *Ulysses*. All I could say as an assessment was that the fun was so intensely wonderful it was like levitating—if this wasn't religious music I wouldn't know what was.

Can you say *forever indebted*?

He was a fanatic about music, Max. I remember he spent a week that summer—at *least* a week—dropping acid and listening to every album in the Beatles catalogue. He'd been talking about it for months, like some great ambition, and an image of him stretched out on our floor wearing nothing but boxers and headphones is permanently emblazoned on my memory.

'They started out as talented ... *lads*,' he announced once the experiment was over. 'But post 1965 their true nature came out.'

True nature?

He nodded. 'They weren't musicians, they were *visionaries*. Visionaries who happened to make music.'

Ah.

Me, I was so happy to be done with dorm life I would've roomed with a cannibal, and Max was no cannibal. He was a cool, good-looking, straight-A student whose confidence carried over to anyone he deemed worthy of his company. If a guy like Max thought you were worth hanging out with, well then, maybe you were. And it didn't take him long to pick up on the situation with my parents, either, which he was able to assess and articulate without any help from me. One night we're hanging out getting high (*Revolver* our soundtrack) and he says, 'Remember, Hoss, you ain't your parents. No reason you have to be anything like them. There are no rules.'

It was like he could see straight through me.

What mattered most, however, was that I had a private bedroom in my own apartment now, and all I cared about was getting my girlfriend Meg into it. We forget how significant such a thing is, but all you've got to do is ask any high-schooler and they'll give you a good reminder. For most of us, at least pre-college, the awkward backseat confines of a car was as good as it got with regard to privacy, and hey—I'll take it. Fact is, it was there that a girl I'll never forget generously claimed my not-at-all-prized virginity.

I was sixteen, a nobody, whereas Susan Marker was a cheerleader (believe it) who had her own car (Chevy *Nova*), not to mention was popular enough to pick and choose who she screwed in it. At the time she seemed sexy beyond measure, but nowadays the word that comes to mind is *cute*. Adorable, really.

And she lived in Oakdale, the neighborhood next to mine, so her house was literally less than five minutes away—her curfew might've been midnight, but she could drop me off at 11:57 and still make it home on time.

We didn't date long (a few months, maybe?) but in those blessed weeks we had sex every chance we got, even on school nights. She'd come over to visit, stay for a couple of hours pretending to watch television or study, then when I walked her out to her car we'd climb into the back and have at it right there in front of my house. My parents sitting inside oblivious in their booze-fog. Nowadays, I'm well aware there's no way she could've climaxed during these quickies, but she never complained. Hell, she *instigated* them, more often than not.

As for me, sex seemed like the key to something, something important. Freedom.

To hear Brenda tell it, freedom costs money. Three weeks prior to this particular coffeedate, she'd announced that she needed to drum up some cash to move to Greece. Why? Because a psychic told her to.

A psychic? I couldn't believe she was serious, but Brenda's *always* serious.

Serious as she is about reiki, she's also pretty serious about painting. When she found out I'd majored in Art History, she announced that this was one reason 'the Universe brought us together. Come on, Nate, I'm a painter and you studied it in college. You want to tell me that's a coincidence?'

I wouldn't dare.

I've not seen any of her paintings in person, but she brought out her laptop once and showed me pictures of some of them. Garish, awful-looking abstractions, gaudy-colored amoebas swirling all over the place. Not my cup of tea at all. But hey—god love her. She's doing her thing, and I couldn't make anything palatable from a paint-by-numbers kit. Now, I knew the day I met her that she wasn't from around here, and in fact the only reason she'd left Northern California and come east at all was to visit her ailing eighty-year-old mom. But from the get-go it was clear that Brenda was a different breed. I mean, she'd left California for her mom—understandable, even admirable. But it's open-ended: when I ask how long she plans to stay in Ansley Heights, she doesn't know.

'Six months or so? Not sure. I gotta figure my next move.'

But what about her home in California, her friends? And doesn't she have a profession, a *job*?

Neither. She'd been living with a man, Greg—they'd shared a house but she made no bones about the fact that the place was his, that she moved in with no intention of staying. Work-wise she did reiki on her own—she had some regular clients and would go to their place whenever they wanted a session.

Given what I was hearing, not to mention what I could *see*, I supposed she had money.

But I was wrong. Brenda *needed* money, bad. 'Everyone thinks that,' she says with a look of puzzled disappointment when I confess to this. 'There's something about me, the way I look or something. People just assume I'm loaded.' She shakes her head. 'I wish.'

Guilty as charged. She says enough to convince me that no, she doesn't come from money, nor does she have—like I envisioned—some fat mound of it somewhere from which she feeds herself in doses, a few thousand here, a few there. Fact is she's on the hunt for it, seriously stressed about her financial situation. 'I've gotta get something going,' she says.

Which is where her painting comes in, and the psychic. Recently she's sold a few pictures through a dealer in Santa Monica, and has a contact in New York who's offered to see if she can help. Only problem is Brenda's blocked, can't seem to complete a canvas to save her life.

'It's weird,' she says. 'No, really. This is *truuuly* bizarre. I've been painting since I was a kid. Well, what kid doesn't, right? But I'm talking *way* more than is normal. All through adolescence and right into college I painted anything that didn't move.'

A remark I don't get, so out comes the laptop. More photos, these of her childhood bedroom, various apartments she's lived in. And indeed everything's painted—all these funky colors and shapes covering everything: bookcases, tables, headboard of her bed, even the telephone is all groovy.

'I didn't start making actual canvases until senior year, and then the stuff started coming out faster than I could paint it.'

So what's going on now?

'I wish I knew. I finally start selling, and all of a sudden I can't paint. I mean, *nothing*.' She reflects. 'I don't think it's an accident, though. There *are* no accidents. I'm sure it has something to do with selling my creative spirit, some discomfort about it maybe. But I need to break through that. The Universe *wants* me to paint—there's *no* doubt about that.'

Must be nice to know what the Universe wants of you. Other than good coffin-filler.

Meg. Margaret. My best friend. I met her junior year of high school, which is when we started dating. She's the only woman I ever got serious with. Margaret knew me, really *knew* me. (The me I was then, at any rate.) She accepted the fact that I lack ambition. 'Who says you have to have some Great Calling to lead a happy life, Nate?'

She also accepted the fact that I have wacked-out parents.

And less than a year after we'd married she sat at our kitchen table on a Thursday night and listened to me fuck our neighbor on the floor of her living room. By Sunday, she'd moved out completely.

Nothing can come
of this   nothing can come

Of us: of me with my grim techniques
Or you who have sealed your womb
With a ring of convulsive rubber:

Although we come together,
Nothing will come of us. But we would not give
It up, for death is beaten . . .

Sure I was scared. I hadn't slept alone in ages, to say nothing of getting out of bed in the morning. But neighbor Rebecca had given me a glimpse of something. I'd made a mistake, sure, even a bad one. But prior to that I'd been good for years—what's my recourse? One mistake cost me my marriage? My best friend? Where's the logic here?

In no time at all I turn it around: I get mad at *her*.

Did she really see herself as the mature one, giving up on our marriage—on *me*—so quickly? Who was breaking our commitment? Who was refusing to forgive? Falling into the guilty trap she'd set for me was too easy, and each day subsequent to her departure—each day she didn't call to say she was sorry, would like to reconsider her actions—I grew more determined not to do so myself.

Sure, I'd screwed around, and I'm not saying it was right, right? But that was one weak moment, *one*, compared with who knows how many other moments when I watched Opportunity stroll by wearing a sundress I only longed to see her slip out of . . .

You want the truth of it? What I was really sorriest about was that Rebecca had already left for London.

I ditch the catering job, even though Margaret had quit when she moved out. It's too weird, awkward. Everyone looking at me like a creature they pity. Jeffrey and Dennis seem to get it, though—the night of my last gig (an early cocktail party that ends at nine) they have me over for drinks and I get too tight to drive home, so end up crashing in their guest bedroom. By the time I get up the next morning—badly hungover—they've already gone, and a *Good Luck!* note confirms that my quitting hasn't hurt any feelings. They even signed it J.D., which I take as a victory of sorts.

Less than a week later I land a bartending gig at a local Irish pub.

Sumpton's claim to fame (what little it has) is its historic district, specifically what's called the River Walk, a long row of three-story red-brick buildings situated on the Sumpton River, the main artery through which cargo ships come to port (it's where cotton and textiles flowed into the city in the 1800s). Nowadays it's nothing but shops and restaurants and bars, which a steady flow of cash-toting tourists support on their sojourns in an 'old Southern city.' After the split with Margaret, I take up residence down there, rotating between bars in the hope of meeting someone who might need "showing around," and Kerry's Pub is the place I frequent the most, little knowing they'd end up offering me a job.

The owner is from someplace south of Dublin, and he rags me for drinking Bushmills, an Irish whiskey I love. But it's made in the North, Bushmills being the name of a town some distance from Belfast. Which means, he seems to be suggesting, that I'm supporting with every sip the terrorist bombings of the IRA.

I eat my ration of shit regularly and keep drinking Bushmills because I love it.

But one night he butts in when I recommend the stuff to a couple of women who say they want to 'try something Irish.' They'd had an Irish stout (Murphy's, on tap), but want something more adventurous. We'd been chatting a bit because it was pretty slow, and these two were nice, seemed to dig me.

I'm thinking I'd like to take on both of them, show Margaret how much fun I can have without her.

So I say, 'Leave it to me,' and just as I'm about to pour them each a shot of Bushmills 'on me,' Mr. Lucky Charms comes over and starts spouting his tired sermon about supporting Jameson's instead, a whiskey made in the South, "Ireland proper." He's got the accent, so with no effort whatsoever convinces them it's the 'right' thing to do. I see the spot they're in—who do we disappoint?—so shrug and say, 'He's the boss,' as I switch bottles.

But pouring the shots I throw in, 'I'm sure he's right. The Bushmills distillery is probably nothing but a covert terrorist operation. Probably the whole town's behind it, even the women and children. Unlike all those churchgoing Catholics in Dublin—'

'Hey, mate,' he interrupts, grabbing me by the arm. 'There's no need for all this. These ladies just want a drink.'

I walk around the bar before telling him to go fuck himself.

A shrink might say (did say) that my proclivity for walking out on such situations is a form of cowardice, or denial, like I'm refusing to confront something important. The hell with that noise. Regardless of her theory's validity, that Irishman wasn't going to change his mind about Bushmills any more than my dad was going to change his mind about the wife he didn't like or the redheaded son he didn't want. Mind you, if these people bothered to ask for input I would've been all too happy to supply it (why stock Bushmills in your bar if you don't want people to drink it, for instance).

My dad was another matter. Obviously.

He ragged me for anything and everything, like it was his *raison d'etre*, and when bored with bullying me he bullied my mom, stomping around the house looking for someone to dump on. Hell, she *chose* the rat bastard, but I sure as hell didn't. So whenever he went on one of his drunken rampages, I walked, pure and simple. Got any better ideas?

Up the street from our house was Hearst Elementary, where I went to grade school, and behind Hearst I could cross a small creek by way of a rickety wooden bridge and lose myself in what at the time looked to me like the Big Woods. Really, they seemed to go on for days, like if I kept walking and eventually came out the other side everyone would dress differently and speak in a foreign tongue.

I remember it took me a long time to go into those woods. In the early days, I'd bolt from home during one of my dad's bad bouts and hide out under the bridge by the ditch, eventually carrying a long pointed stick that I'd use to gig crawdads in the creek. The woods were too scary, too imposing, to imagine penetrating—what if I got lost, stumbled into Bigfoot?

So instead I'd spend hours stalking the ankle-deep waters of the canal, my shoes off and pantlegs rolled like Huck Finn, stabbing those poor two-clawed creatures just because I liked the cracking sound of their armored shell, the mustard-colored fluid that fogged the water at my feet.

If karma's a true thing, I started screwing myself early.

But eventually I braved those Big Woods, headed in there to get as far from where I'd been as possible. I was ten (never forget) and my parents were going at each other like gangbusters, me trying to get lost in *Gomer Pyle* while they hurled insults in every direction. Who knew why, who cared? Even then I realized it didn't matter, that whatever it was didn't explain or justify their behavior. I didn't like my life any better than they liked theirs, but was I yelling at anyone for it? And the fact that they didn't have the common courtesy to take their fight into another room is indicative of how clueless they were.

When I turned and saw him hit her, I walked.

Or ran, in this case. All the way up the street, over the dusty red-clay diamond of the school softball field, and over the bridge into the woods before I even knew where I was headed. I remember a stretch of tall grass—knee-high—bordering the trees, and a little trail leading in. Despite the fact that I'm on a trail, clearly carved-out by the feet of the countless people who preceded me, it feels like I'm the first person ever to venture into these treacherous environs. I move fast at first, but pretty soon realize what I'm doing, where I am, so slow it down, keep turning back to see where I've come from, make sure no one is tailing me. Bigfoot's crafty—why else haven't they caught him?

The gutsy adventure provides its reward in no time: a fairly-elaborate tree-fort emerges in the green ahead of me, built by someone who obviously knew what they were doing. The thing is amazing, and I approach it with caution, even trepidation, not sure if someone might be in it at that very moment. But there's no sound, no movement, and soon enough it's clear there's no one up there. So why not climb those tree-nailed two-by-fours and take a look inside, see what it's like?

One room, that's all. Why'd I expect more? But there's a prize for my cat's curiosity—four cans of beer, the two vacant loops of a six-pack attesting to its tastiness.

Treasure!

Think I drink one? No way—I drink two, hot and foamy though they may be. Then move hurriedly, if wobbly-legged, out of those woods feeling finer than ever, not even concerned about my parents finding out.

What a joke even to think it. Naturally, back home it's like no one even noticed I was gone—they don't say a word. Still I go straight to my room, lie on the bed and stare at the ceiling for a long time. The ceiling was as easy to get lost in as anything else.

So don't tell me—right from the get-go I learned that hitting the road when things turn ugly not only can be a life-saver, it can be a blast.

Everyone's got their ways. Some people are going to do their own thing regardless of what anyone else thinks of it.

Dig: some artists who find themselves unable to paint might go to a shrink. See what's happening internally, emotionally, that might be blocking them. Not Brenda. She contacts a psychic.

Brenda.

Once we start seeing each other regularly—usually for coffee while I'm doing laundry next door—I lose all interest in Brenda as any kind of romantic prospect: we're way too different to ever make a go of it. But hey—she's fascinating as hell, and great looking (to say nothing of just plain *nice*), so planting myself in the midst of the Pretty People and hearing the stories of her always-gutsy life is—usually—a gas.

But a *psychic*?

Seems she went to see this woman in Philadelphia, someone she dealt with a few years prior. Says Brenda: 'She's pretty good,' which leaves me wondering . . .

How does one deem a psychic 'pretty good'?

'There's no question she's got psychic ability—I could tell you some stories.'

But we don't get around to that. On this occasion, Brenda isn't satisfied with the reading she got. 'There was a time . . . ' she says. 'But I don't trust her like I used to. I'm not sure she's as in touch.'

The trip wasn't a waste, though, because she also went up to New York to visit the art dealer who'd offered to help her, and that went really well.

'Her gallery is *sooo* beautiful,' she says. 'The second I walked in I could feel how right—I mean *really* right—the energy was in there. I mean, everything in my whole being opened up like it was the place for me. *Sooo* yummy! Like I was home.'

Now all she needs to do is paint, get something going. I offer the pragmatist's angle.

'Maybe you just need some kind of . . . I don't know . . . a place of your own where you can hunker down and get some work done. Between Greg and your mom and New York, you've been running around so much it's no wonder you don't have any new paintings.'

My two cents are quickly spent with a dismissive wave of her hand.

'Oh no, there's something *muuuch* bigger happening here. It's a thing I can *feel*, like there's this lid on my creative spirit, blocking it. Believe me, I know what it's like when that creative side opens. It's like I can't stop the stuff from coming out.'

The thing about Brenda is her aura. Sorry—I know how flaky that sounds, but it happens to be true. Look, I was lonely and miserable when I made that initial move to meet her, but it quickly became clear this was one pretty pie I wasn't going to get a piece of. Yet damned if I still don't find myself drawn to her, like I can't wait to hear what she'll say next. The woman has this way about her, this enthusiasm even a cynic couldn't deny. You can't sit with her for any length of time and watch the way she expresses herself without getting sort of swept-up in it. Brenda's not moseying along through life, she's *living* it. She's not sitting home measuring out her weeks with the passing episodes of a television series—she doesn't even *have* a home, much less a television. She's moving to Greece because a psychic said she should.

Call it what you like: I'm saying the chick's got balls.

Post-Philly, she contacts another psychic in California—he lives in some little town in the north that I've never heard of, what Brenda describes as 'a magical place.' Apparently, he conducts a sort of interview over the phone, just like twenty minutes or so, then does his 'reading.' You never even meet the guy. And his whole purpose, his *job*, is to tell you what place on the planet is best suited for what you want at this particular point in your life, given the energy of the place, the alignment of the planets, who knows what-all? That's it. It's supposedly geared toward getting you in the right physical location to carry out your 'Higher Purpose.'

And it ain't cheap. Brenda doesn't say how much it costs, she just says it's expensive. Which to me means it's probably outrageous. This cat sits home all day giving psychic readings over the phone, never even sees his clients? I imagine a palatial spread on the California coast, him lounging on a patio all day in his bathrobe doing lines, bikinied women working away on him until the phone rings. 'Greece. You must move to Greece. The signals were quite strong . . .'

Cha-ching!

'But *sooo* worth it,' says the Seeker. 'He's known all over the world. He's been doing this for eons. I mean this guy has *sources* . . . he really taps into what's going on Up There. He said where I am now actually isn't bad, but if I'm really serious about what I want to do, Crete's the place. He said the signs were very clear about this.'

I'm just trying to keep up. '*Crete*? And you're going to do it?'

She nods and closes her eyes, looking determined. 'Should take me ten to twelve months to make it happen.'

Bailing on the Irish pub felt fantastic for about an hour, then the bind became obvious—I'm divorced and jobless, to say nothing of bored out of my mind. Add to the mix the risk that everywhere I go there's a potential for running into people I don't want to see—my parents, or Margaret's (nice people who liked me, at least until I became the scumbag who cheated on their daughter), or even Margaret herself, maybe holding hands and smooching with some lucky bastard who's convinced her he wouldn't possibly screw her over like that sorry sack-a-shit she made the mistake of marrying. So what's a brother to do?

What but get the hell out of Dodge.

I move to Ansley Heights, Max's corner of the world—a three-hour drive. I'm twenty-four and finally leaving my hometown. My mom's not happy, but she's never been happy. And I've never been able to do a damn thing about it.

Being a savior, Max has offered to let me stay with him until I can find my own place, and spots me some money, too—he gave up being an acid-dropping Beatlemaniac, got a Master's in Accounting to become a CPA, and assures me it's no sweat, he's happy to help.

'But we should get busy finding you a place.'

What Max means is that he likes me being here, but the fact is he's recently started seeing someone (Catherine, a pharmacist) so doesn't want me settling in, getting too comfortable.

God forbid we get too comfortable.

Fortunately for both of us, things start falling into place almost immediately, making me wonder at the way of things. In just a few days I get another bartending gig, this one at a cool music club called The Cellar, whose owner Tim alerts me to an apartment he's renting—I can move in first of the month, if I like.

Once I see the place, the icing's on the cake. It's a garage apartment, high up, completely separate from the main house where Tim lives—I can make as much noise as I want without bothering anybody. Sure, it's only two big rooms (with small kitchen and bath), but it's not like I have a lot of stuff anyway—other than my bed and a chest-of-drawers, there's no furniture to speak of, only clothes and books and music. And Tim hooks me up with a loaner sofa, which is all the place really needs to feel lived-in.

I dub it The Penthouse. Max helps me move in on the third, after which I take up cigarettes. Start diving out of airplanes.

Not to toot my own horn (not much horn to blow) but because of skydiving I've been to bed with some *seriously* sexy strangers: the generosity of women never ceases to amaze me. The fact is it's not really me (much as I'd like to think otherwise); it's the job that does the wooing—they're turned on by the risk, the rush, like the rest of us. They relish the thrill-seeker I represent, and like connecting themselves to him, at least for a little while.

Trust me when I tell you: being a skydiving instructor is the next best thing to being a rock star.

This woman comes in to jump—what a looker. It's like she stepped out of a magazine. She's in her mid-forties, and alone. Most people show up at Psycho with a group, or at least in pairs: friends or lovers coaxing each other into courage. Strength in numbers. But this busty brunette with the best lips I've ever seen is all by her lonesome, and Yours Truly gets the luck of the draw—something we do, draw straws to pick tandem-master whenever there's a dispute over who wants a particular client. There are seven instructors, five of whom are married, so if Mike and I are working the same shift and see someone we're both into, we compete to see who gets to go with her. Draw straws, rock-scissors-paper, pick a number, you name it. Granted, it's mostly dudes and their buddies who come skydiving, lots of college joes, but the women's numbers increase every year, and those who do make the trip—and are alone—must be given their money's worth.

With Mike, our tastes are different enough that oftentimes there's no competition necessary. But Hot Lips? She's a doozy. You're not into lips like hers, you better get someone to check your pulse.

Her name's Cynthia, but she says to call her 'Sin'—a line I'm sure she uses every chance she gets, even if it's spelled C-Y-N. When she busts out the line on me, she gives me the crippling grin that goes with it.

She's not the least bit nervous about her jump, even while we're on the plane, which is when the brave shell on the cool ones typically starts to crack. Once we're falling, I let her lead a couple more turns than usual, and just before deploying our chute I call out that I like the way she drives. Then, once we're situated and enjoying the drift-down, I lay on her the line about liking my office, thinking it's sure to seal the deal. The *coup de grace*.

'Nice,' she says casually. 'But my job has put me in stranger places. *And* positions.'

Boomerang!

'Oh yeah? What do you do?'

'I'm a hooker.'

A laugh squirts out first. 'No way,' says the Unbeliever. But I'm a believer by thirty-five-hundred feet. She corrects her confession by admitting she's 'supposed' to say she works for 'an escort service,' but that sometimes she just calls a spade a spade.

I make a joke (obvious) about needing an escort myself on occasion, conveniently omitting that I've been sleeping with someone for the past year (albeit a half-cocked someone—a situation I'm looking to get out of anyway).

'Sorry, but you'd have to take out a loan to afford me.'

I laugh again but it's clear she's not kidding. So I just joke right along, tell her I'll go to a movie instead. And she jokes back that maybe she'll give me a discount if I buy dinner.

Only she wasn't joking.

Being back in the same city as Max is cool, but I'll confess it causes me to miss the *old* Max, the one who didn't give half a thought to money and always seemed to have something up his sleeve. When I recall the cat I met in college, particularly that first semester we were living together, it's like I'd been in Paradise without really knowing it. Max was just *immensely* fun, such a cut-up, a prankster. Dig: he used to hide his alarm clock under my bed, set it to go off at some ungodly hour. He got me a couple of times before I caught on, started checking under the bed every night before I went to sleep.

But Max was way ahead of me, always. The crazy bastard had actually gone out and bought more clocks, hid them all over the room, set to sound at varying intervals. We'd drunk heroically one night, Max fixing gin-and-tonics that could take down a giant, and before turning in I checked under the bed just to see, found a clock there and figured that was it, safe to sleep.

But that was just the decoy, set to throw me, and it worked with a vengeance.

I was blasted awake at two-thirty, completely out of it not only because of the hour but also the gin. What the hell? It's my own clock on the nightstand, which I hadn't thought to check—

too obvious. I wasn't even convinced he'd done it—maybe I'd somehow set it accidentally?

An hour later, renewed slumber's shattered by the next one, sort of faraway-sounding. I'm not even sure what I'm hearing, but as I lay there trying to discern the source it becomes clear, and intolerable. Up again, staggering around the room with the residual drunkenness making mush of my legs, I finally get clued-in to the closet. And there it is—he'd actually rigged up an extension cord, run it in there. I yank out the plug, and right then another one goes off. I can't believe it—how's this possible? I'm so out of it, crawling around looking, and follow yet another extension cord to a clock tucked behind the bookcase. Jesus.

I sit there, back against the wall, and start laughing. I can't help myself. I mean the guy's nuts, right?

'You crazy *bastard*!' I call out, and here comes another. No shit. I just laugh and laugh, crawl towards the sound and finally find the fucker on the floor of the bathroom, behind the toilet. The bathroom's between our bedrooms, and through his door I can hear Max cackling like a chucklehead. Doesn't even matter that he ends up losing sleep, too.

Says he: 'Anything for the fun.'

He's a wiseguy, Max. By which I mean he has *wisdom*.

My solution to the moral quandary mentioned earlier? I finally told my mom I worked at Psycho, but didn't tell her I was training to be a jump instructor.

That time I showed her the dvd of my first solo jump (my *only* solo jump, as far as she was concerned) we were both drinking wine, a *lot* of wine. She's the one who turns the conversation

Michael Hanson

toward my dad, saying that nobody got it, even her best friend Dottie. No one really understood how hard it was to lose him, because they'd borne witness to so much bad stuff. They figure his death will be good for her, actually, once she gets over the shock of it.

And I'm with them: it *will* be good for her. How could it not be? Toward the end, supposedly sober, he was so boozed up and out of it that he never even bothered with the pretense of working. Being in business for himself (marine surveyor, meaning he measured the cargo on some of the big ships coming through port) allowed him to take on as much work as he wanted—or as little. And calls from disgruntled clients started ringing in with more regularity than he could conceal. Pre-cell-phone days, these. He had a second line, a business line, and he never answered the thing. The calls went straight to the machine, and I'd hear these stern, irritated voices asking for figures that were due last week, last month.

Eventually that phone just stopped ringing altogether.

Which meant, of course, that whatever money came into the house was from my mom's job. She was a hair stylist, worked in an old-school salon called *Marjy's* that managed to make do for over thirty years, and though I don't have a clue what she made it couldn't have been much, you know? Meanwhile, he's passed out on the couch all day.

Add to all this that he was such an abusive bastard and you get an idea where people like Dottie were coming from.

'But there was this whole other man in him,' my mom says that night, and starts crying. 'There was this sweet, gentle man in there who loved me. And I lost him, too.'

I'm not sure how to respond. Is this the wine talking?

But then she really starts to bawl—I mean her whole body's shaking from it. I go grab a roll of toilet paper from the bathroom

48

and bring it to her. Kind of kneel on the floor next to her chair, wondering what I can do.

'He was in there,' she says. 'He really *was*.' And she lifts up her ruined face and looks me right in the eyes and says, 'But *we* know, Nate. *You* know.'

I nod. But what I really know is that I'll have to take her word for it.

Seems lousy fathers are a dime a dozen. I'd only known Brenda a few weeks when we were having lunch at Shady's (pizzeria), a junky joint that caters to the underbelly of the college crowd— not the jocks and coeds, more the Goth types, pale-skinned people with lots of black clothes, tats and body piercings. The walls of the place are peppered with album covers—The Dead Kennedys, The Ramones, you get the idea—and graffiti, which the owners don't discourage. But Brenda, over fifty and committed to her spiritual quest, doesn't mind meeting me there, slumming with the underdogs. (It's only later I'll learn that, despite appearances, she sort of sees herself as one of them, a go-against-the-grain type.)

On this particular day I make a crack about my dad (nothing specific, just that he'd been a challenge), which I suppose opened the door for her to make some father-related cracks of her own—the fact that she was sporadically slapped being among them. 'And that's not the half of it,' she says.

I don't press for specifics, even though I'm curious as hell. She just makes it clear he was a man who did his share of damage, and that since his death (massive heart attack, over twenty years ago), she and her mother have made the most of their time with regard to healing all the wounds he inflicted. Took them a while to get started, but Brenda went into therapy and that got the ball rolling. She tried to get her mom to go but no dice. Still, that didn't stop the woman from being open to communicating when Brenda brought her all the stuff that was coming up in her sessions. All the questions about their history, how her father had acted on various occasions. She says her mom was ready and willing to talk about this.

A year later, though, Brenda had had enough of therapy.

'It was good for me, on many levels. But they want to hook you in, keep you coming. Not that they're not helping. They are. But if you get better and stop coming, they're out a hundred-and-twenty a week, you know? So I got the lessons I needed, then started working on *myself*. Because ultimately that's what it comes down to, Nate. It comes down to *us*.'

The job at The Cellar saves my ass regularly, but taxes me, too: sometimes that line between what we need and what we have is tricky to navigate.

It would take a few years to get enough jumps to be licensed for skydiving, so I was out there every chance I got. I worked my tail off at the bar, skipped movies and clothes and dinner out, all the stuff people spend their money on, so I could keep jumping. It wasn't cheap, but even then I knew it was the healthiest habit I had, and though it seemed like a longshot I dug the idea of doing what these guys did—making my living jumping out of airplanes.

Make no mistake, though: I didn't believe for a second I'd ever get there. It was one of those lies I told myself—not to mention everyone else—so I could get out of bed every day.

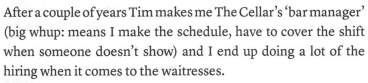

After a couple of years Tim makes me The Cellar's 'bar manager' (big whup: means I make the schedule, have to cover the shift when someone doesn't show) and I end up doing a lot of the hiring when it comes to the waitresses.

Finally—benefits!

Kimberly is among my first hires: a long-legged, fine-assed looker I set my sights on the second I see her strut through the door. She's older—won't tell me exactly, just says 'over forty'—and within a week of her start-date I end up in her bed for a late-night post-work romp that curls my toes just to recall it. I'll admit being a little apprehensive, the *older woman* and all that, but she makes no secret of having been satisfied with my first go at her. Sitting on the john afterwards, her head between her knees, she calls through the open door—'I'm *done*. I can't fucking *move*.' A couple more nights and a couple more romps later, it's clear she wasn't just jiving, digs the sex enough to keep it coming.

So keep it coming I do, if you know what I'm saying.

Call it a new hobby, call it whatever you want, but I'm happy as all hell to have found Kimberly—and her endless legs—to hang with. We're both cool with the arrangement—friends with benefits—and enjoy the added freedom of other company whenever the opportunity presents itself. Kimberly says she's not interested in anything serious, having recently ended a long-term gig with an unnamed guy she calls 'The Drunk.'

He's a drunk? Must drink like a champion. I have to work *hard* to keep up with Kimberly, and usually am ready to call it a night long before she is.

'The Drunk's rich,' says she. 'Bought me everything I wanted.

All this stereo equipment? Shit—*all* this stuff—he bought it. But it was just bribes to keep me. I caught him fucking around.'

I dare inquire about her own 'fucking around,' given what I already know of her.

'Oh, I wasn't doing it then. Well, okay, a few times. Just to get back at him. Grudge fucks. He didn't care. I had to find other ways to get to him.'

Other ways?

'His music, mainly. He's another music geek, collects vinyl. Walls of records. So when he pissed me off, I'd wait until he left and break a record. Just pick one out at random and break it, throw it away. He never knew, but it'll start to drive him crazy at some point, when he can't find things. We were together five years—that's a lot of broken records.'

She snorts a fat line off the coffee-table, hands me the straw, wags a finger at me. 'So don't piss me off.'

I like Catherine, Max's girlfriend, but it's obvious when meeting her that she's a straight line, and more or less limits his movements likewise. So when she goes away for a weekend to visit her parents in Michigan, I have My Lovely Man all to myself, first time in a while.

We make a great occasion of it, just cooling out—like the old days but better, because we're aware of the luxury, the rarity. They have a sweet, breezy house that's within walking distance of downtown, and I show up early in the morning on his first day of freedom with a backpack, a big bag of grass, and a pitcher of bloodymarys I mixed the night prior (so it could season overnight). We sit on the porch armed with each, Max packing my pipe and saying, 'Here's to the first hit of the day.'

No teenagers (or college students) could have more fun: the guy still makes me laugh so much I sometimes think I'll crack a rib, but I know it's adding years to my life. Far as I'm concerned, laughter's the Great Liberator: I even wonder what might-have-been had I gotten my dad high. Liquor only seemed to fuel his anger, whereas I'd wager a little weed would've had the opposite effect, loosened him up a bit.

Hey, can't hurt to wonder.

Max makes this insane breakfast, some crazy skilleted concoction involving eggs, potatoes, onions, and beets. Red Flannel Hash, he calls it.

'Sounds like something you get when your ass breaks out in red bumps because you've been wearing golf pants.' (This ridiculous joke keeps us giggling for many minutes.)

I'm skeptical, in other words (come on: *beets?*) but high as a kite at 10 a.m. means I'll eat damn near anything that's put in front of me. Besides, I'm grateful he's cooking, and the fact of the matter is Max's concoction tastes like the best dish I've ever eaten. Who knew I liked beets?

Needless to say, we don't spend the day on the sofa eating chips and watching reruns of *Beavis and Butthead* (not that I'm above it). We go to a show at the museum—a Jean Dubuffet retrospective—where the grass we'd smoked beforehand helps us better appreciate the French badass' primitive, playful renderings. This cat's stuff purposely looks like some little kid's class project, glorified stick-figures with crooked features, the paint often mixed with pebbles and sand. One in particular I can't get away from—a large rundown apartment-building whose occupants wave out the windows. There's this weird sweetness about it, adorable to me. Innocent and sad and big-hearted, these poor sots are stuck in tenement housing but still smiling and waving to the world outside, like they're trying to tell us something. I'm really mesmerized, riveted by it, until finally Max gets impatient and pulls me away. 'A five-year-old could do that,' he says like a smartass. 'Just ask those Pollock-bashers from our class.'

At lunch in the museum's Conceptual Café, Max moos like a cow as we shuffle through the chow line with the art-loving herd, and I giggle so much I can hardly stand, my laugh-weakened knees threatening to buckle.

That night we hit the Mad Hatter to see a band, but the music falls flat so we don't stay long. Instead end up back at The Cellar—I'd taken those nights off, but the place is my home away from home. Everyone knows me, so I savor a rare sense of myself as Someone, and George slips us every other drink on the house so we end up spending half the dough.

On Saturday we spend all afternoon sunning on giant rocks in the middle of the Broad River just east of town, smoking and drinking white wine from a bota Max bought back in college when he went through a Hemingway phase, then that night a friend of Kimberly's has a bunch of people over after work, so we hit that for a while. What a scene. Everyone's high on something, lots of skin showing and eyes roaming. The whole vibe screams *sex!* But I've got Max in tow: there's no way he'll stray, though he doesn't make any bones about the fact that if it weren't for Catherine . . .

I can't leave the guy in the lurch, consequently we have a few drinks, smoke a little of someone else's grass and get the hell out of there. Kimberly tries to coax me into something with her and a girlfriend, the thought of which is as thrilling as it is unsettling—I won't lie. Men think it's the dream come true—two women!—but the reality requires a courage I can't seem to summon, at least at the moment.

I point out the Max problem.

'Who says we have to leave him out?' slurs the Temptress. 'I think Gina'll go for it.' She casts a glance at her girlfriend across the room, a pale-skinned blonde with a great body, kinky hair, and a scary amount of dark eyeshadow. Then she takes my hand and inserts a few of my fingers into her mouth, licking them lasciviously.

Against my will I imagine Max with a hard-on. It nauseates me instantly.

My ambition fails—let's just leave it at that.

'Tell me I can take a raincheck.'

She says she can't make any promises, drawing out her words as if to say I'll be sorry.

'I'll have to take my chances, I guess,' and just then Max comes back from the bathroom and says, 'Listo?'

He grills me the whole way home. Seems Max thinks I should cut things off with Kimberly, get out of what he calls 'an unhealthy relationship. A good time, maybe, but something about her gives me the willies.'

'Beats the hell out of jacking off,' I say. 'Pun intended.'

'I hear you—those legs look like they'd be worth it. I'm just saying. If I were you, I'd at least get regular check-ups.'

I crash at his place again, wake up first the morning following and fix coffee. Smoke the rest of a roach sitting in the ashtray. A cello concerto by Haydn lulls me into longing, and the sudden thought of being curled up in bed with a woman is bad enough to send all the blood in my body straight to my groin. I cross my legs and tighten up, press down with my hand which causes a momentary wave of pleasure. Then distract myself by getting up to look in the fridge, see what there might be for breakfast. I'm starved.

I hear his steps on the hardwood, turn to see Max standing beside the sofa looking like a trainwreck. A knot of curly hair spirals from his forehead. One look at him tells the tale. He collapses onto the couch.

'I don't guess I could interest you in going out for breakfast?'

He says he's too hungover even to consider it.

I decide to take myself out, let the poor bastard go back to bed and sleep it off. 'What time's Catherine due back?'

'Late this afternoon. Thank Jesus she's coming home today.'

I'm moved by his romanticism, his attachment to that quiet life of love and domesticity that sometimes looks like Hope to me.

But then he clarifies: 'Two days of this is plenty, Nate. One week of your life would kill me.'

The last time I talk to my mom she says she's finally heard the tapes (or, actually, only part of one) and thinks I should hear them. Recordings my dad made with a microcassette player, one of those little silver gadgets no one has anymore, about the size of a cellphone. I never saw him use the thing but apparently he did, and mom says she tried to listen to one of the tapes but couldn't get through it—'Awful,' was all she'd say about it. But she believes I might benefit, so is putting them in a shoebox for me.

I hear the wine in her voice.

We'd found the tapes the week he died, put them aside with some other stuff she decided to deal with later. What a week that was. I remember Margaret's reaction to it all, for it laid bare the madness in that house. Things toward which my mom and I copped a casual, business-as-usual attitude, left Margaret incredulous, shaking her head.

'How could your mom live like this?'

This on the day we found the traps.

Wooden mousetraps with the metal spring, the ones that'll crush a rodent's skull (or a wife's frail fingers) when sprung. Since my dad was supposed to have been sober those months near the end, and since he wasn't, my mom made what turned out to be a token effort to curb her own drinking and nurtured a new habit for combing the house for his concealed liquor (which she'd of course unearth in abundance), and when he got wind of this he boobytrapped his hiding places. Tried to teach her a lesson.

Some teacher.

Fortunately she never found any of them, but the day after the funeral, going through stuff to help her out, I opened a drawer of his desk and damn near lost a finger to one of those fucking traps—trust me when I tell you, they're not to be toyed with. Hateful. I put a pencil in the thing just to see, and sure enough it split that pencil with no problem. All said, there were six of them tucked away in various places—in drawers and on the floor of closets, a couple of them adorned with a handwritten post-it: **Mind your own business!**

Such is where thirty years of marriage got them.

The place was still bugged with booze, too. Half-pints hidden in the pockets of coats in the closet, slipped inside his shoes, tucked behind books in the bookcase. Even his shampoo was a ruse, unless he was washing his hair with vodka. He concealed the stuff with the surreptitious skill of a terrorist.

Margaret was beside herself, causing me to chuckle, head shaking.

'I can't believe you're laughing. It's not funny, Nate. It's tragic. How can you make light of all this?'

She's smart, but my answer was how could I *not* make light of it? I laughed at him, otherwise I'd want to kill the bastard.

And he was already dead.

My old reptile loves the scotch,
the way it drugs the cells that keep him caged
in the ancient swamps of the brain.
He likes crawling out at parties
among tight-skirted girls. He takes
the gold glitter of earrings
for small yellow birds wading in shallow water . . .

The fact of a standing lay with Kimberly doesn't stop me from mixing it up from time to time. Hey, she couldn't care less and I could be dead tomorrow, so why not? One is a dreadlocked black honey named Darlene I meet at a party thrown by Cellar-owner (and landlord) Tim. We'd run into each other on a Friday afternoon when I was coming home from the laundromat, and he says he's having people over that night and why don't I stop by. So at ten o'clock—when I can see from the Penthouse that his place appears to be packed—I walk over, dosing myself with a couple of good bong-rips beforehand. Kimberly's at the Cellar working, so when this chick strikes up a conversation that seems headed in one direction (true north!), I'm right there with her.

I don't know what she's high on, but she's having *serious* fun.

People are making out all over the house, so I don't think twice when she lays a heavy kiss on me. And what a kisser—my word for her is *lushalicious*. After only a few minutes of this, I follow her into a large bathroom with a sunken whirlpool and a big mirror covering one whole wall. She says she likes to watch, hops up onto the counter beside the sink and opens her skirted legs to reveal no panties underneath. She's shaven completely clean, too, and I'm further shocked to see two words tattooed around her puckered lower lips: **THE DEEP**.

I dive in without a mask.

My god does she buck. She has these really muscular thighs squeezing the sides of my head such that I hardly have room enough to work, so finally I force them apart with my hands (not easy) and hold them open with all my might.

Says she: 'That's right, boy, get in there. Make it happen.'

I won't lie to you—I work my ass off. My tongue's going to need a sling by the time she's finished.

But finish she does, grandly, and with enough of a racket to assure me my hard work has paid off. And just when I'm thinking *my* turn, imagining those luscious lips lapping me up (and down!) she hops off the counter, tears some toilet paper to wipe herself and says, 'Thanks, baby. I gotta get back out there or my man's gonna freak.'

When I tell Max this story, figuring he'll get as much a laugh out of it as I do, he asks if I make a habit of locking my door at night.

Come again?

'You spend a party going down on some guy's girlfriend, don't be surprised if you wake up one night with a gun to your head.'

Geez, talk about a buzz-stripper.

But I guess he's got a point—truth is it hadn't even occurred to me. Since such things are cool with Kimberly, I just make an assumption that if someone is doing the driving . . .

'I wouldn't bet on it, Hoss. You don't know someone from Adam, why would you "assume" she's on the up-and-up?'

So I make a new rule. Unless I know the chick, or can confirm her status as single, she'll not get near the sacred grounds of The Penthouse. It's her place or no place. I even alert George, the Cellar's other bartender, and Tim—let them know not to give out my address to anyone who might come asking.

'You going undercover?' George asks with a wink.

Of course, a cute little brunette named Tyler, who shows up at the Cellar one night shortly thereafter, could've gotten me to break that rule in a blink.

So much for good intentions—I'm on a roll.

Instead, she coaxes me to her place once we close (not much coaxing required—I was blasted) and I wake up the following morning on a mattress on the floor, my hands—and midsection—caked with dried blood. It's enough to startle me, but only briefly, before I figure the obvious.

My god, the things we do.

She's not in the bed (likewise soiled) and damned if I don't hear children's voices. I don't remember her mentioning kids, but truth is I don't remember much of anything from last night. I remember she's *tiny*, and agile as a gymnast. I remember a bright-purple tattoo of a peacock feather on her forearm. Otherwise the brain's a blank, my mouth sere as a desert, my head heavy as a bowling ball. Atop me squats a devil daring me to move. I take the dare only for fear of the alternative, sitting up slowly and moving my feet to the floor with a mighty effort. The room is a wreck—a trashpail in the middle of it, chest-of-drawers drooling clothes, kid coloring book pages litter the place like bloody rags—and I find my clothes in a clump amongst a bunch of blouses and skirts strewn on the floor. Dress quietly, ease out of the room into a darkpaneled hallway.

Nothing's even remotely familiar, and nausea rolls around my belly like an egg-yolk made of mercury. Tyler's voice, and that of two kids (boys), spill out of the hallway's other end into a square of light on the floor. I listen for a moment—flatware clanging in cereal bowls—before making a left into the living room, also dark, all the blinds drawn. A big-screen tv, candy-colored toys everywhere, brown shag carpet threatening to gag me. I hurry out the door into searing sunlight and to my car before retching in the driveway, once, and make a getaway like I'm fleeing a crime scene.

I'm in the projects—'affordable housing'—an area of town I wouldn't even consider coming into were it not for a head full of drugs and a sweet piece of ass like Tyler. I need to piss like a racehorse, but can't even consider stopping anywhere: my hands look like I spent the night cutting up a corpse.

Suddenly wondering, I look in the rearview, see that the skin around my mouth looks as bad as my hands. Shocking—like the Joker with a bad make-up job—and it stirs something. This is crazy—for the life of me I can't remember *anything*, I can't even believe what I'm seeing. But there it is, sure as the blood-smeared face in the mirror belongs to nobody but me, and all I can think is that something's seriously wrong here. What if I hadn't woke up at all?

I shiver to shake it, a rabbit jumping over my grave, and decide I'd better keep mum about the whole business. Max gets wind of it he'll wash his hands of me, and I won't even be able to blame him.

Next time Kimberly calls me over I decide to take it easier, maybe even talk to her a bit about how the night with Tyler rattled me a little, like maybe it's time we consider toning things down. And what are we up to, anyway? The thing is, we've set ourselves up as a no-strings sex-only partnership (of sorts) and it's been cool with both of us—after all, the sex is admittedly off the charts. It hasn't even bugged me that I've been sharing the space with someone else, even *many* someones, because in the thick of our own encounters, just when we need a little something extra, we'll share experiences we've had with others and before you know it we're both getting off in serious ways.

Big time, Brenda would say.

But maybe it's time to re-evaluate, lest we both end up ravaged by some vengeful STD. This is the notion I carry over to her place, the gift of logic, only one look at her when she answers the door and it's clear she's in cloudland, not a place where a 'serious conversation' stands a chance of breaking through. Not surprising, I suppose, business as usual, but there's something different going on, I can't put my finger on it. Kimberly typically likes cocaine—check that, she *loves* the stuff, creams to do lines off my hard-on—but it makes me grind my teeth so I generally stick with grass. Tonight it's something else, though, and her tongue's in my mouth before I know what's hit me, her hands climbing up and down me like squirrels.

'Close your eyes.'

She's all woozy-sounding, her words dripping, and I can't deny being curious as hell. I do as instructed, feel her fingers grazing my lips, so I open them a little to let her in. And it's then that she puts something on my tongue, real small, barely noticeable, and I swallow without a second thought, figuring what the hell.

Who would've guessed (not me) that I'd just dropped acid. So much for toning things down—blast-off is now imminent, and the launch that'll occur in the next twenty minutes or so will take me on a ride that'll last hours.

Fucking Kimberly—why's it always have to be *something*?

She jokes that I need to hurry up: her ride's already well under way and she's anxious for me to jump on board. Hands me a lighter and her little blue, prick-shaped pipe, loaded, to get me going, makes a ridiculous suggestion: 'Let's go to Clayton Lake, do some skinny dipping. Think you can drive?'

Well, what do I expect? But in truth I'm pissed. Is she serious? We'll both be tripping our asses off and she wants to get behind the wheel of a car and drive ten miles out to the lake?

No, of course not. That's *my* job, naturally.

'Damnit, Kimberly. Driving sound like a good idea to you?'

Already she's shooshing me. Puckers pretty painted lips and blows a little sexy breeze over my tense brow, runs longnailed fingers through my hair.

'*Eeeeeaasy*,' she whispers. 'Eeeeeaasy. Don't spook the horse.'

She's right. I might be pissed, but the fact I'd better face is that if I don't turn it around I'm in for a long, bad ride. It's a trick of the mind: I know this. So what'll it take to switch it, turn things around?

'Help a brother out,' I say.

She presses those lips to mine and gives me a deep, creamy kiss that could soften a statue. Come on, she says, taking my hand and leading me into the dimly-lit living room, the lamps muted by scarves she's draped over the shades. On the coffeetable is a plate of fruit, peeled mango sliced into wedges. She picks up one of them and, smiling, begins to paint my lips with it, kisses me, paints, kisses, feeds it to me. It's rich, sweet, delicious. She turns and switches on some music, obviously planned, the satiny sound of Sade oozing in while I take a seat on the sofa, Kimberly slinking into some kind of dance, that amazing body sliding into a sinuous rhythm with arms over her head and eyes closed. Next thing I know she's peeling off her shirt, no bra, her nipples pointing toward Heaven and her hips swaying in a way that slays me. I reach for another slice of mango but she calmly intercepts it, takes the golden wet wedge and begins caressing her breasts with it, painting those perky nipples first and then smearing the fruit all over. Crooks a 'come here' finger at me.

I'm so swept up in the fruit and what she's doing with it that, before I know it, I've gone right past the acid's initial speedy stage into the vestiges of a trip beginning, and by the time she starts coaxing me into deeper waters I'm so overwhelmed by stimulus I can't focus enough to rise to the occasion—it's the damnedest thing.

Kimberly says not to sweat it, her words coming to me as through a long tunnel. She rolls over and heaves those holes before me and says, 'I bet your tongue can do the job.'

Well, might as well give my tongue *something* to do. Conversation is out of the question.

'I've put your name on a shoebox, with the tapes and a few other things in it,' my mom says. 'You may not want them, but I'll let you decide.'

I say okay.

'It's a shoebox. You know the kind of box I mean?'

Is she kidding? I'm not sure what she's getting at. Maybe my cell's signal is sketchy, or maybe she's giving me some idea of size, or how *much* stuff there is . . . ?

I assure her I know what a shoebox looks like.

'And I've written your name on it. So we won't forget.'

She must be drunk, thinks we'll forget about the box. That's what I decide.

But two days later, when Dottie calls to tell me, I see why my mom had been pressing. It was me, not my mom, who was being slow-witted. And maybe that's because I was tanked up and high as a kite when we talked.

Unlike when my dad died, my mom's funeral was pretty crowded, but I can't recall much about it, just snippets. I remember telling Dottie there was someplace I needed to go before the service, someplace private (implying that it was a solemn errand, important), and I drove to Kerry's Pub on the River Walk, where I'd made my grand angry exit three years prior, only it's now called O'Neill's and Mr. Lucky Charms has moved on—the place has a new (American) owner, though he's sticking with the Irish Pub theme (never mind all the neon, the lame pop music piped in). I remember the super-cute redheaded bartender (freckles, green eyes) and the two Bushmills she served me (*sans* guilt trip), with a Caffrey's chaser. I remember getting high in the car once I left for the funeral, and how Sly and the Family Stone sounded like they were saving my life.

I remember how funny it felt to be in a church, first time since I was a kid, and how none of the service seemed to have anything to do with my mom. Every time I'd duck out—to the car—to take a quick nip from the flask I'd filled that morning, I'd think how smart my father was (sneaky bastard) to have been a vodka drinker: I was sucking on mints the entire time to make sure no one smelled the whiskey.

I remember missing my old neighbor Rebecca, recalling how she'd 'consoled' me after my dad's death, wishing we still lived in the same city. The same country! For all I knew she was still living in London, knocked up and talking Cockney.

And I remember that my best moment of the day was arriving back at O'Neill's after the graveside service, sitting on a stool where the same great-looking bartender with long curly red locks had a Bushmills in front of me before I'd even ordered it, complete with the beer back. Which is when it hit me that I'd done it: I'd managed to get through all the required rigmarole despite being fairly shitfaced. Sitting there at the bar, finally comfortable, at last relaxing and letting go and satisfied with where I was, I understood for the first time how my dad had been able to carry on a life as a drunk. Because I proved that I could do it, too: could do what I *wanted* to do, even while doing what I *had* to do. And this time Margaret wasn't around to give me grief for it, say I wasn't taking everything seriously enough. Margaret. Truth told, though, I'd take your grief, Meg, in exchange for your company right now. I started wondering where she was, what she might be doing and maybe had she heard about my mom. It even occurred to me to call her, see if she might be willing to come have a drink. Celebrate my orphanhood.

But I couldn't, no way. Too far gone to carry on a conversation.

And later, back at mom's house—what once was Home, a place ever emptier but for me crawling into my old bed with the room spinning a bit, a room that had hardly changed despite my not having lived there for eight years, my Hardy Boys set still taking up an entire shelf—I remember it occurred to me how strange it was that I'd spent the entire day dealing with my mom's funeral, but all I could think about was my dad, what all this would be like if he were around. Even though the guy'd been gone for years, it's like he still butt into my business every step of the way. Like there was no escaping him.

The day I get back from Sumpton I meet Max for a late lunch, Marston's. We sit outside on the patio, and since no one is around, I take a quick hit off my pipe right there at the table. He says to take it easy, his tone barely tolerant. Asks lots of questions.

I give him honest answers, and he says he's sorry he didn't go with me: 'I could've kept you in line.'

I take a sip of my first drink of the day (mimosa) and say that being in line is overrated.

He doesn't even grin, grumpy bastard. 'Look, I don't mean to sound like your big brother or something but . . . I mean . . . are you okay?'

You want the truth of it? Once I got back to O'Neill's after mom's funeral, I set my sights on that redheaded bartender. One look at her was all it took to convince me she could turn the day around, get my mind back where it belonged.

On *life*, not death.

But it wasn't my day. I'd laid some good groundwork—sharing the singularity of being redheads, telling her about the funeral I'd just attended (for a *friend's* mother)—when I got caught-up in that weird loop about my dad. A couple of cats at the other side of the bar had started chatting her up, too, meanwhile my wheels were spinning, not just about my father either because suddenly Margaret started creeping in to make me miss her, and by the time I was ready to bail I just couldn't summon the energy or enthusiasm to clinch the deal.

Call me slow, call me clueless. Call me whatever you damn well want. But at least I can see clearly now that this to me should've been a sign.

Kimberly has a surprise. 'To take your mind off things. Cheer you up.'

Fact is, I can use it—I'm in a funk, so all that stuff about having a sit-down with her, clarifying whatever it is we're doing, needs to take a back seat. I don't have enough energy for the drama.

She tells me to put on nice clothes because she's taking me out to dinner, someplace 'fancy'. It's a little Italian place, and before we walk in to claim our reservation she gets me high with some hash she scored. She's all dolled up, a little black dress that leaves those long legs looking like something I'd die for, every head turning to take a peek as we're led to our table, the chicks just as jealous as their dates. Kimberly spends the entire meal talking dirty to me, saying how hot she is, that she can't wait to go home for 'dessert.' Wet painted lips, smiling in that way she has. My hard-on burns a hole in my thigh, and she strokes it under the table, the fabric of my slacks feeling fantastic.

You should see the way she eats her shrimp.

On the way to her place afterwards, she proceeds to tell me about some new guy she made it with while I was away.

I'm driving, she slides to my side and one hand goes over my shoulder while the other snakes its way to my slacks. She says it was such a let-down, says no one knows how to fuck her like I do. Her tongue caressing my cheek, my ear, between confessions. Her hand leaves me and lifts her dress to expose a pantyless pussy shaved to a thin strip of fuzz like a feather. She touches herself, moaning. Wets my lips with the tips of her fingers to give me a taste.

I won't lie to you—she's delicious.

Outside her apartment she stops and lays one hell of a kiss on me before swinging open the door. Her friend Gina sits on the sofa smiling (at least I *think* it's Gina, the kinky hair the giveaway), surrounded by candles, the silvery sound of jazz. She's holding something I'm not sure of, but when we get all the way in I see that it's some kind of video camera.

'Gina's got a new toy. Remember that raincheck?'

I've yet to encounter the sadness that sex doesn't cure. At least for a little while.

Dottie takes care of everything. Everything. The house is mine, but of course I don't want it, so she enlists the services of a realtor-friend who's able to sell the place in no time since it's in a good neighborhood and the house is in decent shape.

In a matter of months I'm loaded. Well, what I get Mick Jagger could piss away in an hour, but to me it's a windfall, like

I won the lottery. Max admonishes: 'Don't do anything crazy, Nate. Will you let me help you?'

I tell him I'll make him my official financial advisor on one condition, hand him a 15%-off coupon for a trip to Psycho so he can pick up that ball he dropped back when we were nineteen. He agrees to it, says he's always been sort of sorry he hadn't gone through with it the first time, but has one condition of his own: he wants one of the others to be his tandem-master. At the time I brushed it off with a joke—'I'm not sure they're as qualified, but hey, it's your life'—when in fact his demand made more of a mark than I was then willing to admit.

Which is among the things I take bar-hopping that night—I'm gonna burn it out. I start at the Cellar, but after a single drink decide I don't feel like dealing with the small-talk that comes with familiar faces and places, hence head out to explore uncharted watering-holes. And I find plenty of them—take any downtown in the country and I'll bet there's enough booze on every block to drown the entire populace.

Lucky me.

By one a.m. I'm shitfaced to a degree that would've put my dad to shame—the distance from one barstool to the next (like someone in a bad country-song, or a *good* one, for that matter) was but a wobbly walk and another couple of hits from my pipe away, and that bastard father of mine couldn't have handled it, the lightweight. This latest joint I've landed in gives me the willies, though, as Max would say. Max who doesn't trust me enough to take him skydiving, even though I do it for a living. Countless strangers come to me every day, trust me with their lives, but not my oldest pal Max. What the hell?

I pull out my cell to call him—I want to hear him fess up, tell me what it's all about, why it is my best friend is shutting me out. I'm right, right? Makes no sense at all, nor does this fucking phone I can't seem to work. And, as if suddenly,   the whole room is off balance, whirling. I plaster what little focus I have on the phone in front of me to find a still-point. It works, sort of. I manage to navigate to my Contacts, then Max's number, but naturally he doesn't answer, probably avoiding me. So while his voice-message plays I get ready to let him have it, come clean and tell him the truth about how he hurt my feelings.

But that's not what comes out when the beep sounds. It's like I can't speak a simple sentence, much less compose a coherent thought, and all I really want to say is come get me, take me home.

'Everything's turning on me,' I mumble into the phone, hoping he can hear me over the obnoxious music this place is playing. But then I just disconnect because it's too much, everything's too much, and I just need to be home now.

I don't even know what I'm doing here. There are so many people, and it's so loud, that it's like I'm suffocating. My head weighs a ton, tensed-up with this weird pressure like it's about to burst, but I lift it with all my will to look around, find some air, which is when I notice that next to me stands this tall blond guy trying to get the bartender's attention. He's big, this guy, wears a tight black T-shirt that can't cover his sizable biceps shoving out fat blue veins, and on the left breast of which is one word stenciled in small white letters: **DADDY**.

Is that right, is that what it says? What does it even *mean*? I squint into focus and find the word **DADDY** spelled-out atop some guy's tit, and the second I'm sure of it I notice that I'm staring, just dumbfounded. So I try *not* to notice, stare.

But it's not easy.

Up walks another guy, standing to the big guy's right, saying something to him. The second guy's rail-thin, pale. A sickly-looking creature with the same blond haircut and the same black T-shirt, identical—only his shirt hangs loosely on his lank body, and the white stencil over the left breast is slightly amended: **DADDY'S BOY**.

How the hell did I get here? More importantly, how the hell am I going to get *out*? Professional cyclists use the word *bonk* to describe the complete depletion of their energy, that point when they can't possibly pedal any faster, the body's resources entirely tapped-out. And I'm realizing that I'm bonked, that my head is reeling and heavier than lead and I'm in a weird sort of trance, staring at Daddy with my mouth hanging open and a thin line of drool dripping from my lower lip.

I don't even notice the drool until the musclebound blond does, and despite the fact that a part of my brain is screaming, *Look away! Look away!* I can't move, I'm frozen, and this guy's staring straight back at me now with pretty blue eyes, eyes filled with razorblades.

'I think it's time you called it a night,' he says.

'Daddy,' says I, why I can't even tell you, wondering even if he made it out since the word was mangled, mumbled without lips. I sense the spit, wipe the wet mouth with a hand, turn away, back to the bar, alone again. Hear myself repeat it: 'Daddy.' My head's too heavy to hold up anymore, so I rest it on the bar thinking I just need a nap. If everyone can leave me alone maybe Max'll be here any minute to pick me up. But my mouth keeps talking, saying 'Daddy' over and over again into the wood of the bar.

'I'd leave it if I was you.'

The words have an edge like a serrated blade, but I don't even care because I just want to be left alone. Can't he see that? Can't he see that this is an absurd, fucked-up life, filled with best friends who don't even trust you and parents who fight all the way to their funerals, and all I really want is for someone to take me home and put me to bed? Is that so much to ask?

Apparently, because next thing I know a hand that could crack walnuts grabs me by the back of the head and lifts, the roots of my hair searing my scalp. I give up, I surrender. I'm just ready for it to be over. All of it.

'Fuck you, Daddy,' I say.

He slams down, my head banging the bar, and I hear a commotion, a lot of *Heys!*, figure that's the end of it. This guy's going to beat me senseless and drop me in a ditch to die, and in truth I couldn't care less. He'd be doing me—the *world*—a favor.

PART TWO

The Wonder Of Alice . . . S² . . . Breaking Kimberly . . .
Magic Moment . . . Fender Bender . . .
You Call That Penance? . . . Benton And Carson Save
Blackwell Middle School . . . el Camino de Santiago . . .
Enter Sadie . . . Kidnapped! . . . The Surprise
In The Shoebox . . . The Marvels Of Non-Dating . . .
Run For Your Life . . . Shrink Rap . . . Tripping The
Cosmos Fantastic . . .

On a previous coffeedate like this one (talky), Brenda said I needed to embrace the notion that my moves are all exactly right, what they're 'supposed' to be, despite the pattern of disaster in my past. That my life is what it is by *necessity*, the soul seeking by whatever means the very specific lessons it needs this time around, given what it got last time. And the time before that.

Me, I'm not so sure—*people*, after all, are the ones contriving these theories, and as one of them I've a right to be skeptical when someone says they know how all this works. Part of me hears Brenda, even wants to believe what she's saying. But another part thinks it's a necessary lie she tells herself (me) to keep going. No different from a Christian saying Jesus died for your sins so now you owe Him.

I'll admit that Alice's words haunt me, though, add another measure of ambivalence: 'You may not speak that language, Nate, but it speaks to you.'

She's the first woman, Alice, to whom I'm drawn in a way that feels *fated*, and the more I get to know her the less it matters whether it's Fate or the whims of a random and chaotic Universe. She improves my life exponentially just by her presence in it, so what difference does it make whether it's 'meant' to be?

Says Alice: 'If you ask me, it's no accident we met.'

This, regardless of the fact that there's no romantic current between us. Close as we are, and as important a part as we play in each other's lives now, we somehow recognize right from the get-go that romance isn't in the cards.

Granted, the fact that she's already married might influence all this.

The party where we meet is one at which—I'll later learn—neither of us knows a single soul save the hostess, a boyish French woman (Estelle) I met a week prior when she and two friends showed up at Psycho for a jump. After, they extend the party invite to all the jump masters, but I'm the only one who takes the bait, even Mike doesn't bite. I spend most of her party hovering over the food table, the only thing to do when you don't really know anyone, and the drop-dead brunette I'm soon to learn is Alice stands there as well, directly across from me, slipping squares of cut cantaloupe into her mouth.

My god she's astonishing—all I know in that moment is I want to jump her bones. A wild head of miraculous dark hair piled up high with a pretty pin and spilling over both shoulders, and a long red dress that ties behind her neck, her cleavage like something I want to drown in.

But her smile is what makes my knees weak.

Both of us stand there talking to no one—including each other—for ten minutes or more. I'm not even hungry at this point, yet I'm not about to move away—clearly this is the place to be. Fact is, I'm feeling so superfine I'm ready for the gamble, especially given the potential payoff across the table.

Endorphin rush from running—this very day I did twelve miles in preparation for a marathon, a crazy new notion Max concocted, having once run one himself. On top of which I haven't had a drink since the scene with 'Daddy' three months back. I'm still guilty of the stray cigarette, sure, but grass intake has been significantly cut and I haven't caved-in to calling Kimberly, a habit every bit as hard to break.

I mean it: a body like Kimberly's? My god, that's kept the world turning forever.

But I can't deny these Max-inspired changes have some fairly dramatic effects, some of which surprise the hell out of me. I mean, I'm always game for some fun, especially when it's a party loaded with lookers like the one across the table. What's weird, though, is that I'm a nervous wreck, can't seem to summon the courage to speak to her, make my move. I'm guessing it's all this clean living— who knew that booze and grass made life so much easier.

I did.

Of course there's also the flipside, and even I'll admit those old reliables had started to work against me. So I'm trying to turn it around, get my shit together, and it seems to be working. Want to know how I know?

This crippling brunette at last comes around to my side of the table, but not for the crudité. She walks straight up to me and says, 'You have about the most beautiful head of hair I've ever seen.'

No matter what you think, it can always get better.

Oddities from my mom's funeral keep coming up, insisting that I look at them—why I can only wonder. Dig: there were all these supposed friends of hers making an appearance despite the fact that, other than Dottie and a couple of others, she didn't *have* any friends, not to my knowledge, anyway. Certainly she didn't *see* anybody, spend time with anyone. And this hermit-like habit started long before my dad died, even.

So who are all these people?

I remember some tall cat in a suit coming up to me at the Visitation and introducing himself by saying, 'I was nibbling on your mom's ear before you were even born.'

Great, want a medal?

He goes on to say my dad 'snatched her up. He was good at that, your dad. A real ladykiller.'

Could've fooled me.

He hardly talks about my mom at all, just goes on and on about my dad doing this, doing that. My dad was in the Air Force blah blah blah, he was on Tinian when they dropped The Bomb blah blah blah, and when he returned from the war he fell under FBI investigation blah blah blah.

I mean, you should've heard the guy. He talked about my father as if he'd actually lived a life.

'Daddy' doesn't drop me in a ditch to die after all: instead, two guys are walking me, one on either side, and my legs are mush. I can hardly move, and feel afraid of where they're taking me, what they're going to do.

But there's something soft in their voices.

'Easy now, just a little further...'

Next thing I know I'm in a sort of stock room, like a giant pantry loaded with boxes, and a desk. I'm sitting in a metal fold-out chair someone's fetched, and I'm making a moaning sound—I hear it like it's coming from someplace else, and I can't stop it. I rub my right temple to dry the tears wetting my face.

Weird tears. Warm.

I look at the wet stuff on my fingers and it's red.

The wastebasket is in front of me just in time and I vomit into it.

Twice.

It takes more than twenty minutes of arguing, kid you not, to convince Kimberly there's no way for me to screw her while skydiving.

This is one of those conversations that makes me wonder.

In three years (plus change), I get fully licensed for skydiving instruction, and almost immediately they hire me at Psycho. I knew after my second year of training there was a good chance I'd get in, because one of the instructors, Phil Herndon, let me know that he was planning to leave, and if I was serious about pushing through that last year he'd work it out so I could move into his slot. Phil was among the original instructors when Psycho started, over twenty years ago, so with him on my side there was little chance they'd deny me the job. He made sure I understood this, great guy that he is.

Besides, they liked me there—proof that anything's possible. They knew how far I'd come. What a mess my life was, sure, but how getting licensed became such an integral part of my pulling it together.

Psycho was started by a married couple, Michelle and Bill Purvis, and Michelle said to me once, 'I worried about you, Nate. But I could see the transformation start to happen, after that time with the helmet. Like you were coming back to life. And when I see someone like that, see how hard they're working to change, I want to help them. Any way I can.'

At this point I'm still the skeptic, and all her talk about *transformation* and *coming back to life* only confirms that I'm fooling everyone, if not myself. Don't get me wrong—what she's saying *is*, in essence, the goal, what I'm after, but it seems a hell of a longshot. I mean, 'that time with the helmet' is only one of many examples of how willfully determined I was to ruin even the one thing—skydiving, to say nothing of my *job*—that was good about my life.

I was on my way up for a jump—taking some young guy, seventeen, whose dad had brought him—and on this particular afternoon was not only pretty hungover, I was still slightly drunk, having had a few swigs from a bottle of Bushmills before I left home just to level-out. And on the flight up, these waves of nausea started rolling over me, relentless.

I got my helmet off just in time to heave into it.

No jump this go round. I pleaded a vicious gut virus, me and that poor kid watched the others dive out and just rode back down with Stewart, the pilot. Back on Earth, Michelle said one of the others would take him up on the next round, but the kid said he'd come back another time. She gave him a coupon for a free jump, but sensed we'd never see him again, as indeed we never did.

Bill sat me down a day later, said, 'We're only going to have this conversation once, Nate.'

Which turned out to be true, miraculously. I mean, when I recall my history at Psycho, particularly those first couple of years post-Margaret—how I was working the bar at night and jumping during the day (whenever I had the dough)—it's a wonder I didn't dive straight to my death. Fact is, plenty of those days I'd show up still sluggish and buzzing from the night before. Everyone at Psycho saw me as this reticent guy who kept to himself, when in reality I just didn't want anyone to know how fucked-up I was. That even as we were packing chutes to jump out of an airplane, I was making trips to the toilet to throw up, my hangover hammering me. That sometimes I'd jump with booze in my system because I *had* to—some days that was the only way to stop the shaking, calm my body down.

So. A shot of something first thing up. Just the notion makes me nostalgic now.

When I meet Alice, it's like I've finally found something to shoot for—she sees a different me than the one usually running the show, and seems genuinely interested in *that* guy, wants to see more of him. I'm not at all sure who that guy is myself, but her interest creates some curiosity, makes me wonder. Sure I'm bummed she's married, but it's like we blow right past that in no time and I'm just grateful to've met her.

'*You're* grateful? I've been looking for someone like you ever since we moved here.'

Turns out Alice and her husband Leo relocated to Ansley Heights less than a year ago, when they both accepted teaching positions at the university. Alice is an anthropologist, as is Leo, and not having found many friends (outside of colleagues in their department—not what she calls *close* friends), she makes a point of reiterating how happy she is we found each other. She treats me like I'm special, and I won't deny digging it, especially the way she uses the word *found*, like we'd actually been looking all along.

Leo, turns out, is currently doing fieldwork somewhere in Africa (don't ask me—she said the name but it didn't stick, my brain pretty much a big blank whereas geography is concerned), so Alice and I start spending virtually all of our spare time together. Hanging out talking, going to dinner, seeing movies, whatever. Perfect, given my abundance of free time in the wake of Kimberly. I try to coax her into a trip to Psycho, 'on me,' but she'll have nothing of it. 'Appreciate the offer, but when I get on a plane I'm staying *inside* it.' Does a part of me wonder what's up, is she looking for an affair? Well, I can't help but wonder.

I mean, Alice is *beautiful*.

But it's not happening, which I read in no time. She doesn't treat me like a lover (would-be lover), she treats me like a pal. It's the damnedest thing—I can't claim to have experienced it with a woman, ever, yet it's a feeling I recognize nonetheless. Easy to relax into, like family or something.

Not *my* family, mind you, but you get the idea.

In truth, it's hard as hell to describe the fun strangeness of it all, how simple things are with Alice. How we're like old friends even though we've only just met. Her explanation is that the two of us are on similar paths, but we're each at different places on that path. Not one for all this 'path' talk, I still know what she means. That *is* the sense of it. This is the kind of thing that happens constantly with Alice: she has a knack for pinning down feelings that are otherwise vague to me, elusive. But she just says it and it's so. So *right*. Since day-one we've shared a sense of never, ever having been without one another.

And when I thank her for breaking the ice that brought us together, she gives the credit right back to me. When I say she's the one who walked around that table to compliment the carrot-top, she says I'm the one who asked her out.

'Only because I wanted to get inside that dress,' I say, laughing.

She even digs that I still flirt with her, married though she may be. So the bottom line as far as *both* of us are concerned? Run the risk, damn the torpedoes. Always.

I learned pretty early that risk is a means to tapping into something resourceful, serious. A sense of myself as a living, breathing animal. An animal who, like all others, will die. So get it while you can.

Where's a kid pick up intimations of mortality? Not from *living*, I can tell you. I got them from reading.

In fifth grade kid detective books became my obsession. The Three Investigators, The Hardy Boys, Brains Benton. These guys felt exactly the way I did: imprisoned by rules put on us by everyone from parents to school-teachers; that life as a kid just needed to be gotten through, and in the meantime spiced-up by adventure of some kind, the riskier the better.

Around the time I hit eight or nine, I was on the hunt for *anything* different because I felt like a complete misfit (maybe other kids did, too, but I didn't get that impression). You didn't have to be a genius to see that the journey to Adulthood was going to be an endless, tricky course to navigate, littered with every hurdle imaginable for me to clear en route. Hearst Elementary may have been right up the street from my house, but I was this loner, shrimpy kid, with no connection to the others in the neighborhood who went to Hearst with me. And hell, the ones who took notice of me were the belligerent wise-crackers taking pot-shots at the runty redhead.

Hey, I'm not asking for sympathy—it's just a fact.

So I spent a hell of a lot of class-time daydreaming about the woods behind Hearst (what I liked to think of as a *forest*). I mean, you going to tell me school wasn't dull as church, sitting dutifully in your desk while some button-down type droned on about math or social studies? I wanted *experience*, man, even if I wouldn't have known to call it that back then. And it was my fifth grade teacher, Barbara Montford, who clued me in to reading as a means of finding the fun my life was seriously lacking.

I was at a new school, Blackwell Middle School, which necessitated a twenty-minute bus-ride with scads of students who all seemed to know each other already. But the teacher only then known as Mrs. Montford proved that the new stomping ground might have an edge over the tired environs of Hearst. She was a passionate reader, she told our class, and looked it: she wore big blackrimmed glasses with thick lenses like you'd expect. But she was sexier than I could stand—my fantasies during an average day in her classroom could've gotten me put away forever.

How could an eleven-year-old win the affections—the body!—of his teacher? He'd *read* his way in. Well, such was the schoolboy strategy, and my first foray into fiction (en route to Mrs. Montford's bed?) was one of a series of books advertised as Alfred Hitchcock and The Three Investigators, discovered at the school library. I recognized Hitchcock (maybe from TV or something—can't say I'd seen any of his badass movies at that point), so between that and the book cover—three kids at a table with some kind of turban-wearing swami, a huge scary-looking serpent swimming in the air above their panicked faces—I decided to give it a go.

And what a trip it turned out to be! Jupiter Jones's father ran a junkyard, in the back of which was an abandoned trailer buried behind a bunch of trash. Our clever threesome converted the trailer into a headquarters for their detective agency, only you couldn't get to it just by walking through the door, oh no—the trailer was accessible only through a secret tunnel the kids constructed themselves.

Show me the eleven-year-old who wouldn't cream over this kind of thing, and I'll show you a kid who's already beyond help. It was badass.

Compared to the crazy shit these cats got involved with, my life was downright ludicrous, a bad impersonation of living—being only a kid didn't blind me from the fact. School, ridicule, homework, miserable parents, and endless hours devoted to the even-then ridiculous dreck offered up by television. Lather, rinse, repeat.

To hell with that. These kids dug deep. They crawled on hands and knees through a secret tunnel into headquarters and concocted the schemes that turned life into a *serious* experience, a dangerous one, even. Where a kid could die if things went awry.

What was real? What I witnessed in my life, or what went on in these books?

These guys weren't sitting around after school with bowls

of cereal, their brains buried in the idiot-box. They started a *detective agency*, for christ's sake. They had business cards!

I burned through those books like nobody's business, and suddenly was more alive than I'd ever imagined. I'd bombard Mrs. Montford with details of all the exploits of The Three Investigators, and she listened. More than that, if I failed to mention my reading for a few days, *she'd* ask *me*. She'd actually pull me aside and say, 'What, Nathan? Are you not reading any more of those great books you found?'

Devouring them is what I was doing. Every day I'd race home from school to read, and when my parents were around (*danger, Will Robinson!*) hole-up in my room and read some more. I did this every day, despite repeated cracks from my dad about ruining my eyes, how unhealthy it was for me to spend so much time indoors.

'You oughta be outside.'

Nowadays I get it: even then he was starting to slip, work-wise, so wanted me out of there. I was cramping his style, bearing witness to his alcoholic lethargy.

Sometimes I gave him what he wanted, took my paperback and hid under the bridge behind Hearst, too afraid to return to the tree-fort where I'd once found treasure. After all, I *stole* some of that treasure—by now they probably had the place boobytrapped.

Once I'd exhausted the school library's collection of Three Investigator books, I moved on to the Hardy Boys. Not quite as good, but still pretty badass, still pushing life pretty far compared to the kids around me.

All that shit they try to sell you about reading, how it's the best way to educate yourself?

Believe it.

Mind you, my parents did what they could to create an adventurous environment. When my mom discovered my dad was having an affair (I'm still not sure how she found out), she locked him out of the house. Twice. And twice he kicked down the door.

I was eight, slept right through the violence. Got up the morning following to find the front door leaning against the wall in the living room, the sun-lit carport seeming like it was right there in the room.

'Your father got locked out,' says my mom casually, like it'd been an accident. The eight-year-old brain accepts this—what? doubt my *mother*?—doesn't wonder why his dad didn't just knock, wake someone to let him in.

Then it happens again.

'Your father kicked it down. His girlfriend must be on the rag.'

The eight-year-old brain accepts this—what? doubt my *mother*?—but hasn't even the vaguest notion what it means, the word *father* not typically used in conjunction with *girlfriend*.

And what's this *rag* all about?

Knowing I'm safe in the back stock-room of this weird bar, having vomited twice and survived 'Daddy's' wrath, doesn't make me feel any better: I never had such a headache, and I've had my share. Nothing like this. My brain feels like it's going to split my skull, and Mercy is the one who'll cut off my head and be done with it, put me out of my misery.

Max comes to the rescue sometime later (who the hell knows what time it is?) his being the last number dialed on my cell: apparently someone called him and explained the situation. The two guys who'd carried me to the stock-room are Steven and Stacy—kid you not, one of the guys is named Stacy. I learn all this later (obviously) because they actually call to check on me a few days after the fact.

'Just call us S-squared,' says the S known as Stacy, chuckling.

So they're nicknamers, like someone else I know. Turns out the place was a gay bar, which I hadn't even realized, already three sheets to the wind by the time I staggered in there. Not that it would've mattered—all I wanted was a bartender to bring the goods.

'That fellow you had the run-in with, he's a strange one. Always kinda dicey. Steven missed most of it, but I got the feeling you weren't really making fun. Like there was something else going on.'

Making fun? Yes, there definitely was something else going on. Now if only I knew what it was.

The thing is, maybe the world's not necessarily working against us, but my pattern of seeing it that way started early. My parents, sure. Bullies at school. The like.

But I'd even invent enemies who weren't there. Third grade, lingering at the Hearst playground, I'd spot a car coming down Lee Avenue and imagine they were after me. I'd go tearing down the street toward home, the car turning the corner and headed straight for me. I'm running as fast as my feet will carry me, like my life is on the line and if I don't get home before they reach me I'll be toast—they'll throw me in the trunk of the car and take me somewhere to be tortured. Chest heaving, brain running as fast as my feet, I can almost hear the urgent soundtrack in the background . . .

Up the driveway I collapse onto the grass of the front lawn just as the car passes our house, the driver oblivious to the drama. I'm dizzy, my legs all quivery and my knees stitched with strawberries, but my brain at last beginning to relax.

I made it!

Something's happening, I'm sure of it. At least that's what I tell myself.

A week after the gay-bar debacle, the bump on my head is still obvious, but not as sensitive to touch. My showers aren't so painful anymore, my Psycho goggles not nearly as uncomfortable.

Kimberly's told the tale to everyone at work and they've taken to kidding me about it, making me sorry I told her. When I come in they say, 'Good to see you, Bruiser.' When I leave, 'Don't go picking any more fights—you could end up with brain damage.'

I don't stop them, I play along. I smile and shake my head. Sometimes bring my fists up into a fight stance, like a boxer ready in the ring.

But what I'm thinking is they don't get it, they don't know me. And this is the rut my brain starts getting stuck in. I notice, as if for the first time, my interactions with people. Any people, all people. Customers at the bar, my boss, the guy who pours my coffee at the café or the chick who takes my money at the market.

None of them know me. They may *think* they do, given that they see me all the time. Given that we can go on and on about this job or that movie. Given that they know how I dress, what foods I buy, how I take my coffee.

And Kimberly, whose long legs have me locked in? She thinks she knows me. And why shouldn't she? We've been going at it for a year now, screwing each other senseless and stripping off our clothes damn near any place at any time without so much as a second thought. How could she not know me?

Well, wonders the redhead, how could I not know *her*? But I don't. I could tell you at least a dozen ways guaranteed to get her off. What she likes to drink, snort, or smoke. I can tell you that she'll eat anything, *anything*, but that she eats next to nothing because she's afraid of spoiling that super-sweet figure of hers.

What about my parents, my mother and father, did they know me? Not a chance. Nada. They didn't even know feeding me raisins gave me diarrhea.

A rut. This business of knowing each other, *really* knowing— does it even matter? And if not, why all of a sudden can't I stop thinking about it?

The phrase *panic attack* is one I'll learn later, in therapy, but on this particular Wednesday afternoon all I know is that, out of nowhere, a vague terror overtakes me in the laundromat—I honestly can't say *what* I'm afraid of, but am shaking so bad it's like I'm having a seizure, and figure that any minute now the few people who are in here are going to get wind of what's happening, pin me to the floor and call the cops. I'll end up in a sanitarium surrounded by a barbwire fence, strapped to a table getting electroshock therapy. So what do I do in this moment? Ask for help? Call 911?

No, this is America. I get behind the wheel of a car.

I drag from the dryer the heavy cluster of still-damp clothes, dump them into my laundry basket, then jump into the car and tear off like someone on the run from Johnny Law, or someone whose wife is about to have a baby in the backseat. I don't care—I flip on the flashers and haul ass. The thought of getting arrested, or plowing into a telephone pole, doesn't slow me down because it's like I'm bound by a mission, a serious one. All at once *everything* is serious. Risking my neck—god forbid someone else's—seems necessary, because being on this bad ride alone will be the death of me. I want a witness, if nothing else. I'm shaking and sweating, praying I don't heave.

What I'll later try to interpret as a sign—blind luck?—gets me where I'm going: one of those godawful 'office parks' about ten minutes out, a cluster of ugly buildings with a big phony lake in the middle. (How did the words *office* and *park* end up next to each other, anyway?) I pick what I'm pretty sure is the right building (having been here only a couple of times) and hurry inside, run into an elevator and push the buttons in a panic, suspecting the ground is going to open up at any second and swallow me whole. Out at last and through double doors I instinctively navigate a labyrinth of cubicles, head down, not even nodding at the people I pass, until I'm standing in the doorway of Max's office.

If I die here, at least My Lovely Man will be the last sight I see.

'Jesus,' says Max, stunned out of an Accountant's number-crunching trance. 'What's going on?'

'Do you know me, Max?'

I'm all out of breath, my face sweaty. I want to throw up.

'Do I *what*? Damn, man, you're white as a *ghost*.'

'Do you know me?'

I'm standing on the edge of a cliff no one can see, like my future, my fate, rides on his answer. I've never been so scared in my life, a clam without a shell. There's no air, and my chest feels this tremendous weight—pressure—bearing down on it. It's hard to breathe.

But scariest of all is the look on Max's face, a look that might push me right over the edge of that cliff I thought no one else could see.

'I know you're burning yourself out, Nate. Jesus. I know that if we don't figure a way to rein you in . . . ' but he doesn't finish, just shakes his head.

Which is when I lose my legs and drop to the floor, crying.

Max is over me in a second asking if I'm on something, asking what the hell, his voice alarmed in a way that relaxes something inside me. I'm looking up at him and what I see is something like a savior, and all that'll come out of my mouth are the words *thank you*, over and over, thank you, I say, thank you.

A woman appears behind me but Max assures her everything is alright. 'His mother died,' he tells her, justifying the carrot-topped basket-case.

I throw my arms around his neck and hold on like I'm clinging to a life preserver, say, 'Please don't leave, Max. Please don't let go.'

He doesn't. He holds me. He holds me.

And he doesn't let go until I do.

I remember that right in the middle of my mother's graveside service the priest stops, puzzled, one hand holding the open Bible from which he's reading and the free hand patting the sides of his vestments. Do those things have pockets?

He announces he's missing his vial of holy water.

So he walks over to his car, all of them in a long line right behind us on the little road that snakes through the cemetery. He finds his keys (pockets!) and suddenly there's the loud three-beep blast of him disarming the car's security system.

We're in a cemetery, having a funeral. I could spit on the fucking car from where I'm sitting.

He opens the passenger door, finds his holy water, closes the door. And then—the *coup de grace*—that three-beep blast as he resets the security system. This priest takes no chances, you dig?

So much for faith.

If life is a treadmill to the tomb, sometimes that treadmill seems to speed up, move us along faster than at other times. Such is what I see when looking back to the period immediately subsequent to my divorce. I can't honestly claim to have recognized it then, but it's almost like things were happening so fast that three years went by in a buzzed-out blur, and what I'm left with now is a sense of having been on a bad trip.

Or, put another way, I woke up one morning with such a profound hangover that I never wanted another drink from the same bottle.

I take up running, quit The Cellar. Ironies abound: nearly licensed, I'll start as a Psycho instructor next month, only I'd intended to keep working at the bar part-time to cover the winter months when we're not skydiving (Psycho essentially shuts down November – February); now, with the money my mom left me, I'll be able to get by without a part-time gig, albeit barely, and with a will toward frugality. Mom may not have known her son was a skydiver, but now she's financing it.

I don't even give Tim proper notice, just say I'm sorry, I don't have a choice. It occurs to me too late that he's also my landlord, might throw me out of The Penthouse for bailing on the bar. Instead, he does two lines right off his desk with a rolled up bill and says, 'Well, whatever, man. You gotta do what you gotta do.'

Kimberly, on the other hand, wants nothing of all this, ignores me when I say I'd like to back off a bit, take a break. She's in front of a full-length, free-standing, oval-shaped mirror, trying on a new pair of jeans, twisting her torso so as to better see her backside.

'Damn, does my ass look *good* in these or what?'

Regrettably, it's an undeniable fact: her ass looks *great* in those jeans.

I remember when she bought the mirror—an admittedly beautiful piece of furniture, in an old-fashioned sort of way—which now stands in one corner of her bedroom. She called me at work to tell me about it, how she'd found the thing in an antique shop downtown and paid a pretty penny for it.

'But it's gorgeous. I can't wait for you to fuck me in front of it.'

Despite the persistence of this memory to undermine me, I try to stay the course, to explain that I want to make some changes. That I *need* to make them. And this means going it alone for a while.

'Oh, so now you're going to drop me like a bad habit,' she snaps, a scary edge in her voice.

Exactly.

But I take my share of the heat here, and gush in a way I can't stop, weird. I tell her it's my fault my life's such a mess, no one else's. Certainly not hers. I tell her all this will be hard, *real* hard, that part of me is completely terrified because what I'm intending will require more discipline than I can imagine, something I severely lack. But there's this sense of jeopardy to everything, and I'm compelled to take some steps, make changes.

'I'll miss this,' I say, not lying.

'So why quit? Can't we just have some fun every now and then?'

Why quit? I wish I could come up with an answer, simple words that'll make it all clear. But I can't. I haven't even got it straight in my own head—how the hell do I expect to explain it to anyone else?

I just *know*. Some kind of instinct. Something in my bones. Something new.

For over a thousand years people have made the journey across Spain's northernmost margin, on *el Camino de Santiago*. Though started by Christians (who made the march to the burial place of St. James in Santiago de Compostela as a kind of penance for their sins), the hike has become a popular pilgrimage for people from all walks of life, making the trek for their own personal reasons.

I read an article on what's called 'The Way' in a travel magazine at Psycho, one of a half-dozen periodicals littering our little waiting room. I hardly ever look at these things, but one afternoon when Mike needs a lift I hang out waiting for him to finish up and find myself thumbing through one, whose cover of Spanish mountains lured me to take a look.

And by page three I'm knee deep into those mountains, to say nothing of the notion they're espousing: that the ancient pilgrimage has a powerful pull on people trying to sort out certain difficulties in their life, spiritual and otherwise. The idea of *me* making such a trek seems every bit as insane as anything else I've been doing, but there's something weirdly enticing about the prospect, some attraction I can't quite convey when I call Max to talk about it.

No matter, to Max—he thinks it's the best idea I've had in a coon's age. He helps me do the research, outfits me with an old backpack of his, goes with me to get the all-important boots and nails down an approximation of what the whole shebang should cost. After all, he's helping me pay for it.

'It's as important an investment as I've ever made,' says My Lovely Accountant.

And two months later he drives me to the airport on the day of my departure.

'You lucky bastard,' says he.

I miss my parachute. As we shoot across the Atlantic Ocean in a steel tube that means to drop me in Europe all by myself (Xanax keeping my heart from pounding a hole in my chest), I work hard to hear Max's voice the whole way. I repeat his words over and over again, a mantra, trying hard to hear them, believe them.

I'm a lucky bastard . . . I'm a lucky bastard . . .

Contrary to what some might say, there *are* constants in the universe, things you can count on (for good or ill). Among the things I've learned from skydiving, this is one of them.

I'm regularly asked by clients if jumping has lost its edge since I started doing it for a living. Does it ever get old, they seem to be asking. Has it become mundane?

Though I don't actually say this, there are degrees to which even skydiving has indeed lost some of its luster. The getting ready, packing the chute, all the preparation. Even the once-astounding drift-down has lost much of its magic.

But there *is* something that hasn't changed, not one iota: the moment immediately prior to plunging from the plane's open door. These few seconds, I tell people—looking out at the vast emptiness with the knowledge that I intend to hurl myself into it with nothing but a chute to stop me—are every bit as intense now as they were to the nineteen-year-old who entrusted his life to jump-master John that very first time.

The moment illuminates the miracle we've become blind to.

Lots of guys just go diving out. Me, doesn't matter if I'm taking a client or flying solo, I grab that overhead bar and savor the moment. It's what's most significant, precious—I don't care how corny it sounds. Even during my darkest days, when I felt like the walking dead, I could grab that bar above the plane's open door and *know* that this was one hell of a ride, and I was *alive* for it. A lucky bastard to be sure, even if I wasn't quite ready to believe it.

People take their plunges—I think now this is exactly what my dad was doing when he moved out of the house. I was eight, and to this day know remarkably few of the details that motivated these moves, save that he decided to pursue his affair, me and my mom be damned. But according to what mom said later, it didn't pan out (maybe he got dumped?) so he was right back home within just a few months.

And that's not the weird part. What's weird is that not one single thing seemed to have changed in the interim. They were at each other's throats in no time.

Years later, when I ask my mom why she'd let him come back, why not just stick it out without him, she says point blank, '*You*, Nathan. Our family.'

Ah yes, our all-important family.

Therapy is what first starts me thinking about all this family stuff, looking at our history as if maybe it matters.

Not to sound unsympathetic, but we'd have been better off if my dad had just gone his own way. Well, me and my mom, anyway. Or *me*, anyway. And maybe even him.

As it was, he just seemed like the angriest man on Earth, like this meanspirited stranger who sponged off the family and hawked his unhappiness on us from a comfortable seat on the couch. Even the most elementary parental responsibilities—teaching me to drive, say—fell to my mom. My grades (Bs and Cs, generally) confirmed for him my worthlessness—'You'll end up in a fast-food apron.' He'd hound me to mow the grass every week, wash the car he didn't want me to drive. Stretched out on the sofa with a bottomless vodka-and-grapefruit, he'd remind me how easy I had it. How later I'd learn what a bitch this life can be.

Thanks for the warning.

Only once did he hit me—sophomore year of high school—though it was more a slap than a hit. I'd used the car to go out with a classmate, Lester Coursey, and gotten home around midnight, pretty tipsy from a twelve-pack.

At some point the morning following I'm yanked out of bed—literally—by my dad. He pushes me out to the carport in my shorts, points out our car's right rear bumper and says, 'Want to tell me about *that*?'

There's a papery crease in the metal, like someone backed into a pole. I'm confused, and hungover. The sky's real blue, sunny. My neighbor, Mr. Markowitz, is next door raking his lawn and I'm on the carport shirtless, just shorts. My dad sways somewhat, has a familiar hangdog look on his face, his eyes hazy. The usual. Spews a stringy glob of phlegm while waiting on me to answer—a gesture for making sure I'm properly intimidated. Gradually, I begin to put two and two together, but have no idea what to say.

Which is when he slaps me. Once. Hard. I can feel the coarseness of his hand as it crosses my face, steals air from my body. In an instant my eyes fill with water.

'*Answer* me!'

It's sometime in the wee hours when the phone rings. I'm sound asleep, real disoriented when I answer, but Kimberly's voice brings me back in no time.

'You shoulda been here,' says she.

'Are you okay?' I ask, scared she's in some kind of trouble. Who knows what madness she could've gotten into since last I saw her?

'There were two of um . . . they were workin on me from . . . from everywhere . . . all over . . . '

There's that lazy drawl in her voice, lets me know she's come down from all the lines.

'Come on,' I say. 'I don't need this.'

'Why not? *You* don't want me. I'm not good enough for you. But you'll like it—it's hot. So listen up . . . '

I do, don't know why. Maybe it's a crazy kind of penance, or maybe I'm overestimating myself—could be that she's right. Because in fact the erection's there before she even gets started.

Blackwell Middle was just as lame as Hearst Elementary had been, and once I'd plowed through everything the school library had in the way of junior sleuths I decided to take drastic moves—trudge the longish way to a shopping center where there's a used bookshop. Lots of parents hardly let their kids out of their sight, but the (lone) perk of my own was that I could head out the door in the morning and no one cared where I was until dinner that night. So walking all the way across town to some second-hand bookshop was no big deal, especially given the payoff. Because this is where I'll be introduced to Brains Benton, of the Benton and Carson International Detective Agency.

The book's called *The Case of the Counterfeit Coin*, and the cover features our dynamic duo—one a redhead!—gaping at a shrunken head.

Oh yeah, this is the stuff.

Benton and Carson, like the Three Investigators, have a headquarters. At the rear of the Benton family garage, Jimmy (code name Operative Three) presses the third nail on the fourth board from the bottom, activating a hidden amplifier from which Brains' voice beckons: 'State your name and business.' When Jimmy offers his code name, the garage door opens, a secret panel slides to one side and, as he steps inside, the door shuts automatically behind him. A faint blue light illuminates a hidden staircase, and as Jimmy climbs those stairs they fold up below him. Entering, headquarters would seem to be empty, but that's only because Brains sits behind a two-way mirror to confirm his cohort's identity, after which the mirror will swing wide to reveal the 'inner sanctum.'

Like I tell you, this was the shit. These cats didn't give a rat's ass about wandering around the mall after school.

With the benefit of hindsight, coupled with enough literature classes to obtain a bachelor's degree, I've come to view Headquarters in all these amateur detective stories as a sort of sacred space where one's fantasies are allowed to flourish. Sorry to sound like some college prof, but it's true. It could even be argued that these books were young-adult postmodernism (not that anyone would've used the word, thank god)—that these kids never did any of the stuff told in the tales, rather spun all the elaborate plots from prodigious imaginations, freed from the dull constraints of 'real life' and allowed to run wild whenever they entered the *head* quarters.

Back then, though, all I knew was that I needed to start taking some chances, the way these cats did. But where's an eleven-year-old find risk?

Same place a seventeen-year-old does. Or a twenty-eight-year-old.

Girls.

Paula Meyer not only was the best-looking girl at Blackwell, and not only did she share my fifth-grade homeroom, she actually lived in my neighborhood. A Jewish goddess with full lips and feathered black hair parted in the middle, she and her best friend Diana lived on Marengo Street, which ran parallel to my street, and every day I had the luxury of walking home from the bus stop tailing the two of them. But one day—emboldened by all those boy detectives—I decided to damn the torpedoes and do something audacious . . .

I get off the bus before they do and walk ahead of them. But not too far. And as I approach Marengo, I accidentally-on-purpose drop a note on the ground, a folded piece of looseleaf paper on which I've waxed poetically (ha!) about my secret profuse love for Paula, how she'll never know of my undying adoration. I keep walking, too afraid to turn and see if they've discovered my dropped note, before taking the left toward home with the question still unanswered.

To this day I've no confirmation that Paula Meyer read my note, but two weeks after I plant it she invites me to a party at her house—a first. And there, on a couch in the corner of her parent's living room, lots of awkward adolescent dancing all around us, this goddess of my dreams asks me if I've ever french-kissed anyone (what?) before graciously giving me a personal demonstration.

I could've died of happiness on the spot, sometimes wish I had. Moral of the story? Those boy detectives taught me something important—live dangerously every chance you get.

My European odyssey first lands me in the City of Love, but only long enough to take the metro from the airport to the train station, then with *beaucoup* help hop a TGV to the French town of St. Jean Pied de Port—white cottages red-shingled and red-roofed—where I'll spend one night before walking into the Pyrenees mountains at eleven a.m. tomorrow.

The world traveler? I can't even believe it.

With Max's backpack providing vicarious company, the first day on the trail has me ascending from 300 meters to nearly 1,400, through verdant hills patched with pastures for cow, sheep, horses, every now and then a thickly-wooded stretch like something out of the Southern Appalachians. I won't lie to you: there's something scary about being so far away from 'civilization.' At least back home—where crime rates are through the roof, every city rife with thievery and murder—being a bit suspicious makes some kind of sense. But damn: even out here in the middle of nowhere I imagine predators surrounding me. I think about where I am . . . crazy . . . alone in the mountains of the Basque country, paranoid about being kidnapped by ETA terrorists and held captive as a political prisoner. It's unfortunate that I read a bit about this stuff in the travel guide tucked in my pack: the ignorance-is-bliss notion might've served me better.

The flip-side, however, is being treated to one breathtaking vista after another. Summiting the high hill, I literally straddle the border between two countries—France and Spain—the boundary marked by an old wooden fence with three strands of barbed wire, like something supposed to contain a farmer's flock. I mark the moment. I say out loud, 'Bonjour,' then walk through the old gateway and say, 'Buenos dias,' heading down off the ridge into Spain.

The remainder of the hike is essentially an easy walk downhill, and seven-and-a-half hours later I arrive in the Spanish town of Roncevalles, where I go straight to the patio of a café, heave the heavy pack off my sore shoulders and order *uno cerveza*, happy to have survived my first day in the wilds.

Nervous? Scared shitless is more like it. I'm in a foreign country where I don't speak the language (save to say hello or order *una cerveza*), armed only with a travel guide, a phrasebook, and a confused heart regarding my real reasons for being here.

From an adjacent table, two butchy German women who speak impeccable English strike up a conversation, having pegged me as *el peregrino* and saying they too are hiking el

Camino. They tell me there's a hotel, expensive, which is where they're staying. Or I can go to the old abbey where 'pilgrims' are allowed to stay for free. Already I'm relaxing, this whole *pilgrim* business clearly putting me in special company: less than ten minutes in town and already strangers have helped me. Like the pilot of a crippled plane, I coach myself: *You can do this. Just keep calm. It'll all work out.*

The decision is a no-brainer: the expensive hotel might be where my heart wants to hang, but my wallet knows better.

The abbey is a large multi-floored fortress, imposing to approach for being buttressed by the mountains behind it, but when I check-in, a kind *senora* who speaks 'un poco Ingles' sets me up with an official booklet for hiking el Camino: a *Credencial Del Peregrino*, a sort of passport that I can get stamped at each stop as proof of my pilgrim status (as if the clothes, the smelly boots and backpack aren't a dead giveaway). She leads me up three flights of stairs to a large open room filled with wooden bunks, points the way to the bathroom where three showers and two toilets are shared by all. Tells me that Mass will be held in the Chapel in about an hour.

Mass? I slogged all this way to share toilets and go to church? Guess I should've splurged on the hotel after all.

Long before Alice got her doctorate and became an anthropologist; long before she married Leo and secured a tenure-track teaching job; and at least a lifetime before she approached me at a mademoiselle's party to tell me I had the most beautiful head of hair she'd ever seen, my 'soul-family friend' (her words) did the same thing that I'd just done. And what, pray tell, was that?

'Ran off to Europe, looking for what was missing.'

She was twenty-one at the time, went to Montpellier in the south of France.

'It's where the college sent people as part of the foreign exchange program. But I didn't bother applying, just went on my own. And what I found was my*self*.'

Given that a mere month ago I was on my own trip, I say, 'Damn, isn't that crazy? That we both—'

She's already shaking her head. 'I told you, Nate. It's no accident.'

'You ever used those Turkish toilets?' says a good-looking young guy as I stretch my sleepingbag on a bunk.

'Can't say that I have.'

'It's an experience in and of itself.'

Carl is Scottish, from Edinburgh, another in a series of kind souls I'll meet on el Camino who are plenty willing to help me however they can. Share their own story, say why it is they're in a foreign country recreating the pilgrimage of ancient Christians.

We go to Mass together, and bizarrely I end up kind of digging it, despite my inner cynic. Something about the small eleventh-century church—with its belfry and steeply slanted roof, its stone sides still pocked by French cannon-fire, courtesy of Napoleon—or maybe the fact that Mass isn't in English, ratchets up a sense of mystery about the whole ritual. If only Mass back home was as strange and otherworldly I might actually go every now and then.

Afterwards, a whole group of us gather near the bunkroom around a long rectangular table cluttered with bottles of red

Rioja wine, crusty baguettes, and Basque cheese bought off a street vendor.

Carl speaks Spanish, periodically translates for the embarrassed (me), but eventually we fall into our own conversation in English while the others chatter on around us. He's just recently graduated college, but doesn't know what to do with himself, can't find his calling. Hence he's here, plans to do the whole hike, which should take about three months, he says. His parents are footing the bill.

Sure, we're both in Roncevalles, this tiny village in Navarre, northern Spain, same point on the path. But by my reckoning Carl's already way ahead of me. He's focused on figuring himself out, getting it together, whereas I don't even know what I'm doing here. I'm only a few years older, but meeting him makes me feel ancient, clueless.

When I tell him I'm only doing a part of the hike—three weeks, tops—because I've just gotten my skydiving license and have been hired on as a tandem instructor at Psycho, he nearly pisses himself with excitement, can't believe it. Says it's the coolest thing he's ever heard.

The playing field levels.

He asks a million questions, and talking about it makes it more real to me. Despite the hundreds of jumps and the two tests I had to take to get licensed, part of me still doubts what I'm doing. Like I'm not really accomplishing anything, am just dicking around. His interest helps.

Since he's so curious, I tell him about my inauspicious first jump with John, watch his amazement with new satisfaction.

'That is in-*sane*,' he says, clearly astonished. 'And you actually kept jumping? You don't have a death-wish do you?'

I raise my eyebrows, shake my head. But I'll confess his question causes me to wonder.

'The thing is, my mom knows none of this stuff,' Brenda says. 'Even the move to Greece is . . . well . . . let's just say I didn't tell her the reason. I didn't tell her about the psychic. She thinks I'm going just because I'm interested in the culture there. Which isn't entirely false.'

My kingdom for a cup of coffee.

'Hey,' I blurt before I even know it. 'I hate to interrupt, but I gotta pee.'

'No, that's good,' she says, snatching the bait. 'I'll get another coffee.'

'Oh, that too.'

Mission accomplished.

Of course, I don't really need to pee, but I go to the men's room for the sake of the facade, plus it gives me a well-needed break from Brenda's Big Story. There's no one in there, so given the privacy I let go of what little I've got. The sudden thought of sex with Sadie (the only woman I fantasize about anymore, even though I haven't seen her in six months) produces a sinking feeling, like someone's letting my air out. Maybe I'll never have sex again, and even if I do it's doubtful it'd be anything but a disappointment after Sadie. When a breathless desire to cry surges up like a wave, I distract myself by reading the manufacturer's label on the back of the urinal. Then the sign over the sink to my immediate left: **Employees Must Wash Hands Before Returning To Work.** Some genius has taken a pen and scratched through *Hands*, scrawled *Pecker* above it.

People.

Moving over to the sink (to wash my *hands*) I see in the mirror that sadness has bunched itself beneath my eyes. It didn't used to be this way. Time was when I could conceal the truth—now everyone knows whether I tell them or not. Who knew aging started so early?

I splash cold water on my face, coax myself to suck it up and get through Brenda's saga. I don't mean to come off like I don't care, because I do. But today I just want to crawl back in bed and disappear. It's entirely possible that nothing's ever going to work out the way I want it to—that's the reality I have to face. I made a mess of everything, it's all my own doing, and just because I've taken some steps toward coming clean doesn't mean everything's now going to fall into place. Losing Sadie's proof of it.

And all Brenda's hot air about 'creating my own reality' seems like just that, another lie to kid me into hopeful longing. Maybe I thought seeing her this morning would help, would pull me out of the funk, but she's not even making a dent. Today's just *murder*, nothing coming easy, and Sadie's dogging me like a depression I'll never shake.

Not that I blame Brenda or anybody else (given my track-record), but no one really gets it: I honestly believed Sadie was different, was the one I'd make a *real* relationship with, maybe even a marriage. Believed she could be the prize for putting my bad habits behind me. And I still believe it—the fact that she bailed doesn't mitigate my own sense of its being *right*, or as right as anything can be in a world run by randomness.

Clearly she has other ideas.

Brenda, on the other hand, doesn't believe in random. Everything in her world happens for a reason, and while that might be something to which I aspire (maybe not) today it won't help me to hear it. Besides, the sky's black above me, and Brenda's only going to blather on and on, bragging about this latest trip to California to see Shuly. How this *huuuge* thing happened that I'm not going to believe.

Believing is only part of the problem—*giving* a damn is the real challenge on a day like today. Much as I love her, my heart's just not in it. There's this part of me that wants to shake her and say, *Sometimes we're just fucked and there's no rhyme or reason to it! And while you're courting the 'divine feminine energy,' how about giving her my number . . .*

You know what I'm saying. Making it through her story will take some doing.

And coffee.

Out of the bathroom I see she's already gotten her refill and settled back at our booth. I retrieve my cup. 'Need anything?'

'You!' says she.

No escape. I'd hoped maybe she'd pick up on my struggle this morning, let me off the hook and send me home. But that ain't happening. So much for all her 'intuitive sensibility.'

God I'm a grumpy bastard.

I refill my coffee, add some honey to spice it up. Maybe it'll be just what I need to get myself going. Pouring the cream I take conscious deep breaths—one after another—readying myself—air traffic control checking in—*You can do it. Hang in there.* I recall this exact scene the very first time I laid eyes on Brenda, so anxious to meet her I made a mess with the cream decanter. Now here I am, actually *with* her, and all I want to do is run. Nothing's enough, never is.

'You look *tired*,' she says when I sit back down.

Part of me appreciates this—she sees!—while another part is saddened by it—I look like hell.

'I'm afraid I'm a bit out of it this morning,' I say, tempering the truth.

'Well, you just relax, sweetie, and I'll do all the talking. When you hear this it's going to cheer you right up.'

Lucky me.

Enter Sadie. Damn, how I love the sound of that, and all it conjures. She's the first woman I dated who got my guard down (such is how Alice says it). What's sad to admit now is that, regardless of all reassurances to the contrary, I'll forever wonder if that's where I went wrong.

One day at Psycho I mention to Doug that I'm considering a professional massage, which I've never had, because all the running I've started doing has me sore as hell. And he refers me to Sadie Weston, whom his wife sees regularly for acupuncture. 'But she does massage, too,' he assures me. And when I call to make the appointment, jotting down directions to her office, something about the way she talks to me gets me a little excited. 'I look forward to meeting you,' she says, and I find myself wondering if she says that to everyone, or did Doug maybe tell her about me . . . ?

Her office is in Foxborough, an old southern mill-town about ten miles south of here that's become a sort of satellite of Ansley Heights. Like lots of these little historic towns (I'd wager), Foxborough has been bought-up by the wealthy and refashioned into a "quaint village of old" (albeit a gentrified version of one). Town Hall still sits squarely in the center, its brick clock-tower restored to tell the correct time, only now it's surrounded by antique and gift shops, fashionable clothing boutiques and frou-frou restaurants whose menus boast pricey entrées, wine lists with no bottle under fifty bucks. The place is also home to lots of alternative health-care practitioners like Sadie, whose office is in a big old house with high ceilings and hardwood floors, a space she shares with two other massage therapists.

One look at her is all it takes—I'd be a gutless fool not to give it a go. She's a tiny thing, fit tightly in a blue body-clinging dress that's shaped like a dream. She has thick black hair, shortish, adorable, and a smile that makes her blue eyes light up.

It's really something, that smile. There's ebullience in it, and warmth, but it's the hint of sadness that sets the hook in me.

Stripped down and stretched out on her table, I actually worry an erection will sneak up and shame me. But it doesn't. Fact is, what I feel while she's working on me seems deeper. My god the *smell* in this place is heavenly, some kind of incense, and a trickle-sound leaks into my hearing—like peace— from a small stone fountain in the corner. Even the cheesy music—undoubtedly produced in a slick, high-tech studio, but fashioned to sound like some primitive tribe buried deep in the Amazon rain forest—sounds luscious, like it's opening up a big space inside me.

Long before she's finished, I've resigned myself to taking the plunge.

She leaves the room after an hour, sixty minutes that seemed an eternity, and allows me time to dress before returning with a glass of water she hands over with a smile. 'How are you feeling?' I don't even answer the question, just jump out the plane's open door by asking if she'll meet me for breakfast sometime, breakfast seeming safer than dinner.

She's shocked—it's obvious—but not necessarily in a bad way. 'I'm not looking for someone to date,' she says, puckering her lower lip in a gesture that says she's sorry to disappoint me. But her bluntness is a turn-on, so I take it as a *Maybe*.

'Yeah, but don't you eat breakfast?'

She does, so we do. Knowing she's not interested in dating, and figuring this is probably the only chance I'll have to talk to her, I throw caution to the wind and ask every question I can think of to piece together her picture, coloring the spaces I can't see. I get the essentials first—age, rank, and serial number—before pressing for more personal stuff: why is she single, why the no dating, has she ever been married, does she have or want children, the like.

'I'm not kidding. You're absolutely beautiful, yet you're single, and don't date. It's just . . . confusing. Not to embarrass you.'

If you ask me, these questions aren't disrespectful—they're what I'm wondering, given the gorgeous mid-forties woman before me, beaming with sprightly warmth. The fact that she's fifteen years my senior might freak another guy out, but as far as I'm concerned it's completely negligible.

And rather than running, she answers my questions without equivocation. No kids, never wanted kids. Lived with a man for seven years, separated when she caught on to the affair he was having on the sly.

The usual.

And we laugh—a lot. She's funny. I don't know if I'd say sparks fly, but something's definitely simmering.

Feeling courageous, I press the dating issue. She says her energy goes to her work—acupuncture and massage. That romantic relationships take more time and energy than she's willing to devote to them.

'I hear you,' says the Suitor, not really buying it. 'But the thing is, *I'm* looking for someone to date.' I smile to underline the joke, ask if she'll humor me, consider having dinner.

We meet downtown the following Friday. Sitting in a windowseat at the Wine Market, I order a Caesar salad with chicken to convey a health-conscious sensibility that's a sham, while she has fried calamari and a side of steamed spinach. She says that during our breakfast date she'd spent the entire time answering my questions—'You hardly let me eat!'—so now it's her turn to find out some things about me.

It's still hard to talk about myself like it matters, but I'm trying. And with Sadie—like Alice—it's easier. I figure she'll want to know all about the skydiving, which will give me the opportunity to impress her with my nonchalance, the casual way I can talk about such a 'dangerous' profession. Win her over with courage, show her the thrill-seeker and risk-taker we instructors represent to those caught in the dull confines of the comfort-zone.

But she surprises me, steers clear of those questions by prying into my past instead, specifically my family. So I tell her about my dead parents, what a disaster I was when they were still alive. I say my dad's death was overdue (given his alcoholism) but that I hit some kind of weird bottom when my mom went, and it was friends who helped me turn the corner. I started taking stock, I say, set my sights less on drinking and drugging, more on relationships with the people around me. 'That's when things really started to . . . *shift*,' I say, tossing off Brenda's word like it was my own.

This kind of talk does something to me, though. It takes on its own momentum, and I don't stop it—all this disclosure to a virtual stranger seems part of it somehow.

I say that *humility* and *gratitude* are becoming my favorite words in the language (who cares if it sounds cheesy), and how I regret not being able to share this side of myself with the people who brought me into the world. Sure I had my problems with them, particularly my dad, who topped the shit-list. Doesn't mean I wouldn't like another shot at getting to know them, at least learn a little more about what made them tick. I have a feeling my mom wanted this, too, maybe even tried—in her way—to make it happen, especially once my dad was out of the picture. There was the night she got so worked-up, that whole business about the nice guy buried beneath the booze—I wish I'd taken the time to encourage the conversation, hear whatever it was she wanted to say. But I guess I just wasn't ready for it, hadn't figured out what my dad's death should've shown me. Because they're gone now, history. 'The whole reason I'm here on this planet is gone,' I say, noting the enormity of it as a hollow spreading inside my stomach.

Suddenly there's a grapefruit clogging my esophagus and my eyes are full. It's like I'm saying all this stuff straight to my parents.

'I'm sorry,' I say, blindsided, embarrassed, wiping wet cheeks.

But Sadie just reaches up and touches my tears with a strange delicacy I can't describe, like something that could cure cancer.

'You're beautiful,' she says.

In my mind, all the stuff I'd read in the travel magazine at Psycho had taken root—the pilgrimage as lonely spiritual quest, an opportunity for relentless self-reflection—and, longshot though it may have seemed, I wanted to make the most of it, give it a sincere go. The messy scene in Max's office had given me a scary glimpse of something I never wanted to see again, and all of the subsequent moves I'd made toward getting my shit together sent me to Spain determined to learn something, *anything*, that might improve my life in the long run.

This is what the trip was supposed to be, and it was. But it was also more than that, not at all what I had in mind. And in this way taught me one of its important lessons—

Things rarely happen the way we want or expect them to.

Maddening to some, I've come to see this as a good thing. Great, even. Life's nothing if not a series of surprises. Not all of them *nice* surprises, but still . . .

Nearly a year after el Camino tried to teach me this lesson, I continue to forget. I set my heart on a fantasy—Sadie, say— carry it around as a dream and wait for Life to deliver it, leave it on my doorstep like something ordered up from room service.

Or I'll actively pursue the dream: map out the route in my mind, the one guaranteed to get me where I want to go. Then stand scratching my head when it turns out the landscape looks nothing like I'd imagined.

The trick is not getting attached to The Way—just walk it. Shoulder that heavy pack and take one step after another, grateful for what's there in front of you rather than regretting how different it is from that picture in your head.

So all that lonely walking I imagined doing? There was a lot of that, sure. But the surprise is that I met more interesting people on el Camino than I'd meet making drinks by the dozens on a busy night at The Cellar. Kind people, fascinating people. People who all seemed to be on a mission of some kind—any kind. Like maybe we're *all* on a mission, and it's not necessarily supposed to be this private thing.

Maybe, more so than we realize, we're all—*all* of us—in it together.

Carl the Scot becomes auspicious detour *numero uno*. That morning in Roncevalles, we wake to the otherworldly sound of Gregorian chants, echoing throughout the high-ceilinged abbey all the way to our third floor bunkroom from a single stereo speaker sitting in the lobby downstairs. Carl and I breakfast at a local restaurant, café con leché with toasted bread and butter. Then—unplanned—we spend the next two days hiking together. We walk through Burguette, and Zubiri, but by the time we make it to the walled city of Pamplona on the third day I'm hobbling along like a near-cripple, both feet seared by blisters from my boots.

Guess I won't be running with the bulls.

I spend three days there, healing up in the plush comfort of sneakers Max wisely insisted I carry, seeing some sights, relaxing. Spain is *old*. You hear this, right? How old everything is in Europe compared to back home? But you've got to come here to *know* it. There's this sense of history I've never experienced before—not just the old cobbled streets and structures, it's like history's floating around in the air. You breathe it in and it gets into your body, your bones, so you start to understand it on a visceral level. Carl's curious about this notion, never having been to the States, so I tell him that everything in America seems new—we're so *young*, a child. And, just like a child, the country I'm from is sometimes clueless, careless, and can act in shockingly selfish ways, as if its own needs matter more than anyone else's.

But hey—it's cool, too, I tell him. 'I'd love to do a hiking trip like this back home.'

'I'll come visit!'

Carl knows a lot about hiking. Along with showing me better ways to load the backpack (putting my socks in plastic bags so they won't stink-up everything else, for instance), Carl also teaches me a blister trick: he takes a needle and a two-inch length of thread, sews it through my blistered skin and leaves the thread there, dangling from my feet. Sleep this way, he says, and the thread will draw out all the gunk, dry-out the blister so it can heal faster. By the time he finishes with me that first night both feet are hairy with all the thread hanging off.

On the second day, after breakfast, Carl hits the trail. He's got months of walking, so can't afford to linger too long in one place. I'm sorry to see him go—he gave me confidence somehow. In the sentimental moment of goodbye, I say as much, make a self-deprecating remark so he'll know how much I've appreciated his help.

That's how much I like the guy—I want him to know.

'You'll be fine,' says the Scot. 'Anyone who makes his living skydiving has a few things to teach the rest of us.'

See what I mean?

'Buena suerta,' I say, having learned a tad of the native tongue, and he walks out of my life.

Sure we exchange addresses, just in case. But that's not what it's about, not really. Chances are I'll never hear from him again, never know if the three months of hiking helped him find the calling he'd come to seek.

No matter. He was in my life, I enjoyed his company, and now he's gone.

The Way.

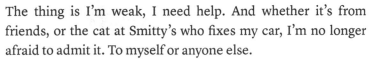

The thing is I'm weak, I need help. And whether it's from friends, or the cat at Smitty's who fixes my car, I'm no longer afraid to admit it. To myself or anyone else.

Therapy coaxes this confession.

Despite some decisive moves—taking up running; quitting The Cellar; ending the affair with Kimberly; even curbing the drinking, the drugs—still I'm drawn to the old ways. What drives me there is loneliness, insecurity about my worth—with guidance I've learned to see this. But also a fatalistic sense of life as fragile, made up of minutes that can end at any given moment. There's this internal quandary: if I truly believe that every minute could be my last, why not live that way, take every risk imaginable? You know what I'm saying?

Why deny myself *anything*?

Says Alice: 'Take risks with *people*, Nate. Live dangerously by being vulnerable, honest. Honest enough that it scares you.'

Subsequent to the surprise wee-hour phone call, the woman who won't go away makes her next appearance on a Wednesday night while I'm home watching a movie. I've not spoken to Kimberly in two weeks (blocked her number from my cell, so she can't even text me) and abstinence—hard as hell, those legs lingering in my memory like the teeth of a trap—has at last started to gain some ground.

Naturally that's when she knocks at my door. What the hell? Unexpected, someone knocking at ten-thirty at night, and the sight of her standing there when I open it is even more so.

She's got this black scarf tied over her face with only her eyes exposed, like those bank-robbers in old movies.

'This is a kidnapping,' says the muffled, pseudo-serious voice behind the bandana.

You want to know the truth of it? Something in me sinks because I'm actually glad to see her.

But damned if I'll say it.

'What the hell are you doing here?' says the supposedly-reformed redhead, feigning incredulity for all he's worth.

She doesn't break character, says to keep quiet, not a peep. Turns me around, takes my hands behind my back and ties my wrists together, me letting it all happen.

Cracks in my armor, sure. I'm digging her antics (to say nothing of my own grave). I remain still while she ties me and—further—puts a blindfold over my eyes. Why not? I'm curious as the cat who gets killed for it.

She leads me out (locking the door for the handless), says not to give her any trouble. Her tone mock-tough. 'Hard or easy,' she says. In the car, she drives me down more lascivious roads than I can see coming, blind on the edge of the passenger seat.

'I'll tie you to the chair first,' she says, then describes fellatio like something she's been deprived of, is starving for. 'But don't get any wise ideas—there'll be no Happy Ending. Not for you, anyway.'

I won't lie to you: there's a new edge to all this, like maybe she's gone over the deep end, is going to drive me out to the lake and drag me in, blind and tied . . .

But her talking reassures me, because it's all the usual stuff. You know the usual I mean?

'I'm so hot I can hardly drive,' she says. 'I'm treating myself to a full dose tonight.'

Of course I'm right there with her. She reaches over and strokes my jeans long enough to see for herself.

'Just as I expected,' says my captress.

When we arrive wherever, she has to help me out of the car. Kisses me deeply, rubs me right there, my knees wanting to buckle, then leads me down a walk of some kind before helping me up a couple of steps.

It's her place: I can feel it.

'Remember the two guys I called you about?'

Long kiss, lots of wetness, a snake-flicking tongue. Now I'm truly nervous, if hotter than hell. I hear the hiss of a lighter, the intake of her hitting it. When she kisses me again she shotguns the smoke to me.

'They're waiting inside,' whispering now. 'Once you're tied to the chair I'll take off your blindfold so you can watch.'

Her tongue takes breaks from the talking to taunt me, and the grass hits me like a shot of heaven.

'Not your hands, though. You'll just have to sit and watch what they do to me—*two* of them. I never knew what I was missing.'

More stroking. My hard-on feels like it's going to break the buttons off my jeans.

'You'll be begging to join us, and if you're a good boy I might consider it—next time. Not tonight. Either way you're gonna thank me, 'cause I like it to last. As lonnnngggg as possible . . .'

Who contrived the notion (save The Church, a bunch of dudes in robes) that there's something inherently valuable about a life of asceticism, of discipline and denial, when instead we could be burning our way through all the booze and women—the endless bounty!—the world has to offer?

I ask again: why say No—to anything that's fun, gives you pleasure—*ever*?

S-squared frequent a bar I'm comfortable in, teetotaler though I purport to be these days. Maybe it's crazy, like putting myself in the path of a freight train, but damnit I need to take *some* chances, and the fact is I like the challenge. Resisting temptation leaves me that much stronger.

Or so I tell myself.

Bars tend to be generic—neon and overloud music (the worst), and countless TVs aiming down from every conceivable angle, the flashy epileptic editing begging for attention no matter how hard you try to ignore it and focus on a conversation—but this place is different. There's not a television in sight, for starters. And the music, though not my flavor, is at least volumed low enough for conversing without screaming. Blue deco fixtures cast a cool glow over lots of black-leather sofas and snug chairs, giving the place a cozy atmosphere.

And they don't allow smoking—keeps me from caving-in to the cigs.

It's not a gay bar, per se, but they account for most of the clientele. I don't linger all that long usually—there's only so much club soda and lime I can stand—but damn near every time I go I get hit-on by nice, even nice-*looking*, guys. Boosts the ego. And when I tell them the truth they don't bail, oddly enough. We often end up having decent conversations, like they're actually interested in me regardless of the prize they won't get (though of course there's the occasional young buck who thinks he can woo me, get me to switch teams).

'I told you,' says Stacy, like a sweetheart. 'Catch of the century.'

Not feeling like the catch of the century, I ask how these two got together. Somehow, hearing the romantic success stories of others feeds a hopeful appetite.

'Just a lucky flip of the coin,' Steven says.

I chuckle, but it's no joke.

'I moved here because it was tails.' Stacy has hands like birds, constantly fluttering around when he talks. 'If the toss had come up heads, I'd be living in Miami right now. Never would've met my saner half.'

I'm looking at both of them trying to figure out what they're telling me.

'Can you believe that?' Steven says. 'Actually, who am I kidding? It's perfectly believable. Just like him. So im*pulsive*.' He sits back in his seat, case closed.

'You really flipped a coin to choose where you'd live?'

Stacy raises his right hand, swearing-in on the stand. 'Mea culpa,' he says. 'But look what happened.'

'Lucky you,' Steven chimes in. 'Not only did you get *me*, you know deep down you're happy not to be living in Florida. You and all those reti*rees*. And can you imagine your wardrobe? I shiver to think about it.'

They get a good laugh from this. Then Steven turns to me.

'But you know, he still loves to flip that damn coin. Whenever we have trouble deciding where to eat, which movie to see, next thing I know he's got a coin out and ready to flip.'

Stacy pulls a coin from his pocket, puts it before us like a priest offering the Eucharist. Then he lifts his wine glass to Steven and says, 'I'd say it's served us quite well, wouldn't you?'

Steven clinks his glass, pecks him on the lips.

Something to shoot for.

I dig into my mom's loaded shoebox, take out the tapes and sit them in the middle of the floor in the living room, like I'm preparing for some important ritual or ceremony. First I fix what for me is a fairly elaborate dinner (pasta with pesto and sun-dried tomato, a salad), after which I wash up the dishes and situate myself on the floor in front of the sofa, lighting a couple of candles Alice gave me. She made them herself, mixing wax remains from old used candles. Alice can do anything.

The tapes aren't labeled in any way and I've no idea how long each one lasts, so just load one into that little micro player and make myself comfortable.

Lots of static at first, then my dad's voice. Very drunk. So strange to hear that voice again, as if I'd forgotten what he sounded like. I have to turn the volume all the way up, and sometimes listen to a statement multiple times to decipher it.

'The Bitch is in everything.'

This is followed by at least a full minute of nothing but silence. Then:

'Everything.'

More silence.

'A nigger's . . . a nigger.'

You get the idea—not a lot of enlightenment. Silence outweighs talking by a longshot, mercifully. When he does talk, it's in cryptic snippets I suppose might make more sense if I was shitfaced. I'm not. I fast-forward through the stretches of silence until I hear him talk, rewind to listen to whatever it is he's saying.

'A miner works in the dark.'

Maybe he thought these were profound observations, but in the warm light of sobriety I hear them as nothing more than the drunken ramblings of a bastard. Sometimes they're bad jokes that say more about the man himself than his sense of humor.

'Give a woman an inch and she thinks she's a ruler.'

Ba-dum *cha*!

I get through the first two tapes, no small task. 'The Bitch' makes multiple appearances, and I assume he means my mom. 'Niggers' get plenty of mention, and it shocks me every time he says it—I never heard him use the word before. Through most of this I'm wondering what the hell my mom thought would be the benefit of my hearing these tapes. Maybe she was as blasted as he when she listened to them, and some black logic led her to the conclusion that this gibberish has some value.

But then I'm blindsided.

Twice.

The first hook hits me right at the beginning of the third tape: I've just fixed a cup of hot tea and am about to fast-forward through the silence when he breaks it:

'I spent so much of my life focused on how different I was from other people. I should've focused on how I was the same.'

What? Did he actually . . . ?

I rewind, listen again.

And again.

He's clearly very drunk—it takes him some time to speak this observation—but every word is enunciated in a way that punctuates what's happening, like maybe he's actually aware of this as a revelation. I notice that he's speaking in past tense, too, like there's no chance to change course.

Which makes his next breakthrough even more telling, given that it's in present tense:

'Wake up and smell the formaldehyde,' he says out of nowhere, breaking a long stretch of silence. 'Your ass is dead.'

He makes this statement in a different voice, clear and emphatic. I rewind and listen again, then stop the tape. Just sit with it. A hollow feeling. I don't know a damn thing about formaldehyde, but there's no mistaking what he means by the remark.

And the more I chew on it, that previous bit about focusing on his differences—that one comment—can't be overstated, not really. Especially given the man who made it. The moment makes its mark on me. I begin to believe that my father was actually learning something. Like maybe it can happen to any of us.

Which would mean the second bit—'Wake up and smell the formaldehyde'—confirms that he was being brutally honest with himself. A first, far as I know.

Of course, I can't claim I *felt* all this at the time. That comes later, once I'm in therapy. I'd been seeing Lynn for a couple of months, and one day without premeditation I launch into the story about my father and the tapes he made.

The guy wanted to be different, I tell her, exceptional. Who doesn't? But he'd go to any lengths to get there, the extremities of brutality and alcoholism included. This helps me connect his comment to the man who wrecked our car, then blamed me for it, standing on the carport in my shorts. Then the slap and the water that came with it. The hatred, everything in me hardening despite a desire to fall to pieces . . .

And Lynn's voice swims through, everything wavy, saying, 'It's okay, Nate. Keep going. Now's the time. Why not share it?'

When at last I leave Pamplona, blisters finally healed enough for hiking, el Camino blesses me with a day to keep. I spend most of the walk on my own, passing a few people but consciously keeping to myself. Something was going on, something different, and I knew it.

This was a chance.

Fortunately, The Way is well-marked—even a lackey like me would have a hard time getting lost. The stretch between Pamplona and the town of Puenta La Reina is twenty-four kilometers, and takes me up four-hundred meters into some of the most amazing mountains I've ever seen. Headed up the trail, I'm surrounded on all sides by waist-high green grasses, waving in the sunny wind like wheat-fields in an American movie set in the Midwest. Once I crest, the land dips briefly before rising upwards again to the top-most ridge, where dozens of gargantuan windmills loom like Don Quixote's worst nightmare. Only these are modern, high-tech windmills, shooting electric power all the way to Pamplona.

Walking amongst them is something. They're wild. And a little spooky, I'll admit. It's impossible not to personify them, these giants whirling their blades at a lone little boy a million miles from anywhere.

My god, *look* at them! The things people do . . .

I catch myself having fun, notice this big shiteating grin on my face for no apparent reason. For *every* apparent reason! My heart races along like it can hardly contain its pleasure, and there's not a single thing in sight that isn't positively breathtaking in its beauty.

Ever get the feeling you're the reason?

> *To feel and speak the astonishing beauty of things—*
> *earth, stone and water,*
> *Beast, man and woman, sun, moon and stars . . .*

From here the trail winds down the mountain, and the view from these upper reaches encompasses all the villages toward which I'm traveling, strung out like destinations ahead of me. I'm surprised to discover that coming down a mountain is harder than climbing it—my blisters start bothering me again despite the moleskin I put on them this morning.

No matter. Today I'm happy.

'I hear you,' I say out loud to my aching feet, promising we'll be there soon. I miss Carl, suddenly wishing I could share the moment. I miss Alice. Which—weird—makes me think of Kimberly, how far away she is, and how one day of this hike would've had her hating me. Kimberly. If it takes a trip to Spain to break the backsliding, so be it.

But her kidnapping's hot on the heels of all my worked-for resolve. I smile to recall it, the two lovers she invented to entice me. Inside her apartment that night, she'd removed my blindfold and untied my hands, me relieved to find us alone.

Hey, even I have limits.

Then she instructed me to put the blindfold on her.

'Do whatever you want—have a field day—and I'll pretend there are two of you.'

Sure, I gave it the old college try—who but a dead man wouldn't? But we'd pulled out so many stops already my trick-bag was pretty much empty.

I shiver even now at the recollection, though, take note of the tingling below. This is her power. It crosses the Atlantic Ocean and climbs the mountains of Spain to find me. It works. I start justifying some ongoing trysts: *What's wrong with some good dirty fun every now and then?*

Then I look around me, feel the sun on my face, reconsider. *Wake up and smell the formaldehyde . . .*

Sadie invites me to dine at her place for our next 'non date.' That's what I call it, making fun of the fact that we're seeing so much of each other but aren't allowed to call it dating.

'I know that's not what you're looking for,' I say, smiling.

Her little house is some distance south of town, in the country between here and Foxborough. There are other houses around, but nothing near enough to call *next door*. Inside, rustic décor betrays her small-town roots—she grew up in Tennessee, the daughter of a school teacher and a father who runs his own construction company, becoming the wealthiest man in town with it, too, she says. (Her father's still there, and a younger brother, but her mom died ages ago, when Sadie was still in high school.) Counter to the country-girl feel of her place, statues of Buddha and Ganesha adorn the rooms, and photographs of her 'spiritual teacher' are all over the place, the way crucifixes and pictures of Jesus might populate a Christian home. I kid you not: this cat's picture is *everywhere*, his robe, matted gray hair and long white beard attesting to his 'wise man' status.

Sure, it makes me wonder. But she says this guy saved her life, that the year she spent living 'in the ashram' got her on course, put her on the path she'd been missing.

This 'path' business I'm getting used to, but Ganesha? Ashram? Guess I'll have to learn a whole new language, but with a teacher like Sadie I plan on being the star pupil. When I'm bad she can spank me with her ruler.

Her dinner is simple but elegant: an arugula salad with mandarin oranges, feta cheese and toasted pine nuts, on top of which rests a spiced pink salmon steak so pretty I almost hate to eat it. Grateful for all the work she's done, I help clear the table once we're finished and dive right into the dishes despite Sadie's suggestion that we just load them into the dishwasher.

'It'll take no time at all,' I say. 'There's not enough here for the dishwasher. Besides, I like doing dishes.'

Might sound like a line, but it's true. Something about washing dishes relaxes me, and at this point I'll take all the help with that I can get—I've wanted to jump her ever since I walked in the door, and the loose-fitting, just-enough-buttons-undone blouse she's wearing only makes matters worse.

Or *better*, depending on how you look at it.

After, we sit on the sofa with cups of hot tea, some herbal stuff she says will be good for me. A detoxifier, she says. Seems all the women I meet these days drink lots of hot tea, so the redhead's joining the ranks.

The fact of everything being so courtly fails to mitigate my ferocious desire to tear off her clothes, ditto the stare of her holy man's picture from the coffeetable, grinning like he knows exactly what I've got in mind. Sadie'd said the guy was 'spiritually evolved,' and whether that's true I can't claim to know. What I *do* know, however, is that under all those robes that cat is carrying the same prick as the rest of us.

Sorry to sound like such a cynic. We all have our strategies, I suppose, and as long as we're not screwing someone over who cares what they are, right? I'm relying on running and therapy, Sadie has her spiritual teacher. And in the words of someone *I'd* say is a sort of spiritual teacher, *Whatever gets you through the night* . . .

Finally I fess up, even if I cut the crudity with a joke: 'Even when I'm sitting down you make my knees week.'

Says she: 'I think I'd like you to kiss me now.'

I have no objection. But once we start and that current runs through me, I know that stopping will be no small task.

So I say as much, take to heart Alice's advice about honesty. I pull back, and confess that at this point she should either send me home or invite me to stay the night. I feel silly for it, like I'm in a Cary Grant movie, but the simple fact is that describing what I feel as *fireworks* doesn't even come close.

Sadie doesn't say a word. Just takes my hand and leads me into her bedroom, where a four-poster bed with all these sheer reddish scarves around the sides looks like a world I'd love to get lost in. Then turns to face me and undoes the remaining buttons on that beautiful blouse, revealing which of my presented options she prefers.

It's crazy, I know, since we've only just met, but I'll say it anyway: for the first time in my life I feel like I'm home.

> Bright petals of evening
> Shatter, fall, drift over Florence,
> And flush your cheeks a redder
> Rose and gleam like fiery flakes
> In your eyes. All over Florence
> The swallows whirl between the
> Tall roofs, under the bridge arches . . .
> Your moist, quivering
> Lips are like the wet scarlet wings
> Of a reborn butterfly who
> Trembles on the rose petal as
> Life floods his strange body.
> Turn to me. Part your lips. My dear,
> Some day we will be dead.

Why I ever quit running is a mystery, but once I start back it becomes as necessary as breathing, or eating. Who—other than Max—would believe it? I'm into the shoes and everything, paying a hefty price for these fancy things that are supposed to be better for the feet, the knees, the back. Now this notion of a marathon. Seems absurd even to consider it.

But when I start doing it regularly, consistently, running gets into my bones. My soul, even. And thanks to my mom I can devote the days to self-improvement. Don't let anyone tell you money doesn't matter—it can buy you *Time*. You selling something more valuable?

The thing is, running *lifts* everything. My body feels better because of it. If I don't run on a given day, I notice the difference: my limbs heavier on my frame, I lug around this weighted-down lethargy. To say nothing of what it does for my spirits. A dark mood can turn to bliss, literally, after putting five miles of pavement behind me. Running becomes the broom that sweeps away the cobwebs.

And it takes the edge off my bad cravings, those that'll send me straight back down the tubes.

So I do it, feeling funny at first. I used to laugh at people, their futile efforts to stave off the inevitable. Not anymore. I run like my life depends on it.

And it was in me all along.

I've never understood cemeteries—a bunch of bodies buried in fancy boxes, using up all that acreage, that space. Big stone and marble markers. What's the point of such a place? I mean, they're *gone*. And thanks to Dottie, I saw firsthand how much all this fuss costs the surviving family—it ain't cheap, this fastidious packing of a dead person into a super-expensive package that'll need one hell of a hole to hold it.

Burn me up—make me a handful of dust—throw me in a river where I can run forever.

But after a couple of trips back home I start to see: the cemetery's a memory, and more—it's a place to go. Admittedly there's something strange about it. I find the spot and sit there, two small arched slabs of stone become my parents. Sometimes I'm silent, just thinking to them. Sometimes I voice what I'm thinking, talk to those stone slabs because they're my parents and there's stuff I want to say now. A lot of stuff.

Do I believe they hear me? Not for a second.

So why do I keep talking?

It's Alice who convinces me to look into therapy.

'You've got the money, what's the downside?'

We're at my place, which Alice is helping me paint. I decided the Penthouse needs a little TLC, and it's Alice's suggestion to paint the whole place white. 'I know it sounds dull,' she says to convince me, even though I don't need convincing. 'But it's kind of dark in here, and white will draw in more outside light.'

This notion of therapy, however, requires coaxing, who knows why? I waffle. I give her some halfhearted rap about wanting to do everything on my own, by myself. If my life is screwed up it's because I made it that way, so I should be the one to fix it.

But she's not buying it.

'First of all, you're not the only one who made it what it is. I'm sure your parents meant well, Nate, and I'm sure they did the best they could but . . . let's be honest—some of that responsibility is theirs.'

I can't say anything.

'Besides, it'll still be your work. That's what you don't understand. A good therapist can help you, guide you to the issues that need addressing. But you're still the one who has to do the actual work. They can't do it for you.'

I hear her, but hate admitting it. I wonder aloud how necessary it is. I mean, I'm doing so much *better*.

'Look. I love you, right? You're a great guy, and there's no doubt in my mind you've done a lot of healing. But you've got a lot of old stuff built up, Nate. It's a heavy load for anyone. You always talk about how you had a first life, back before I knew you—how you were drugged-up 24/7 and all that? That life didn't just go away. I see all you've done to change it—it's obvious, because half the stuff you talk about from back then sounds like a different person. It's hard for me to see you living that kind of life. But a therapist can get to the deeper stuff, really open you up. Take you to the next level. You know I wouldn't say all this if I hadn't experienced it firsthand, right?'

That's what tips the scale: I trust Alice. Completely. And she's seen things in me—possibilities—no one knew were there. More, she's helped *me* see them, believe them. Well, sort of.

So I do it for *her*, to show her. And if it actually ends up helping me—longshot—that'll be icing on the cake.

'Hey,' I say. 'You know I told you how Sadie's got pictures of her guru all over the house? I think I'm going to put pictures of my guru all over the Penthouse. Pictures of *you*.'

'Ha! That's a good one.'

'It's true, though. In theory, I mean.'

'You ask me, we could put up pictures of *lots* of people. Seems like I've learned something from just about anyone I've ever met.'

That's Alice.

Just back from Spain, I call S-squared to check in, find out how things are going. They're the ones who suggest we have lunch, so I meet them at this little Italian place they love. I'm a bit disappointed—a month in Europe means I'm dying for nothing more than a cheeseburger. One thing about S-squared, though, even lunch is a big deal: they'll order a bottle of wine, or bubbles, maybe even appetizers before their entrees. Whenever I join them for lunch, I make sure I hit a bank machine beforehand to pad the pocket.

'Give me the dirt,' I say. 'Do any good consulting while I was away?'

They're both 'business consultants,' whatever that means. I asked them one time and they assured me it didn't matter, would bore me to tears. 'It bores *us* to tears,' Stacy said. 'But the money is plenty exciting. And the fact that we work from home and basically make our own hours.'

In any event, they'll have nothing of my question, not today. 'You're the one who's been around the world. We're all ears.'

I focus on the hiking, say I walked as far as the town of Burgos, about three hundred kilometers total, then pull out my *Credencial* to show them on the map. Point out the stamps I got at each stop. I tell them about all the great people I met, Carl the Scot in particular. And how I hiked the last few days with a group of super-fun Brazilians: Luis, Katia, and Marcos.

'It's like everyone was on a mission,' I say. 'They were there to find something, or learn something. And they made no bones about it. They were talkers, you know? And of course hearing them helped me realize—as if I didn't already—that *I* was there on a mission, too.'

'You mean other than finding some fine Spaniard hunk?' Stacy winks.

'Mucho gusto,' Steven fires back, and they both cackle.

'Tell us a story,' says Stacy. 'Anything. Or something that made an impression.'

I hesitate, wanting to make it good. There's so much. My feet hairy with blister-thread; those gargantuan windmills; the Brazilians singing in Portuguese as we hiked along . . .

Then remember something that's perfect. I describe how, one night at a *refugio* in a town called Logroño, I fall into a brief conversation with a man in his mid-sixties: Alvaro. There aren't all that many pilgrims bunking down this particular night, about ten of us I'd say, but some cat is snoring up a storm and it's keeping me awake. So I get up to go to the bathroom, hoping by the time I come back he'll have stopped, or some braver (pissed off) soul would've waked him, gotten him to turn over or whatever.

Alvaro is sitting alone at a little round table near the eating area just outside the bunkroom, smoking a cigarette and drinking wine from a small straight tumbler. Even out here you can hear the snoring, and when I walk out he says, in English, 'Surprise he no wake him*self* up.' He motions for me to join him, points toward the kitchen with his glass, offers me a cigarette.

I turn down both, heroically. Or stupidly. Wish I knew for sure.

'Why you to walk Camino?'

He's got this great voice, rusty but resonant. I don't sit, just stand in the doorway, say I don't really know why I'm here. 'I read an article about it in a magazine back home, los Estados Unidos,' (as if he didn't know) 'and it got me curious. I've never been a big hiker, but something about the article really struck a chord. So here I am. Y tu?' (I also love throwing in a dash of Spanish I've learned. Un poco!)

'My wife, her heart go.' He says this like that explains it, and when he mentions her heart he brushes at his chest with these big fingers. Alvaro has this intense, weathered face, all these deep lines, and speaks a broken English that makes me want to hug him.

I say I'm sorry about his wife. 'Lo siento.'

'Camino keeps us busy living,' he says.

I'm mesmerized by his hands, which are enormous, fingernails like nickels. Hands I always wanted. The kind of hands that could pry nails from an old board, palms you could strike matches on. With hands like that a guy could do damn near anything.

He says he'd hoped el Camino would help with his grieving, plus he could mark her passing with something other than a funeral. Something *substantial*, he says.

I ask how it's going. Does he think it's helping?

He nods. 'Every step I feel. Every step . . . it has meaning.'

It's quiet and I'm not sure if I should probe, or back off. After a moment more, I observe that the snoring from the bunkroom seems to have stopped.

'You sleep now,' Alvaro says, which I take as a hint.

'Tu tambien?'

He shakes his head, drags one of those big fingers down a thick crease in his face. 'Es difícil.'

So I say goodnight, but throw caution to the wind and thank him for sharing his story with me. Then damn the torpedoes and say how amazing it is that everyone I meet on el Camino is so honest about the motive behind their pilgrimage—the real reason for their being here—even when those reasons are intensely personal. 'Like your story,' I say.

And he looks at me sternly with that weathered face: 'Why does this surprise? What is worth talking about, if not Life?'

I know it's from Kimberly, the handwriting obvious on the padded manila mailer in my box, to say nothing of the smartass sentiment: it's addressed to *Mr. Clean?*, the question-mark punctuating her sarcasm. But opening it I've no idea what she's sent me.

Of course, the second I see it's a homemade dvd something sinks. I'm slow on the draw, I guess. There's a note: *You may fool those new friends of yours, but not me. You're just as dirty as the rest of us.*

Given what I'm now guessing, why should I even bother confirming? Why not just toss the damn thing?

But of course I put it in the player—that compulsive curiosity I can't seem to shake.

I'm nervous, make no mistake. But after only a few minutes with Lynn I start to settle. Her office is in a long, two-story structure in yet another ubiquitous office park, but inside the vibe is very different. It's cozy and pleasant, less like an office than like a room in someone's house. A study, say. I sit on a comfy couch facing her chair, a big bookcase behind her and an uncluttered coffeetable between us (a little wooden stand with her business-cards, a clock with its back to me), and while the wall to our left has no openings save the door I came in through, the wall to our right is taken up entirely by a large picture-window that's as wide as the room itself, nothing but trees beyond it so the light filtering in feels almost green.

This time yesterday I'd no notion that in twenty-four hours I'd be sitting in a shrink's office, but Stacy was insistent enough—once he heard I was considering it—to take out his cellphone right there at the restaurant and call his therapist, Lynn Inman. See if she could take on another client.

'She's wonderful,' Stacy says. 'Changed my life.'

'I'll second that,' Steven throws in, toasting and smiling slyly.

'It's true, Nate. You can't imagine all she's done for me. I'm calling her.'

Next thing I know he's got that damn phone out. She doesn't answer, he leaves a message, and I think I'm off the hook. That is until she returns his call just after we order coffee.

Listening to the way he talks you'd think it was his best friend on the phone, not his shrink. He's laughing and teasing, being Stacy. There's nothing at all formal about it.

This helps. A little.

He tells her why he's calling, says I'm 'a gem.' This helps, too.

'Tomorrow at three?' He lifts his brows at me.

I hem and haw.

'He'll be there,' he says without waiting another second.

It's Saturday, and Sadie has suggested something fun. So fun, in fact, I wish I could claim credit for coming up with it

'Leave it to me,' says the Pretty Thinker.

Before we went to bed last night, she went around her house covering up all the clocks, all save the one on the nightstand, which she simply turns face-down. I think of Max and his clock shenanigans in college, but Sadie's got other ideas.

For one single day we will not be slaves to Time.

And what a day. We make love before the sun's up, linger lazily in bed just looking at each other, like we can't believe our eyes, or our luck. Who knows how long we do this? Who cares?

'Say Ananda,' she says out of nowhere, breaking our long silence.

I repeat the word as instructed.

She tells me this is her 'spiritual name,' one she selected for herself during her year in the ashram. It's a Hindu word, which she defines for me as meaning *full consciousness*, or *bliss*.

'If you're ever having a hard time reaching me,' she says, all serious, 'and we can't seem to hear each other, or *understand* each other, use my spiritual name, Sadie Ananda. Reach out to my Higher Self.'

I'll reach out for any self she offers—the lower one's plenty enticing, too.

Hunger eventually carries us to the kitchen, and once breakfast is made we sit outside on the deck to eat. Already it's gorgeous out, sunny and clear, and another part of her plan is that we'll not wear one stitch of clothing all day. Good thing Sadie lives in the country.

Naked in the sun we sip mimosas from tall crystal champagne flutes. Sadie's not sure about this, now knowing a bit more of my immoderate history. But I promise it's fine, and it is—I know it. Sadie's the drug that can outshine any other, though admittedly the one mimosa I allow myself starts to feel like salvation after only a few healthy sips.

I ask her to tell me what she was like as a little girl. Sure it sounds hokey, but I tell you I'm genuinely curious. I want to know everything. I could listen to Sadie talk forever.

She smiles, humors me. Says she had what could be called a 'textbook idyllic childhood.' She describes growing up in rural Tennessee, near Chattanooga, as heavenly. Her parents were happy people, good to one another. They had land, farmed much of their own food, raised chickens and goats. She and her brother learned early the importance of a healthy diet.

'The way people eat these days would horrify my mother.'

I ask if there was anything she wished would've been different, something missing. Hard for me to believe in an idyllic childhood.

She just shakes her head. 'Sorry, there's no dark secret. Not much of one. My dad worked pretty much all the time, so I didn't get to spend as much time with him as I would've liked. But still—every child should grow up in such an environment.'

She also admits missing the ocean. 'We were in this gorgeous valley, surrounded by mountains. But the first time they took me to the coast I just couldn't believe it. It was the most magnificent thing. And to this day I'm drawn to the ocean in a way that's magical. The mountains are Home to me, the place where my soul just . . . relaxes. Takes a deep breath. But the ocean's different—it's what I'd call a more *expansive* thing. Whenever I start to feel hemmed in, antsy, take me to the beach so I can see the ocean.'

When she says such things, giving me instructions that seem to insinuate a future that includes me, I want to weep. Or jump for joy.

Hey, it's all the same to me.

I tell her I'm glad she had such a childhood. 'Seems like everyone's family has some kind of weird dysfunction.'

'I know,' she says. 'But it's not true of ours. There's not one thing I'd want to be different. Though all that kind of changed once mom died . . .'

Her voice—and her gaze—trails off: I can see her go someplace, and wonder if I'm supposed to follow. But after only a few moments she looks back at me with this big, beautiful smile, her eyes all shiny and lit-up when she says (in, I swear, this dreamy voice), 'Where did you come from? You're not from this world.'

I know—it's like something out of high school. But when was the last time *you* found the love of your life?

I'm thinking I'd like another mimosa, but know better. Instead, I lean over to kiss her, unable to help—or conceal—the erection.

Says she: 'Is that for me?'

Next thing I know we're having another go, only now we're on a blanket stretched in the grass of her backyard. And this time's different. In fact, it's not like any experience I've ever had. Nothing could've prepared me for it.

I don't know how to talk about this.

The thing is I'm lost, or at least that's what I think at first. Once inside her we move together very slowly, nothing urgent, everything quiet and calm and feeling so good I know it won't last long. I shut my eyes, and it's like something releases and leaves me in this immense, wide-open space. It's real dark, but not at all scary. Again, the sense of it is of endless openness . . . *space* . . . rather than the closed-in claustrophobia I associate with darkness.

Expansive is what Sadie would call it.

I keep my eyes closed—though I long to look at her, I don't want to leave this space I'm in. We move together with no sound, mutually lifted into a place I all at once recognize. Some part of me knows that I've been here before.

Is there a collective unconscious, a place from which all souls come and to which all return? There is. I've seen it. I was that soul. I was there.

Label me a loony. There are worse things.

So I'm not lost, not really. I'm *found*. A thin line connects me to the land of the living, and Sadie provides the passage that allows me to roam the cosmos, safely, farther from any earthly feeling than I can travel without dying. Her writhing body beneath me is a beautiful conduit.

I climax and I cry, in that order. And when I hear the sound of Sadie, I open my eyes and there she is. Smiling and looking straight up at me, tears streaming down the sides of her face.

'You're here,' says she.

'*You're* here,' says I.

There's this long pause. I wonder if I'm completely crazy. Then she says, 'We've been looking forever, haven't we?'

Loony times two. She'd been there as well.

The dam broke that day, exploded, and for me,
now, nothing will ever be the same, regardless what
the future brings. Like the greatest teacher of all
Love has given me a glimpse of capacities always questioned
with a quiet skepticism I couldn't squelch, but once we
met in that darkened expanse and admitted—or knew—
the other was someone we'd sought, the sweet agony to
    which I became
so wonderfully subject upon finding you made me understand
the power of those onrushing sentiments the sluice had kept
concealed until we broke through it and bathed in the wash . . .

Here's the problem: the night I disdained my marriage vows on the floor of Rebecca Benton's empty living room, I not only destroyed my commitment to Margaret, I hurt her. Broke her heart.

But what an *experience*. I shiver—in the best way—to recall this, so grateful to have been there. And isn't that why we're here, to wrest what we can from our days?

But more significantly, if I hadn't made that 'mistake,' I never would've met Sadie. Never would've known what it's like to find the missing piece of the puzzle, this woman in whose company I feel something akin to completeness. Wholeness and clarity, beyond anything I ever imagined.

How are we supposed to make sense of such things, these endless contradictions? Are there really good reasons to break the hearts of others? Or am I just like my dad—a selfish son of a bitch who'll rationalize every move he makes?

Fucking insanity. Where I shop, they're on aisle eleven: detergents, cleansers, sponges and mops, the like. Next time you go to the grocery store, pick up one of these things and take a good long look. *Feel* it. They're wrapped in plastic, but still you can try to set it, get an idea of the pressure of that spring. Just standing there in the store I'm hit with this wave of incredulity that makes my blood boil.

A mousetrap, for killing rodents. But the thing would crack my knuckles like twigs, and that crazy fucking father of mine set them for my mother.

His wife.

You see what I mean? Why do we need each other?

How long can I keep sitting in this coffeeshop? Well, with Brenda in charge, this earth-shaking story of she and Shuly and the Divine Feminine Whatever, there's no telling. She'll put a hurting on that seat she's in, draw this thing out for so long it'll make my head spin.

God I'm a mess.

'The thing is, I'm *safe* with Shuly,' she says. 'I can just *be*. I don't have to worry how she's going to respond to something I say, because she just *gets* it. We speak the same language.'

I know all this already. Brenda often gets sidetracked during a story. If she were a writer, her book would jump all over the place. By page fifty, I'd be frustrated and thinking, *Stick to the story*!

'But this is key. I mean huge. *Huuuge*. No matter how bad I feel about not being able to tell mom about Greece—or not being able to tell her the whole story, why exactly I'm going and all—it's not my fault. She just wouldn't get it. And what I learned from my mentor—did I tell you about my mentor?'

No. Tell me we're not adding that to the mix.

I shake my head and say not that I recall.

'Oh that's a *whole* other story. Remind me to tell you. Oh . . . this guy is just amazing. He's just so far ahead of what most of us ever come into contact with.'

'Wow.'

I mean it (kind of skeptical, truth told), but I'm not doing a good job feigning enthusiasm at this point. What am I even doing here? It's not like her story—whatever it is—will change one thing, make me feel any better. She going to tell me Sadie called her, said she wants me back? In other words, why am I wasting our time here this morning?

Because sharing this stuff will make *Brenda* happy—bottom line. Makes it worth sweating out, I guess.

'Anyway, one of the things I got from my mentor is that people have to learn to recognize their real family. I mean, just because someone is blood family, that doesn't mean they're your *real* family. Your *spiritual* family. And I've worked hard to find my spiritual family, the people who know where I'm coming from. Who really get it. Mom's a great woman, and I love her dearly. But our paths are different. It's . . . if I tried to tell her how I really feel about certain things, how I really *am*? It'd blow her mind. She just wouldn't be able to handle it. This thing that happened with Shuly? Whoa! No way. No, no, *no* way. There just aren't that many people I can tell it to, and definitely not mom.'

So what is it? What happened? *Stick to the story*!

It's weird when something like this happens. I pay no attention to news, but when I get to work it's immediately apparent that something's up.

Seems an outfit like ours—outside of Columbus, Ohio—had an accident. One of their planes took off for a routine run and something went wrong. Not long after takeoff the thing plummets— witnesses say they heard a sputtering sound, next thing you know it's down, kills everyone onboard. Six jumpers and a pilot.

The plane was a single-engine Cessna 210. Figures. We have a couple of Cessnas—the 206 and the 182—but I'm rarely on them because I don't trust them. There's something about those planes that just doesn't *feel* right, doesn't feel solid or something. (Mind you, everyone at Psycho says I'm paranoid.)

Fortunately we use the Twin Otters most of the time, the DHC-6, which I like a hell of a lot better.

Anyway, this crash in Ohio sends shock-waves throughout the whole skydiving community. We're all reminded of the different things that can go wrong, and how dangerous the job is when they do. Not like an office printer needing toner. No matter how much preparation I go through to ensure that my client and I will be safe, that damned plane could malfunction and . . .

Six skydivers—all dead with unopened rigs on their backs. Like I say to people who are shocked by my profession: sitting patiently in that hunk of metal while it climbs air to reach the clouds is the hard part. Jumping out of the thing is a breeze.

Not to mention a *blast*.

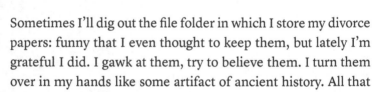

Sometimes I'll dig out the file folder in which I store my divorce papers: funny that I even thought to keep them, but lately I'm grateful I did. I gawk at them, try to believe them. I turn them over in my hands like some artifact of ancient history. All that officialdom, that long arm of the law reaching in and claiming control of our lives. So strange.

Me and Margaret. *Me* and Margaret. That was *me*. The life I made such a mess of. It's right here in front of me—black and white—signed and sealed and delivered.

Never forget. Frailty.

'Well, this was about a year later, I guess. That time he blamed me for wrecking the car, that would've been junior year. So yeah . . . that's . . . this definitely would've been *senior* year.'

My shrink's pushing this, for some reason. So to hell with it. What've I got to lose?

'I was watching television. I don't like to admit it, Lynn, but I watched a lot of television. What kid didn't? It was the device of our day. And this particular time I noticed their raised voices coming from the back bedroom. Well, I should say I heard my mom; I didn't hear him. But I mean, this kind of thing happened all the time. *All* the time. So I didn't pay any attention to what was being said—just noticed they were fighting.

'Next thing I know my mom's in the kitchen. I didn't know what she was doing until my dad came in, and what I heard him say was, "Hold on! Wait a minute." Something like that. It's not so much what he said as the tone in his voice. He sounded . . . well . . . *desperate*. That's the word, actually. He sounded desperate. Like there was something urgent in the way he said it.

'Normally I'd just try to ignore them, same as always. I mean—again—this went on all the time. It just pissed me off that as usual they'd brought it into the kitchen instead of staying in their room. So now I had to hear it.

'But there was that thing in his voice—that urgency. So I turned around to see what was going on. And what I saw, the reason they'd moved into the kitchen was my mom was standing by the sink with this big half-gallon bottle of vodka. Like she was about to pour it out. And my dad said again (with his voice kind of dragging in that way it did when he'd hit The Wall, usually late in the day), "Just *wait* . . . a minute."

'You know, in retrospect it's like I can see all this stuff in slow motion. I remember details that may not be exactly right, you know? Like maybe I'm making stuff up. But that's just the specifics—the gist of it's right.

'Anyway, it looked to me like my mom made a big decision. At that *moment*, I mean. As I say, I could be inventing some of these particulars. They both just sort of stood there for a minute. Nobody moved. Then I could see my dad sway a little bit—this sway he had damn near all the time, because he was always drunk. Just a matter of degrees. And I noticed he sort of leaned on the counter, like he was holding onto it, and I swear it looked to me like my mom's face changed. I mean, I don't think I'd remember this if it didn't happen, because it was so obvious. Her expression seemed to go from being scared to being . . . um . . . *determined*. That's the look. I'm sure of it. And that's when she started pouring that vodka down the drain.

'The rest . . . well, it all happened so fast. I couldn't tell you exactly what he did but I saw him grab at her, and then I just remember this . . . this awful scrabble of limbs . . . it was shocking. And I was right in the middle of it before I even had time to consider where I was headed. On the sofa one minute and the next thing I know I'm standing between my parents.

'But you know . . . I got real clear. I remember becoming *really* conscious of what was happening. My mom was behind me—I'd stepped between them to block him—and it's like . . . it's like she disappeared from the scene altogether. And all the anger I felt was just looking to come out. I can't tell you exactly what I said—I honestly don't remember. But I can tell you it was ugly. I threatened him for sure. Like in a year—from that time on the carport to then—I'd stopped being scared of him. In fact, at *that* moment, seeing him grab my mom like he did? I just . . . I was *looking* for a reason to unload on him. I really was. I goaded him. Again, I don't remember what I said exactly, but I know I told him if he touched her again I'd take him apart. That I know. And I meant it.

'And I *prayed* he'd make a move. I really did. Try to intimidate me the way he always did, the way he'd been doing my whole life. Because then I could do it—I could really let him have it.

'Even thinking about it now, all this time later, I mean . . . I guess it's a good thing he didn't do anything, because there's no telling what would've happened. It's just . . . I was *ready*. He'd always been such a bastard, and genuinely scary, but at that moment I knew the tables had turned. He was just this wobbly old drunk. I could've destroyed him, and the fact is I . . . I *wanted* to. My god I can't begin to tell you. I actually taunted him. I *tried* to get him to make a move. I begged him to give me an excuse to kick his sorry ass because that bastard had abused my mom for too long, and damnit those days were *over*. I was ready to prove it.

'And he knew it, too. It was written all over his face. I was staring straight at him—like I don't think I'd ever really looked him in the eye before—and he looked like this little kid who'd just been scolded by his parents. And while I'm waiting on him to take one step toward me, he just mumbled something— something totally unintelligible—and turned to go back to the bedroom. Swaying like crazy—I'm surprised he didn't fall down. Hell, I could've *blown* him over. And I hate to say it but . . . I was actually disappointed. Because I wanted it to happen. This was my chance. I wanted to just . . . really give that bastard the beating he deserved . . .

'I'm sorry. I don't mean to get all . . . It's just . . . I felt such a *hatred* I can't tell you. I mean it's like I hated him with every fiber of my body and I just wanted to unleash it all on him but . . . I mean . . . what's so frustrating *now*, or what I can't seem to shake no matter how hard I try, is how *sad* it is. Which I can't fucking *stand*. That I can't just stay mad at him. But it's just that . . . it's not like I didn't *want* to like the guy, right? I mean, that guy I hated so much and wanted to . . . to . . . you know . . . that guy was my *father* . . .

Maybe it's obvious to most people, but I'm just now starting to see something.

It's one thing to want to change. Coming to the conclusion is the easy part. But then you have to do it, take the necessary steps to enact it.

You have to change.

Me, I'd always thought there'd be another way.

I put a card in the mail to Dottie, thanking her for all she did after Mom's death. Not only that, but apologizing for having been so out of it, so useless when it came to dealing with the funeral arrangements, the selling of the house. That money still supports me, and I wouldn't have it were it not for Dottie. I should've said these things long ago, but I'm trying to buy that better-late-than-never business.

I also say that next time I make a trip down there to visit the cemetery, I'll let her know, stop in and say hello.

After all, she was Mom's oldest friend, might have a thing or two to teach me. About *both* my parents. And I'm ready now, ready to learn what I can about them. Because when Dottie dies, that world—the world I come from—is gone forever.

'Where did you come from?'

It's the line Sadie continues to give me like a gift, dreamily, again and again. Every day I ache to get to her, she to me. Being apart is a rapturous agony. As I'm finishing up for the day at Psycho, I'll find messages she's left on my phone. 'Where *arrrrrrre* you?' Her voice full of a longing that seems to have my name on it. 'I need you *heeeeeere*. You've turned me into a junkie.'

With Sadie, everything's an adventure. Staying home doing nothing is a miracle. Holding hands sends shockwaves through my whole body and having sex becomes a transport to Paradise.

Inspired, I use her digital camera to make a photo essay I call *The Road To Bliss.* 'Ananda,' I say, showing off. Pictures of our clothes in a clump on the kitchen floor; or strewn over the sofa in the living room; or a long line of stripped garments leading back to the bedroom. She just shakes her head, says I'm silly.

I'm silly? 'You should talk!'

Sadie says that food tastes forty-five percent better after lovemaking. Hence, at three-thirty in the morning—having gone to bed at eleven and awakened three hours later to that entangled ecstasy we can't get enough of—we'll sit in her kitchen gratefully gorging sudden appetites on hot bowls of oatmeal. We find ourselves in that kitchen at all manner of hours these days. So strange to eat in the middle of the night, but—she points out, smiling—notice how the oats taste forty-five percent better?

As do chips and salsa.

Cheese toast.

Ice cream.

Who would've imagined (least of all me) that a woman like

Sadie—older, spiritually minded, conscious of keeping her body and soul healthy by watching what she puts into both—could be such a *blast*? I always thought you had to go one way or the other, like there's Kimberly or there's Marian the Librarian.

And let's face it—a good book (great, even) pales in comparison to the other.

But Sadie strikes a balance. I'm not sure if she knows it, but it's like I'm taking internal notes when we're together. She shows me there's nothing wrong with an indulgence here and there, nor is there anything wrong with taking care of yourself, staying in shape, physically and otherwise.

She shows me we can have it *all*, in other words.

It's not like we don't have our hurdles, though. Says The Lady Sadie, one day out of nowhere, 'I wish you didn't do what you do. Jumping out of planes.'

This surprises me. Usually women *love* what I do.

'What about you? All those men parading in there for acupuncture and massage, naked on your table.'

We make a deal. I'll try acupuncture, she'll 'consider' coming skydiving.

On her table two days later I'm not at all nervous. Fact is I'm excited. A couple of the needles send a current when she puts them in, but it's brief.

And sixteen needles later I lay still, eyes closed, feeling. Just feeling. Crazy, but those needles are *deeply* relaxing, like dropping a lude, and the peace becomes a kind of buoyancy. If a guy like me can pull it all together, get to the place I am now, then there's no limit to Life's potentials. I'm awash in the possibility of *everything*. Every dream coming true, every miracle at once imaginable. Heaven is here, now. The world is generous and bountiful, bestowing its biggest gifts only when we can grasp them. Only when we're prepared to embrace all that is there, all that there is. Within us.

Heaven is *right here*.

After fifty minutes she removes the needles, and tears, sprung from some place she'd penetrated, come without warning. It's like I've been in a trance, gone someplace else, and coming back is scary somehow.

She touches my face. 'What is it, baby?'

'Don't go,' is what comes out of my mouth, no idea why. 'Please don't go.'

When I take the time to dig deep and think about what's going on (not often enough, but more now than ever before), there's this new awareness that I'm no longer on my own, flying solo—I have friends helping me along, not only as company but also leading me toward new horizons I'd never noticed. So just prior to the massage that will add Sadie to the mix, I arrange a big dinner date: S-squared, Alice and her husband Leo, my lovely man Max and Catherine. I want these worlds to come together.

But I'll admit I'm nervous. These people who've done so much for me, who've reinvented the world and my place in it— what if they don't hit it off?

Since the Penthouse is really too small for a dinner party, Alice and Leo host. Leo's just back from his research trip to Africa, so it'll be fun to have people over, she says. I give Max directions, pick up S-squared myself so we can carpool, and by seven-thirty the whole herd of us are gathered around the table like a gang of old pals. Pre-made sushi rolls are passed around on big platters Leo picked up from a Japanese place, and Alice has complemented the sushi with homemade Miso soup and a spinach salad. The rest of us contribute by bringing bottles of wine (though Yours Truly brings a couple of big San Pellegrinos), and in no time at all my nervousness evaporates. Maybe it's their home—warmly-lit, bookcases everywhere, framed maps and photographs on walls dotted here and there by tribal masks they've acquired on their travels—or maybe it's just all these cool people in one place. Whatever the source, I'm comfortable in a way I wouldn't have predicted. Even Leo, about whom I'm a bit paranoid—like maybe I'm the guy who moved in on his wife while he was away—welcomes all of us like he's genuinely excited to meet us. He even makes a point of thanking me for keeping Alice company during his absence.

'These big trips usually backfire at some point, and she gets mad at me for going.'

Alice drops her head, smiling. 'It's true, I hate to say it. The first week he's gone I love it. It's nice to have the space, I can get a lot done, that kind of thing. But then I start to miss him and wonder why we thought him going to do fieldwork on the other side of the world was such a great idea.'

'This time I get back and she's all happy. Me and Nate did this, me and Nate did that . . . '

'Well, it's like the time just flew by,' Alice explains. 'I was so excited to have Nate around. One more academic party with colleagues and I'd lose it.'

Crazy, all this. Admittedly it's a selfish pleasure, given the common denominator connecting the couples. I seem to be the subject of every conversation, these generous people singing my praises as if I'm not sitting right here with them. Like being at your own funeral. But I just kick back and dig it, relish reliving the anecdotes of our meeting each other, the wildly opposing ways we came together. Max knows All, but S-squared never heard how I met Alice at a party where neither of us knew a single person; and Alice never knew about that dreadful night at Boxers, the gay bar where I pushed my luck way past the breaking point before a stranger named Stacy stepped in to save me from a certain beating.

'So you guys knew the *old* Nate,' says Alice.

'We didn't know him, but let me tell you, honey—he was a *sight* that night. Just a shambles. But Steven's my witness: it didn't even matter. You could see there was something going on with this guy. Something different.'

'Oh my god, I felt *exactly* the same way when I met him at that party! It's like I knew within minutes there was something extraordinary about Nate.'

Their exact words. Who's a lucky bastard?

'Of course we hated he wasn't gay,' Steven says, surprising me. 'We've got friends who *need* someone like him. Desperately.'

'Hard to imagine,' I say, not quite believing what I'm hearing. 'Unless they're looking to jump out of an airplane.'

This is met with a general uproar around the table, equally unbelievable even though I more or less asked for it.

Stacy turns deadly serious.

'Listen, it will happen. You know what Steven and I say— you're the catch of the century.'

Steven smiles, touches Stacy's shoulder lovingly. 'It's true. And that's why *I* for one am *glad* you're not gay. I'd have to rein-in my boy here!'

Laughter, but Stacy's right back on me.

'I mean it, Nate. You just keep doing what you're doing. When you're ready—*really* ready—she'll come out of nowhere.'

Alice makes a show of relief. 'I'm *so* glad you said that, because that's my feeling about it, too. And that woman? You know how lucky that woman is going to be?'

Less than a month later I step into Sadie's office for a massage, having been referred by coworker Doug. No lie. My friends are like prophets, pointing out signposts for the blind.

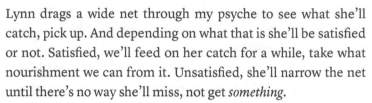

Lynn drags a wide net through my psyche to see what she'll catch, pick up. And depending on what that is she'll be satisfied or not. Satisfied, we'll feed on her catch for a while, take what nourishment we can from it. Unsatisfied, she'll narrow the net until there's no way she'll miss, not get *something*.

The wide net catches my divorce; the dysfunction of my family; my frequent flirtation with unhealthy habits.

The narrow net catches my fear that I'll make a failure of everything I try. That I'm not worthy of Happiness, even were it handed to me on a caterer's silver platter.

Though we spend the stray night at the Penthouse, I spend most nights at Sadie's: the cramped quarters of my place are fine by me (pretty cool, actually), but Sadie's *house* is admittedly more like a *home*, and I know she's more comfortable there. Whenever I show up, she comes running out of the house and throws her arms around me, like I'm returning from The War. Other times she'll greet me wearing something sexy. 'Where have you *bennnnn*?' she says in that voice dripping with longing.

My brain works differently when I'm with her. I think in new ways, an opening-up feeling. Ideas flood me. Big ones, little ones.

We should take six months off, travel in Europe or Asia. We should both make a list of ten things (twenty, fifty!) we want to do before we die, then get to doing them, taking turns from each list. Move to Spain or Morocco, immerse ourselves in a different culture, maybe hike el Camino in its entirety. Take a Thai cooking class, save our money to buy a hot tub for Sadie's deck. Surely I'll be moving in with her in no time . . .

Case in point: when Bill calls a meeting at Psycho to say our numbers are down, my Sadie-sparked brain suggests that a couple of us crash the college campus on a campaign to promote recreational skydiving.

'No way,' says the boss. 'Great idea, but not on campus. It's illegal.'

I won't be swayed.

'So we set up just off campus, like outside the post office, adjacent to the main quad.'

Talk about a brainstorm. Mike and I don jumpsuits (geeky as it seems), load-up a table with flyers and photographs, and start reeling them in. The spot I'd suggested is an artery that connects campus to downtown, so from eleven until three in the afternoon the parade of students looking for lunch takes more people past our table than we can keep up with, answering questions and handing out flyers. We do this on a Monday and a Wednesday, and the weekend following is one of our busiest in forever at Psycho.

Sure there's the coed factor to contend with, what Mike calls the parade of poontang. And on Wednesday there's a theatre-group parked near us, seriously cute chicks, eager and bubbly trying to raise money for an upcoming performance. A magic-markered cardboard sign attached to their table—**The Cabaret Players—PLEASE DONATE**—causes me more than a couple of double-takes throughout the afternoon: **The Cabaret Players—PLEASE DO NATE**.

But if you want the truth of it, I dig the show with no real urge to take it any further than a little flirting. When Mike makes a joke about setting up our table near sorority row, I say I'm done with child care.

'I found a *woman*.'

'Fuckin-aye,' he says. 'She's got you right where she wants you.'

'Correction: she's got me right where I want to be.'

It's true, I don't care who believes it. Or doesn't. When I'm with Sadie—wherever—it's Home. Something I've never known, but I recognize it just the same.

And when I'm at her house, in her space, the possibilities are endless. The Imagination begins to breathe, soar.

Headquarters.

PART THREE

Jam Master . . . Stonehenge Comes To Fox-borough . . .
Even Alice . . . Another Park, Another Saturday . . .
26.2 in 3:18 . . . Cross The Bridge, Or Burn It? . . .
Missing Rebecca . . . Dottie Spills Some Beans . . .
'What's The Downside?' . . . Beware The Soup Aisle . . .
More Icing For The Shitcake . . . Soccer Mom
To The Rescue . . .

And to think I'd almost cancelled on Brenda this morning, spared myself the coffeedate that never ends. Why hadn't I? Well, she'd just gotten back from California, all excited about her trip and anxious to tell me about it, so when she called to suggest we meet for coffee I suppose I was thinking it would do me good to get out, make an effort. Spend time in someone *else's* head since mine was only making me miserable.

But the minute I wake it's clear I'm going to have one of those days, which is when I consider cancelling. Still dark out, Sadie sneaks into my bed just long enough to whisper in my ear what's missing, the thought of being curled up with her enough to sink an already-leadened spirit. I'd make a deal with the Devil, let

God lop-off a decade of my life to have her here. But what I wake with instead is the knowledge that not only is she somewhere else, she'll never be in my bed again. Involuntarily, I recall the first night she spent here in the Penthouse—at this point I'd let myself be lobotomized to wipe it from the memory-banks. Taking a cue from Alice, I'd put candles everywhere, and we stayed up late in the flickering light with me as Jam Master, Sadie asking me to play her some of my favorite music. At some point a big storm roared in, all this lightning and loud thunder, and she insisted we take off our clothes.

'There's nothing like making love during a thunderstorm.'

I'm happy to oblige.

And when I woke later in the pre-dawn morning, she put her cheek against mine and whispered, 'Good morning, beautiful man,' and lightly kissed my eyes, my cheeks, my chin. My god the things she said to me. She talked about my body like a precious object, a work of art.

'Sometimes while you're sleeping I just sit up and watch you, look at you. So lovely.'

I laughed this stuff off when she said it, thinking it was silly, funny. But now I'm realizing it wasn't funny—it was a windfall, my one chance at hitting the jackpot.

Remember *The Road To Bliss*, my photo essay for Sadie, various shots of our clothes in a clump where we'd peeled out of them on our way to Paradise? Well, I take it up a notch by putting together a series of poems under the same title to give her for our upcoming *mensiversary*, our fourth month together.

*Anniv*ersary? Hey, why wait a whole year to celebrate?

The idea is that the poems will reflect my state of mind *before* Sadie and *after* Sadie, so she'll see the shift in my perspective and how instrumental she is to it all. I have a great time poring over the pages of all these books I haven't looked at in ages, glad that I always marked the poems I preferred because now it's saving me scads of time as I try to select ones for Sadie's present. I don't pull any punches, either. The early poems are miserable, lonely, while the later ones are shamelessly smitten, from Hardy and Lipsitz to Rexroth and Lawrence, and for the *coup de grace* I put down some lines of my own at the very end—they're lame, compared to the Giants, but she'll dig that I did it, will see how she's moved me. I copy all of the poems out by hand on real nice paper, eschewing my illegible cursive for careful printing, select as a "cover" a reproduction of Psyche Revived By Cupid's Kiss (thank god I saved art class textbooks). Then bind it all together with thick colored thread rather than routine staples.

I was planning to present it to her on the exact date of our fourth month (starting from our first breakfast non-date) but I can't stand the waiting. So on the Saturday a week prior, when we're just laying low at her place reading our separate books, I damn the torpedoes and do the deed. When she leaves her seat on the sofa momentarily, I move the face-down book she's reading (*Women Who Run With The Wolves*), replace it with my little hand-made job. And when she comes back and finds it she sits with a smile that could melt a glacier and says, 'What have you done?'

Already I can see this was a good idea. Great, even.

I explain my corny little project, tell her I hope the poems will reflect the way I feel. 'Sorry that I need others to do the talking for me,' I say.

She skims the thing, not reading but turning each page slowly and carefully, me watching her face while she does so. What I see convinces me I've done a very fine thing, maybe the finest thing I've *ever* done. 'I'd like you to read these to me,' she says. 'But there's something I want to do first.' And suddenly she's up and moving, coming back with her car keys. 'Don't ask,' she says.

It takes about fifteen minutes to get where we're going, driving toward Foxborough on Highway 89, but it's a beautiful day and passing all these cornfields and horse pastures is pleasant beyond measure, especially with Sadie all excited and beaming in the driver's seat. 'I don't know why I didn't think of this before,' says she. 'I knew you liked poetry.'

I'm clueless, and curious as hell when—on the outer fringes of Foxborough—we turn into a newish residential development called Majestic Oaks, one of those small "intentional communities" where everyone shares a big garden and lives in solar-powered homes—it's an admittedly-nice arrangement, but of course you have to be loaded to even consider living here. Just adjacent to the entrance, out in the middle of this big open field way up at the top of a hill, I can see this strange structure— it's too far away to make sense of, but from where we are it calls to mind Stonehenge as seen in school textbooks.

'What is that?'

Sadie doesn't answer, just pulls onto a little graveled sidestreet and parks off the shoulder. 'Come come, don't dawdle,' holding out her hand for me to take.

Still carrying my present, she leads me toward the hill. There's a small wooden handcarved sign posted at the bottom: **This is private property, but we welcome you to our place of peace. Be respectful. No alcoholic beverages, please. Closes at dusk.**

We hike up, holding hands like Jack and Jill, and cresting the hill at last I discover that it *is* like Stonehenge. Arranged in a giant ring are these enormous slabs of cut granite planted in the ground, each standing tall as the black monolith in *2001*, and each with a poem engraved onto its smooth surface. In the center of the circle is a large granite disk, raised like a table, on whose surface is inscribed a Navajo prayer about the four points of the compass. That's when I realize there are only four of these monoliths, arranged as the points of a compass and therefore giving the *sense* of a circle.

'It's not Stonehenge,' says the Jokester. 'It's *Poem*henge!'

Sadie explains that a sculptor who once owned a bunch of this land created this monument when he sold the property to the developers who wanted to build Majestic Oaks. I wander from one monolith to the next, not yet reading the poems on each—rather just seeing what they are, who wrote them. It's inspirational stuff I've heard of but am not at all familiar with, verses from Rumi, Lao-Tzu, Kahlil Gibran, and the *Bible*.

'Beautiful man,' I hear behind me, and turn to see Sadie sitting stark naked on the table-like disk in the center. I walk toward her shaking my head like I can't believe it, like I've died and gone to Heaven, and she holds up my little book and says, 'As soon as you undress, I'd like you to read these poems to me. Then we'll see where that takes us.'

You know, whenever I wonder if Sadie's just some fantasy, like she couldn't possibly be real, I remember that I couldn't invent such a perfect fantasy. She surpasses any dream I ever had.

Things were happening fast, and I loved that. Like that treadmill started speeding up again, only this time every place it took me was even better than the place before it.

But it goes both ways.

One morning Sadie wakes up moaning, literally. Her whole body aches, her head hurts, her legs pain her.

I massage them. 'But I'm not a trained professional,' I joke, trying to make light.

She doesn't even smile, let alone laugh.

'It's not for sissies,' she says.

'Not for sissies?'

'Aging.'

She battles migraines, too, once or twice a month. When one comes on, it'll take a full twenty-four hours to relent. I'm powerless to help.

Her head back, eyes closed, she says softly, 'There is one thing you can do.'

'Name it.'

A finger in the center of her forehead marks a spot. 'Put a power drill to my brain.'

Instead, at her behest I hide cans of cola all around the house—she doesn't want to know where they are because she'll drink the place dry, and whereas normally she doesn't indulge such stuff, soft drinks seem to help the headaches somehow. She's embarrassed by this, a holistic healthcare provider who uses soda rather than herbs or essential oils.

'Are you kidding?' I tell her. 'Whatever gets you through the night.'

So every few hours she says it's time and I'll dig a drink from the potted plant; fetch the one tucked behind the toilet; pluck one from the pocket of a coat in the closet. Crazy—my dad's booze-hiding trained me for this.

It's new to me, migraines, and clearly the pain is something I can't imagine. When it happens, we have to keep most of the lights in the house off at night, speak in whispers. Sometimes it gets so bad she goes in the dark bathroom and puts towels under the door to shut out even a sliver of light. I hear her in there vomiting.

'I guess the honeymoon's over,' she says during one of these episodes, her sprightly spirit dulled by disappointment.

I tell her that couldn't be further from the truth, and mean it. Weirdly enough, none of this puts me off. I only want to help her however I can. Take care of her. I've never felt such concern for another person, never even knew I *could*.

'Right here.' She marks the spot for the power drill.

Instead I kiss her there, very lightly.

'Where did you come from?'

It's the damnedest thing. I'm on my way home from dinner, having spent a long evening with Alice and Leo, at their place. Sadie'd gone to a work-related gig, then was planning to turn in early, so we'd taken the night off. At some point after dinner I'd confessed to those two sweethearts some disbelief about how well things were going for me, like I was waiting on the bottom to drop.

Alice shakes her head, says this is exactly how she felt once she'd gotten into therapy and turned her own life around. Having wondered about this, I finally brave the question, ask what led her to therapy. 'I mean, you just seem so . . . *together*,' I say. Truth is, Alice strikes me as superwoman.

'Thanks for that,' she says, lifting her cup of tea as if toasting. But she goes on to describe how her own life 'bottomed out' sophomore year of college, the result of an unwanted pregnancy.

I look to Leo, who's already shaking his head.

'Oh,' says Alice, 'this was long before Leo.'

I should've known: Alice had another life, too.

'We did the pregnancy test together, one of those store-bought things, and when it came out positive, his reaction told me everything I needed to know. And it was all bad.'

'You mean . . . ?'

'He was out the door in five minutes.'

I hate to admit it, but my first thought in that moment is to realize—for the first time—how lucky I am not to have landed in that cat's shoes.

My second thought is poor Alice.

'He basically washed his hands of the whole thing, said he didn't want anything to do with that baby. Not that I did, either,' she says.

Of course I make the obvious assumption, given that I've heard no previous mention of a child, and Alice makes it clear that yes, she made the hardest decision of her life.

Alice, even Alice, thinks I, as Alice starts to cry.

'If it wasn't for my mom I might not . . . I just don't know if I'd even be having this conversation . . .'

Leo puts a hand on her shoulder, leans in and kisses the side of her head.

'I'm sorry, Nate,' she says, catching herself, wiping her eyes. 'It's not something I even . . . it's a choice I wouldn't make again. Let's leave it at that. You heard me say it. I'll never get over the guilt of that. Honestly, I don't even think I *should*.'

This is not, however, the note the night ends on. We work a circuitous course back to the fun of the present, with a nod to the miracle of it, and as I'm leaving Alice asks that I please keep to myself the very private information she'd shared earlier.

'You can count on that. I hope you're not sorry you told me.'

'I'm not at all,' nothing but conviction in her voice. 'I'm happy to have you in my life, Nate. You're someone I want to really know me, so this is the kind of thing that had to come out. Just remember *why* I told you: I was at the *bottom*. Really just . . . *convinced* I wouldn't survive it. Nothing to hope for. And here I am. Living proof that things can change.'

She tears up again and Leo, standing behind her, puts his arms around her shoulders and says, 'Say *goodnight*, honey,' smiling.

It's true: me and Alice take forever to say goodbye.

And it's when I'm driving home that the damnedest thing happens. I'm flooded with all these feelings, primarily gratitude for having found Alice. I imagine how scared she must've been all those years ago, pregnant at nineteen, not knowing what to do. Then all the guilt of that godawful act, the self-hatred of her decision. Yet she got through it, evolved, became Alice!

Plus, it's thrilling that she'll talk about this stuff in front of me, like I matter to her.

Which is when it hits me—again—how extraordinarily lucky I am. I mean, I can't tell you. Not only because of Alice, Sadie, and others who seem to have faith in me. But also because it so easily could have been *me* in those dire straits—the fact that it didn't happen seems remarkable, really, given the number of careless encounters I've indulged over the years.

And I say—out loud in the empty car—"Thank you, God,' and chuckle at myself, like God took a break from His busy schedule to make sure I didn't get someone pregnant. I mean, this just comes out of my mouth without any thought, any premeditation whatsoever, like letting out a held breath. 'Thank you, God,' I say.

Which may not seem so strange to some people, but see, the thing is—I've never even *believed* in God.

I'm just back from a jump when Sadie calls. Her father is dead, and that's not even the worst of it.

He's a shotgun suicide.

Holy shit. The shock is something, and it's not even my family. It's like I've just woken up, yanked out of a marvelous dream I'd been having. We were considering a trip to see him so he could meet me, now this.

She'll travel to Chattanooga for the funeral, but doesn't want me to go with her. 'I need to do this alone.'

I buy it—what choice have I got? But I long to be with her. She's lost her last parent, and I relate. We're both orphans. At least she's got her brother, who's just a couple of years younger. Makes me wonder—another first—what it would be like to have a sibling.

It's hard to be separated while all this is happening. I call multiple times, leave messages that go unanswered—strange, because usually she's the one calling *me* all the time. Finally, I fire off a text: *Just remember that Nate loves you, and is HERE, always*. When this elicits the same silence, I feel the tremors for the first time.

Anxious as all hell and wondering what to do about it, how can I be of some use, I drive out to her place, let myself in with the hidden key and clean the whole house for her—vacuum, make the bed, wash the dishes left dirtied due to her hurried departure. At the market, I'd picked out two big bunches of fresh flowers, and I arrange one of them in a vase on her dining room table, the other in the bedroom. These will greet her whenever she gets back. The redolent lilies will pervade the place with a scent that says she's loved whether she's here or not, and the condolence card I lean against the vase on the table will let her know who it is that's doing the loving.

A couple of regular Psycho jumpers—not instructors—like to tease first-timers on the flight up. They'll start telling a story about some guy whose chute didn't open, watch the first-timer's face wane of color. Then they'll laugh, let him in on it, say they're just joking.

They know how I feel about this. After all, I was there.

Besides, why rib some guy who's doing it, going out on the limb? Why not help him out instead, make it a great ride all the way around?

Because the fact is, eventually, one way or another, someone's chute doesn't open. And they're history.

When Sadie gets back, eight long days later, she asks for some time, space. So we spend a second week apart. Then a third. There's never even a mention of the flowers I left, the card.

That's when I start losing it, the tremors threatening to open the ground beneath me.

I call and insist. 'I need to see you,' I say.

She comes to the Penthouse on a Sunday. Atypical, given that I usually go to her, so I'm on guard already when she suggests coming over. And the second she walks in it's like a different woman. She doesn't smile, just sort of scrunches up her lips in an indecisive gesture. She goes straight to the sofa to sit down, doesn't even hug me.

'It's been three weeks,' I say. 'How about a hug?'

'I'm sorry,' says the Serious One. Still she doesn't stand up to hug me.

I tell her I'm sorry about this tragic thing that's happened, but I'd like to be included. I say it's not right, going all this time without seeing each other. I mention having cleaned her house, didn't you get the card I left? But she only nods, doesn't really respond. I keep going, can't stop myself. Pleading. I say I'm not afraid of whatever she's feeling, that what she's going through is obviously really heavy and all I want to do is be here for her.

I've never talked this way before, but the words roll right out of me, like the script's already written.

I say that ever since I started seeing Lynn, I've learned the value of sharing our suffering. Tremendous. The benefits can't be counted. 'It's just . . . it's crazy, you dealing with this alone, going all these weeks without seeing each other when we could be—'

She doesn't even let me finish. 'If you mention that again I'll have to leave.'

She doesn't—then. I don't mention the weeks apart again, but she's gone within twenty minutes anyway.

Something else in Lynn's narrow net: the fear that nothing I do is of any real consequence, so if I disappear no one will even notice.

I'm nothing, not even here.

Says Lynn, 'Let me remind you of your parents. More specifically, your home life when you were a kid.'

'But no,' I butt in, 'I'm talking about *now*. This is something I'm feeling *right now*.'

Says the Shrink, 'Let me remind you of your parents.'

See what I mean? It's like she doesn't even hear me.

Sure I panic some, but console myself Sadie's in shock. This awful thing has happened and it's thrown her off. She just needs some time. I was good to her, kind, attentive. And she made no bones about the fact that she believes we're fated to be together. Not one for all this *fated* talk, I can't deny having been swept up by her conviction, so am figuring once some of this smoke clears she's bound to miss me, and then . . .

Alice encourages me to take this opportunity to focus on myself, find a productive place to put my energy.

'Think about it, Nate. I can't even imagine what she's going through. It's bad enough to lose her father but . . . let's just say suicide adds a whole other level to it. Just remember that it isn't about *you*. It's about Sadie. Give her the space she needs, and let's hope she'll find her way back to you.'

So at Max's prompting I pour myself into training for an upcoming marathon. Five days a week I run seven miles, and every other week I'll do a long run—thirteen, fourteen miles. The fifth week I do eighteen, as far as I'll run before the race itself.

And I make up a mantra, by accident. I'm running one day and missing Sadie so much I have to stop, cave in to crying, scared she'll never come back. Crazy, it comes out of nowhere, what the hell? Seems like this happens more and more, like I never cried before I met her and now I can't seem to stop. Once I pull myself together and start running again, air traffic control kicks in—a syllable at every step—every time my foot impacts the pavement:

Im-*prove* your-*self*! Im-*prove* your-*self*!

Four weeks subsequent to that dreadful Sunday with Sadie, I come home from Psycho late in the afternoon and find two brown bags on my doorstep. My stuff, the clothes I'd relocated to her place.

If she misses me, she's got a hell of a weird way of showing it.

I want to call Kimberly so bad I can't tell you. Screw my way through the grief. It will work. Guaranteed. At least for a little while.

But I know that doing so will take me right back to square one. It's like opening the floodgates, and those waters are poison. They'll drown me.

So instead I lean on friends to keep me in check.

'Use our number as a hotline,' Stacy jokes, not joking. 'When you get that urge to call Kimberly at three in the morning, call us instead.'

Forget calling, I say. I'd rather show up at Kimberly's unannounced, make it a risky venture. Just the thought gives me a hard-on.

'Show up at our place with a hard-on. We know what to do with it.'

Lynn's approach to this particular problem is different. When I say that the old habits are haunting me, but that I recognize how destructive it would be—ultimately—to relent to them, she says, 'Forget about you.'

Come again?

'What about Sadie? Shouldn't you respect her needs? And you say Kimberly wouldn't bat an eye, and maybe that's true. But how would that affect *her*? You're wanting to use her as a Band-Aid for all your hurt feelings—what about *her* feelings?'

Christ, she's right. I'm a selfish sonofabitch. There's no real escaping it.

Im-*prove* your-*self*, im-*prove* your-*self*, im-*prove* your-*self*. Every step. Seven miles.

It's pouring rain. Last Sunday I ran eighteen miles, so the nine to Sadie's place in the country is no problem. But it's after ten and the roads are real dark—anytime a car comes I'm happy when they pass without incident. Horror movies have made me paranoid.

By the time I knock on her door I'm drenched to the bone, between the rain and the sweat. She asks who's there—'It's me.'—and when the door opens it's clear she's shocked, and moved, by my desperate measure. She's naked out of bed, and pulls me to her without a sound, her tongue drinking the fluid from my face. She draws back only long enough to strip off my soaked shirt, then works her wet way down my chest to my belly—starved—her hands squeezing my ass.

Then she moves those hands around front, frees it from my shorts, and is all over it.

But I need *her*, *all* of her, so push her back to the wall and peel off the stubborn shorts and I'm in there, working away with her moaning as much as I am, nine long miles behind me. We're in love, we can't stand it, can't deny ourselves, *o my soul* . . .

Which is when I fold the soiled tissuepaper, flush it down the toilet along with the fantasy. Pathetic, sure. But hey—I didn't bother anybody.

I tell Lynn the sanity of my life is starting to get to me. Make me crazy. I need a bad habit, something off the map. Dangerous.

'More dangerous than diving out of airplanes?'

True enough. But I do that all the time. Now that Sadie's not around, I need something new, or even old. I tell her how good Irish whiskey sounds all of a sudden . . . a bottomless bottle of Bushmills . . . and a night of nothing but dope and sex. A night doing lines with Kimberly. I miss the relief of checking out every now and then.

'Every now and then?'

Okay, granted, I checked out a lot. But right now I'm just looking for a break. Something temporary. Anything. All this sobriety, all this self-improvement—*Mr. Clean*—look where it's got me?

'It's gotten you happier than you've ever been. You said so yourself.'

Sure, alright, I hear you. But *right now*, this *moment*. It's all we've got, right? I could be dead tomorrow. I just need a week—a *night*, even—getting high, letting go. Not wrestling with everything in an effort to make sense of it.

Long pause before she says, incredibly, 'Have it.'

Come again?

'If that's what you think you need, there's nothing stopping you. So have it.'

This throws me, shuts me up.

'But if you ask me, I'm going to tell you that's not what's missing. Not all that long ago you weren't convinced there was *anything* missing, least of all drugs. Now you're looking for something to fill the empty space. The one Sadie left.'

The empty space. How'd she know?

'But Nate, that space has been in you for a long, long time. Drugs can't fill it. You know this. Even Sadie can't fill it. No one can. No one but you.'

And I'm gone, this crying come from nowhere. Why can't I keep it anymore?

It's pouring rain. I'm ready for a marathon, so the couple of miles to Kimberly's is like a warm-up. She opens the door wearing a familiar waist-length shirt—silk, black, unbuttoned—and a red thong that slays me. One look and I can see she's in The Zone. Behind her the room is flickering with candles, satiny jazz luring me in. Without a word she kisses me in a way that'll save my life, then gives me a wicked smile and says in a lazy voice, 'About time you came around. I haven't been properly fucked since you left.'

You get the picture.

Then I fold the soiled tissuepaper . . .

Lynn wants to know why I think I've been so 'successful' with women—sexually speaking.

'Isn't it obvious?' asks the Wiseguy, arms outstretched to

present himself like a prize. Dropping my hands I say, 'Chopped liver's more like it.'

Right now I couldn't feel further from successful, in *any* sense.

'I knew you'd take it that way,' she goes on. 'But that's not what I'm talking about. By your own admission you've been—how should we say?—emotionally absent. And yet it sounds to me like you've not lacked for female company. If not romantically, then sexually. Would you agree?'

'I haven't set any records,' I say. 'But for a redhead, I've done alright.'

'What do you suppose attracts these women to a man who's not emotionally available to them?'

I cut to the chase. 'If I hadn't gotten into skydiving, things would've been different.'

'Skydiving?'

'No doubt about it.'

'Don't you think there's more to it?'

She's fishing for something. She acts as if these are legitimate questions, when what's really going on is that she's made up her mind about something and merely wants me to confirm it.

'It's really not complicated,' I say, set to burst her bubble. 'Skydiving gets these women into my bedroom, the rest is me doing the one thing I'm good at.'

This, at least, gets a smile out of her.

'Look, I know that sounds like I'm bragging, but I'm not. You know what it is? I really *want* to be good at that. I'll do anything to satisfy a woman. Anything. But if it weren't for *them* I'd get nowhere.'

'Meaning?'

'Well, let's just say you show me a woman who'll be straight with me, *tell* me what turns her on, and I'll show you a woman who'll be glad she did.'

I win another smile. Am I flirting with my shrink? Bet your ass I am.

'This is all good information, Nate. But I still think there's more to it.'

I know you do, I think. 'That's where we're different,' I say.

When not with friends, I bury my brain in movies, running, books. Not having been a regular reader since I graduated, it's time to get back to it, give it another go. Besides, reading in public looks good to people, especially women, and at this point I need all the help I can get.

Hey, I'll do anything to stay on the wagon, even read poetry. But I can't deny daily praying for the phone to ring, Sadie saying, 'Come home.'

Never mind that it's her home.

I tell Alice I'm not sure how I'm going to get through this without caving-in to some serious cravings. Unhealthy ones. Even though I only dated Sadie a few months, it's no measure— it's like I don't know how to live alone anymore, like she did something to me. Like she herself used to say, she turned me into a junkie.

And now it's damn-all. I'm a slave to my cellphone, ready for it to ring any second, and every car that passes the Penthouse is hers. I'm at the window every time I hear one, which means I'm running to that window about seven-thousand times a day. And despite the fact that she lives in Foxborough, nearly ten miles away, I'm afraid to leave the house for fear of running into her, maybe catching her on a date.

God help us if that happened—I'm ready to make a name for myself, do something monstrous, newsworthy.

I don't like the guy I'm becoming, in other words. I want the old Me back, the one who didn't bother getting involved, knowing damn well it's not worth it. Nothing lasts.

Says Alice: 'You can do this, sweetie. Get through it. You can. You're one of the most disciplined people I've ever met.'

I look at her like she doesn't know me.

'I mean it. Not only have you kicked a *bunch* of bad habits, look at your skydiving. Didn't it take you a couple of years or something to get licensed? And you were working a job the whole time, right?'

It's true. I'd never thought about it.

'Look, this thing with her dad just threw Sadie. How could it not? You've got to respect that, honey. She's probably re-evaluating every single thing in her life, not just you. And, much as I hate to say it, maybe she really isn't ready for a committed relationship. She warned you of this from the start, didn't she? I'm not defending, just saying. And if that *is* the case we've got to find you a woman who's ready.'

Alice always does this, uses the pronoun *we*. It's a small thing—I don't even know if she's aware of it—and it melts me. Like maybe she's in it *with* me somehow.

But it's a lie—she's got Leo. Me, I'll go to bed praying for a call that won't come, and wondering why Alice got married before she met me.

Then she thinks of something, suggests I try a strategy copped from her folks.

'When I was a teenager, whenever I'd get low about something, or feel sorry for myself, my parents had a rule—do something for someone else.'

Didn't matter what it was, she says, any little thing could do the trick, so long as it truly benefitted another. It could be picking out a silly present for a friend or helping with chores around the house. They even took her to the local soup kitchen sometimes, where they'd spend the day volunteering.

'We'd help with the food, the laundry, the cleaning, whatever. I have pretty amazing parents—I'm the first to admit it.'

The crazy coincidence is that, not long after this conversation, Stacy calls to ask if I'd like to join him and Steven the following Saturday, when they'll go to Chelcy Park and hand out food to homeless people.

I'm not kidding. What the hell?

I meet them at their place, seven fricking a.m., and only when Alice and Leo show up do I realize it wasn't a coincidence, my friends are in cahoots.

People.

We drive to the downtown park together, Stacy saying they used to do this regularly, but lately have been less consistent, which he regrets. 'You won't believe how good it feels to be *decent*. Not as good as it feels to be *indecent* but . . . '

Me, I'm scanning the surroundings for Sadie—maybe she'll show up with a giant tub of 'essential oils' ensuring felicity. Who cares if you haven't eaten in a week?

Me and my mood.

We carry coolers to the wrought-iron benches by a big fountain in the park's center, where more volunteers are gathered, setting up tables and such. At least two dozen raggedy-looking unfortunates are already lined-up waiting. What we're handing out isn't much: the only 'real' food is biscuits gotten from some take-out place, while the rest is little plastic packages of crackers, cookies, muffins. My job is pouring orange juice into small Styrofoam cups, Stacy helping, while Steven and a couple of women I don't know fill cups with coffee from a big portable urn. Alice and Leo are walking around replenishing the stuff we're handing out, making sure everyone has what they need.

The first thing I notice about the recipients are their clothes—they're dirty, and nothing fits right, all the sizes too small or too baggy for the bodies wearing them. Pants falling off or cinched tight with a ratty belt. Teeth are bad across the board, hair not much better.

But at some point I'm struck by something else. Every time I hand a cup of juice to someone they thank me, sometimes a *God bless* as they shamble by. It's a little thing, right? But I mean they *all* say it, meanwhile most of us don't bother. How many times have I failed to thank someone, whether it's a waiter at a restaurant or a clerk at a convenience store? How many thousands of drinks did I fix for people while bartending, yet for a fact the *thank yous* were in short supply. Sure they'd sometimes stick a buck in the tip jar, but at the moment the former is preferable—seems to go further.

Maybe it's just me.

Stacy chats away with people as they pass, and I'm ashamed of my silence, not sure what to say. They'd told me in advance that people don't generally ask for money, but that if anyone does I should just say I'm sorry, point out there's food and drink for the taking. Still, the guilt for being on the other end of that line is quietly crushing. I want to empty my wallet to every other taker, go to the nearest ATM and drain my account—these people need it. Hey, it's only money—the least of my worries.

And the damnedest things occur to me, doing this. Like: every day I deny myself alcohol, the luxury of a drink, fighting that impulse every time I'm near a bar and every time I pass the beer cooler in the market. Meanwhile, more than a few of these cats parading past me today look like they'd sell their souls for a drink, but they don't have the money.

Is this a weird world or what?

'How often do you masturbate?'

This startles me, I'll admit. Among the countless things I've shared with Lynn, this one seems—initially—the most intrusive. Sensing this, she nudges, makes it safe.

'I'm making the assumption you do. You *are* like the rest of us, aren't you?'

Right. My shock at her question having betrayed me as prudish, I overdramatize my answer to compensate.

'Every chance I get.'

'Really?'

'Well hell, I don't know how often. I mean—?'

'Every day? Every week?'

'Probably every day, or damn near. Let's just say enough to have mastered it.'

She chuckles, relieving me. This talk stirs something. Somewhere in her mid-fifties (I'd guess), Lynn's not an unattractive woman. Granted, she's not what most guys would call a looker, but I see it in her, just past the buttoned-up facade she presents to clients like me. Now all this talk of masturbating makes her one of us.

The truth of it? If she undid one button of that blouse I'd tear through the rest of them faster than she could say *Take me!*

None of which happens, naturally. The shrink I'm fantasizing about instead lowers a weird sort of boom on me, says she'd like me to give up masturbating. Temporarily, of course.

'Try a week. If you manage that then we'll go for two, then three. Up to a month depending on how it goes.'

She also wants me to journal during this time. Impressions, observations, feelings. Strange as it sounds, I agree to do it, no idea why. But Lynn I trust—she seems to know what she's doing.

Or else she's just another quack, winging it like the rest of us.

Handing people juice, I have to stave-off an urge to ask them how they got here. Why are they homeless, standing in a long line in a public park for a package of plastic crackers and a cup of juice? I think of my mom, Dottie selling our house, me inheriting a chunk of money to drop into savings.

Is this healthy, being here? Part of me thinks it was a bad idea, only inspires more reasons to feel shitty about myself. But another part of me says to the Other, *Shut your pie-hole. Hand over each cup of juice with a smile, and quit thinking so much.*

Stacy hugs a black woman wearing a floppy purple hat—she's short and round, spiky hairs sticking out of both nostrils, most of her top teeth missing. But that doesn't stop her from smiling to beat the band—you'd think she just won the lottery. It looks like she's a regular, because everyone seems to know her. It's also clear she's crazy about Stacy.

Says he: 'Emma, I'd like you to meet my friend Nate.'

And she has her arms around my neck before I know what hit me. She smells, she really does, but damnit I hold tight, really get a good grip on her. Think I'm kidding? Fact is I don't want to let go—it feels so good for some reason. I'm really holding on, like there's something other than the stench coming off her that I want more of, *need*.

But all at once I get sort of self-conscious, wonder if everyone's looking at me. And when at last we let go, she looks me straight in the face and says, 'You sure know how to hug a lady. That's better 'an any old biscuit.'

I'm speechless, just standing there, everything welling up. Wiping my face, I blurt *Thank you* before she adds, like she didn't even hear me, 'Where'd you get that *hair*? Your momma must have some real pretty hair.'

Swim days.

One of them . . .
may even dream of tears which must always fall
because water and salt were given
us at birth to make what we could of them,
and being what we are we chose love
and having found it we lost it over and over.

The first week is no problem, but beyond that the monastic challenge Lynn laid on me becomes a serious buzz-killer. She insists that I make these stupid notes whenever 'the urge' hits me, and by the time the month is out they convey the contempt I feel toward the whole crazy business.

I read these rants to her every week (*Who the hell decided that staying in shape, or being drug-free, is some great virtue?* etc.), and nearly every entry denies that masturbation—or the lack of it— has anything to do with my mood. Reading them aloud, it's like someone else wrote them, like I'm listening to someone other than me.

That is until the fifth and final week. I'm reading along fine until the following stops me in my tracks: *How do I* feel? *Since you're so curious I'll tell you point blank that I feel useless. Worthless. A waste of skin.*

Hearing myself say this, the hollow stab of accuracy leaves me breathless.

'What the hell's the point of all this,' I say finally, so pissed I'm not even sure how to handle it. 'If your goal is to make me more miserable than I already am, you're succeeding.'

She doesn't say anything, so I let her have it.

'And I *pay* you for this! That's what's crazy. Hell of a way to make a living.'

I'm beyond caring—about *anything*.

'Everyone wants to tell me what to do, how I'm supposed to just suck it up and deal. Everyone's convinced they know what's best, but they don't. They don't even *care*. It's just fooling each other into thinking someone gives a damn, but I'm not buying it. We're all too caught-up in our own . . . *worlds* . . . to really give a rat's ass about someone else's. Just ask my parents—they wrote the book.'

Fuck Lynn and her stupid assignments. Fuck everyone.

But when I look up to see if she's even listening, there are tears on her face. I shit you not—my shrink is crying. It's like she finally sees it's hopeless.

My marathon shorts have these little mesh pockets lining the back waistband, for packets of energy gel. This stuff has the nasty, gooey consistency of you-know-what, but all the literature about long-distance running swears by it. So—nasty or not—I load those mesh pockets with the little condom-sized packs, and suck one down every few miles to get me through the next leg.

Water stations are everywhere, Gatorade, too. And portable toilets, which I use twice before the fifth mile because of all the water I drank this morning before the race. Most people have their number on their shirtfronts, but I run shirtless, my number—**917**—pinned to the front of my shorts.

My friends have spaced themselves along the route, armed with bananas and encouragement. They gather at the start line, then drive up to the 7-mile mark, the 12-mile mark, etc, all the way to the end. When I pass the gang at mile 18, Lynn has joined them, beaming—a complete surprise. I slow enough for her to hand me a banana, and she kisses my sweaty cheek.

Like I say: people.

Do I look for Sadie along the sidelines, wonder if she'll show up to surprise me? Sure I do. The sight of her would have me *sprinting* twenty-six miles.

As it is, I play it safe most of the race, conservative. I just need to *finish* the damn thing, succeed at something. I'm not out to set any records.

But once I pass Lynn, I can tell I've got more than enough steam to get me through the rest, so start pushing, *running*. Really picking up the pace. Not having used it the entire time, I kick in the mantra. I'm passing runners in spades and hope they know it has nothing to do with them. It's not about showing off.

When I hit mile 25—one left!—I really let loose. I'm at an all-out sprint, a gallop, and it's unbelievable. You'd never know I've already put twenty-five miles past me. The sides of the street are packed with cheering spectators—who are they? Does everyone know someone who's running, or are they just cheering us on for the sheer hell of it?

Either way it works a kind of magic—maybe one-tenth of what a professional athlete experiences in a big game, or a rock star stepping out onto a spotlighted stage, but it's one hell of a rush for a redhead. There's this invigorating thrill, running with everyone screaming along the sidelines. Like you're not alone, all these people are pulling for you.

Three hours and eighteen minutes after that starting pistol, I explode past the Finish Line, my legs trying to keep running—takes twenty yards to stop them. A woman I've never seen (part of the race committee) congratulates me, hands me this shiny smock that looks like aluminum foil. A 'space blanket,' she says. I'm supposed to wear it around my shoulders to deflect the sun, help the body cool down.

Despite the hordes, I manage to locate my gang—and Lynn—with no problem. They each hug me in turn, never mind the sweat.

Says Stacy the Sweet: 'Space blanket? Oh honey, ain't *nothing* going to cool *you* down.'

We walk past a big tent: **MEDICAL**. EMTs are everywhere, runners stretched on cots with IVs in their arms, getting ankles, legs, knees bandaged.

Lucky me, I feel better than I've felt in all my life. Endorphins have me high as a kite, and the good buzz lasts all night long. The seven of us—*sans* Lynn—attend a big dinner sponsored by the race. I've been guzzling Gatorade and water for weeks, so at dinner allow myself a congratulatory glass of champagne to celebrate. My friends toast me, and I'm a little loopy after only a few sips, don't even want any more.

Which is when it hits me that I ran the whole race without Sadie.

'We weren't convinced this was the right time to do it. Shuly said she'd had it in mind to try this thing, but felt like the *timing* was important. You know what I told her? Same thing I told you when you were trying to decide about that second marathon. Remember?'

I do. I'd only recently run the race when I met Brenda. It'd gone well enough that I was already geared up to run another one. I wanted to break three hours—confident I could—but worried maybe it was too soon. Maybe I should wait six months, give the body time to rest? But the registration deadline for the race I wanted to run—in Richmond, Virgina, well within driving distance—was only two weeks away.

So, says the pretty stranger I've just met, 'It's the chance of a lifetime. But you've got a lifetime of chances.'

I didn't say it, but what I thought then (still think) is, How can you *know* that?

I've learned to accept that timing is, in fact, important. Which might explain why certain events that seem insignificant can strike us as crucial long after they first made their mark. I mean, if you think about it, it's crazy, all the important stuff we forget. Or forget we remember.

Soon after I start seeing her, Lynn begins asking questions about home, the environment I grew up in—her favorite subject, even if it bores me to tears. Scanning some of the titles on the bookshelf behind the chair she sits in (*Feel Good Now!*, *Creating An Abundant Life*, *Yes You Can!*), I have to wonder if she selected the books strategically, knowing that her clients would be facing them since the sofa on which we sit (anyone ever lie down?) is directly across from her. For fun I'd like to sneak a few alternatives onto those shelves, all with those irritating exclamation points in the titles: *You're A Loser!* Or, *Why Not Cut The Throat and Quit!*

'Were you allowed to express yourself at home, your feelings? And I don't just mean you. I mean your parents, too. Was it an atmosphere where expressing feelings was okay, or were you expected to keep a tight lid on them?'

Is she kidding? I describe my dad kicking down the front door. Does that count?

Apparently not. She gets more specific, and in no time it's clear she's asking if anyone ever *cried* in our house. Well, my mom cried when my dad died, but she clarifies that she means the early days, when I was a kid. No way, I say, because the fact is I can't recall one occasion on which I cried—I'm sure it must've happened at some point (infancy?) but hell if I can dredge up an example for her.

'What about your parents? Ever notice them emotional in that way?'

Immediately I huff it off, like she's crazy to think it. But out of nowhere I'm blindsided by memory. This thing hits me, or *emerges*, and in a matter of seconds I can piece together a picture, something I witnessed when my dad moved out. I was eight.

'How long did you say he was gone?'

'I don't know exactly, maybe a few months? Definitely less than a year. Seemed like he was back in no time.'

Who knows when exactly—on this timeline—my memory occurs. I must've been seven or eight, single digits for sure. But I walk into my mom's bathroom one day and catch her crying. I'd forgotten all about this, like it must've been buried and Lynn's prodding pulls it back to the fore. The door's open (not like I bust in on her), and she's standing at the sink in front of the mirrored medicine-chest, and the first thing I see is her ruined reflection. Grim.

'What's wrong, Mommy?'

Startled, she wipes her face quickly with her hands, sniffs and says, 'It's nothing, honey. Mommy's just having an anxiety attack.'

Exact words.

Crazy how clear it is—now I can see this like it happened an hour ago, when in fact a few minutes prior I had no memory of it at all. It was the way she said this—casual, matter-of-fact. She said it in such a way as to suggest it was next to nothing, like dust or allergies making her eyes water.

And of course I bought it. What? Doubt my mother?

But describing it to Lynn two decades later is like enlightenment. My father—her husband—was cheating and had moved out, left her in the lurch with an eight-year-old. So she was a mess, pure and simple. Who wouldn't be?

In that instant, saying all this to Lynn, I catch myself thinking, *That poor woman.* But what comes out of my mouth is, 'My poor mom.'

'Keep going,' says the shrink.

So I talk it out—what else can I do? I say that, as an eight-year-old, the phrase *anxiety attack* had absolutely no meaning to me, but nowadays it sends a serrated chill up my spine. Memories of collapsing in Max's office. Can the crushing weight of those two words successfully convey their meaning? She was being *attacked* by anxiety, and what could she do to defend herself from such a vague onslaught of terror as those two words connote? What save give it a name, something concrete. Something that can be rattled off to her kid so as to spare his virgin sensibilities.

Mommy's just having an anxiety attack.

My poor mom. Looks like she knew all about the sink-or-swim days. And what becomes clear in that moment of recollection is that, although she was weighted down with more trouble than I can even imagine (her kid not the least of it), she was actually a pretty decent swimmer. Granted, she leaned on the booze, but whatever gets you through the night, right? And hell—what's weird to think now is how easy it is to cut people that slack. Yet it never occurred to me that I should've done the same for my parents.

Well, my mom, anyway.

Sometimes I'll dream my way back to Rebecca Benton's apartment. Margaret—my *wife*—is catering an event with Edwin and Dennis, and I'm sitting on the floor of our neighbor's empty living room, the raunchy eloquence of the Rolling Stones egging me on from a boom box that can barely contain them. She's wearing this white tank-top, no bra, her nipples dark beneath the thin fabric.

They're big around as half-dollars.

I look through the long lens to determine what to do, realizing now that this decision could alter the course my life will take forever after.

'Baby, I'm going to Europe. You think I care how many bridges I burn on the way?'

Magic moment.

I'll bring the fire, thinks I—even all these years later.

Which means maybe I've gotten nowhere, learned nothing from Lynn, my friends, all the advice and support they've offered. Learned nothing from my past save that I'd go back there in a blink, making all the same mistakes and loving every miserable minute of it.

The fact that it's a three-hour drive back to Sumpton gives hardly a hint of how far the trip will take me. I won't lie: I'm nervous as hell, and those hours give me ample time to reconsider the plans I set in stone with a couple of scared phone calls the week prior.

The first of which is lunch with my mom's best friend Dottie. Now half-way through her seventies, she's not in the best of shape, moves slowly, walks kind of hunched-over with a shoulder-burdened stoop. But there's this crass spunk in her manner and speech, an *I-don't-give-a-damn-what-anyone-thinks* attitude (not at all meanspirited) that's genuinely refreshing. She has an energy about her that's enviable.

Brokenhearted because of Sadie, I feel more exhausted than she acts.

We eat at *Harrison's*, one of Sumpton's historic restaurants, about a hundred years old—a staple not only for Dottie and my folks but even the generation before them. It's dimly-lit, all the windows covered with these deep burgundy curtains keeping at bay the sunny day outside. The music moves you back in time—Glenn Miller, Artie Shaw, Tommy Dorsey—and were it not for the "Vegetarian" section on the menu you'd think we'd stepped into a 1940s time capsule. The two of us are swallowed-up in this big padded booth with high backs—it's like having a whole little room to yourselves—and all the waiters are men, older, dressed in black slacks and starched shirts and vests that match the curtains. I order clam chowder, Dottie has fried chicken livers—for my mom—and a martini that looks good enough to make my mouth water.

I swallow hard, order ice tea.

'Your mom loved the chicken livers here,' she says, an innocuous reflection that nevertheless pries the lid off the rabbit hole and sends us both scurrying down it.

It only takes a couple of questions to get her going, and she tells me more about my parents than twenty-eight years taught me. How they met after "the war," my dad "dashing" in his Air Force uniform.

'We went to a place called Peyton's Place, because that's where the boys hung out when they got back.'

'A bar?'

'Kind of a pool hall. A great jukebox. We didn't really drink, us girls—mainly sodas was all we'd have because we were young. Sixteen. The boys drank, but not really—just a glass of beer, maybe two. Anyway, that's where your mom met Jeff. Music's what maybe brought them together. They both loved music, Sinatra especially. We all did in those days.

'But you know, Nate, they were just buddies for a long time. Years. It took a while for them to actually date because they were always dating other people. Jeff had a reputation for girls, and your mom didn't do so bad, either. She was so pretty, you know. Once they finally got together, Jeff used to joke that he married Gail to get her off the streets. That's only a joke, honey. We dated a lot, but we weren't what anyone would call promiscuous. Not at all. And even after they married, you know, it took a while before they decided to have you.'

I ask her about what that cat told me at mom's funeral, something about my dad being investigated by the FBI.

'Oh yes, that's true. It sure is. God, I haven't thought about that in ages. I don't know if he was really being investigated, but they definitely questioned him. Came to the house. Scared the dickins out of him, too.'

'???????'

'It was all about the Bomb. Since your dad had been on the island, I think they were just trying to find out what people knew. But it shook him up. Gail called me, I remember, just after they left. Two of them I think came to the house. And she said it was just like the movies—they were in suits, flashing badges. All confidential business. But that was the end of it. They didn't bother him anymore after that.'

She bites into a big olive from her martini. My mouth waters some more.

'Really your folks had a pretty good marriage until the stroke. That started the trouble, far as I can remember.'

'Stroke?'

'You don't remember? Gosh, you were maybe in your early teens?"

This rings the bell. My dad went into the hospital when I was eleven or twelve—I remember because I was at Blackwell by then, surviving only due to a steady diet of boy detective books. But I had no idea it was a stroke. Memory serving, I was told it was kidney stones or something.

'Well, I didn't know they never told you,' Dottie goes on. 'He'd had a stroke. Not a major one—what they called a pin stroke.'

But that's not the punchline.

'What nobody knew—nobody but your folks—was that it ended his sex life forever. I'm sure no one told you *that*!'

I'm so shocked I'm not even sure what she means. But Dottie just plows on like it's nothing, nothing but the truth.

'He couldn't get an erection. Never had another one after that stroke.'

I try doing some quick math to figure the chronology, but give up and just ask outright.

'But when did he move out? How did he have an affair if . . .?'

She shakes her head. 'Vicki. That was a couple of years before the stroke. Your mom was convinced it was the cause.'

She chuckles when she says this.

'You mean . . . ?'

'Well, the stress for one. But you know, Nate, Gail had some funny ideas about that whole affair. After Jeff had the stroke, part of her believed God was punishing him.'

'Really? She told you that?'

She nods and lifts her eyebrows at the same time, a look that convinces me she's as skeptical as I am. 'People believe what they need to believe,' she says.

'Did you think Daddy—?'

'Oh I've no idea. I doubt he even knew that I knew. But those were such different times. Gail didn't even tell me about the affair until Jeff moved out. That's when I heard about Vicki and all.'

'Did you know her? I mean Vicki?'

'Heavens no. Remember—she was twenty years old or something. A kid, half our age. Which made it all the worse. That whole thing nearly killed your mom. She was a real mess for a while there.'

'And the stroke happened after he'd moved back?'

'Few years later, I think. And that was it. Jeff had always been a drinker, but after the stroke it was like drinking was all he lived for. I hate to tell you, but I think it was his only real pleasure. I really do.'

'Do you think . . . I mean, how did they . . . ?'

'They didn't. The cheating was bad enough. After the stroke they were pretty much done. Couldn't get past it. And divorce wasn't an option, not really—we were old-fashioned Catholics, remember, and even though divorce was coming along, we just didn't consider it. Not like now, when it's the *first* thing people think of. We lived in a different world than you do, Nate. So you can't really blame them. Nowadays they could maybe get some help—my goodness, there are enough drugs out there now to give a dead man an erection.'

I'm just trying to keep up (no pun intended).

'Mom told you all this?'

'Oh sure, eventually she did. Look, Jay and I never had any real trouble in our marriage. Nothing outside the usual. And he was gone before his sixtieth birthday, God bless him. Come to think of it, I don't think *Jay* even knew the truth about Jeff. The impotency part.'

My dad—that mean bastard—couldn't get a hard-on. No wonder he was a mean bastard.

The sad truth of it? Part of me still wishes I'd known so I could've rubbed his hateful face in it.

'I know you're not a drinker, Nate,' Dottie says, 'but I'm having another martini.'

'You know, right from the beginning I could tell something was happening. Almost like everything was aligned for this. And the Energy was just waiting to see if we'd pick up on it. Take the opportunity to bring it in.'

No more coffee—I'm done. Brenda's working overtime to draw me into this, but I'm a million miles away, can't do a damn thing but feign interest. At least it seems like she's getting to it, finally. I sense the "all important" climax coming.

'At first I kept my eyes closed. Shuly's doing this séance kind of thing, inviting the Divine Feminine Energy to reveal itself, saying we're a safe haven. She repeats over and over that the Energy is welcome here.'

I just want to go home, crawl back into bed. I could sleep forever.

'And *something* was going on, changing. It was palpable. Started in my feet, this warm, tingly thing. And I could feel it move up my legs, slowly. I mean, it was so *clear*, this line of warmth moving up my body. I could've taken my hand and traced the progression as it rose all the way to the top of my head.'

She does so now, to show me: her flattened hand—palm down—moving upward. But I'm not really there, or even here, with her. I'm thinking I let Sadie put all those needles in me, yet she never came skydiving. I bet she never even considered it, because it would've meant *needing* me (at least long enough to deploy the damn chute). And she couldn't admit such a thing, that she might need a guy with a normal name, wearing blue jeans instead of fancy colored robes. And nearly thirty or not, I've never been able to grow so much as a mustache, much less a long beard like her bigshot guru.

I mean, how much wisdom could a nobody like *me* have?

Thinking back on it, I got the sense that Sadie thought skydiving was a frivolous way to spend my time in the world, not important like being a healthcare provider. Sorry—a "healer." Just a feeling I got. She used to say how proud she was that her job was healing people. She said this multiple times, almost like she was trying to convince a skeptic, which may not have meant me at all.

Made me wonder.

And one Saturday morning I was helping her mix 'essential oils.' She sells these tiny bottles of the stuff—pricey. We mixed various things together, herbs or whatever, then used a small funnel to get it in those little bottles. The doubter in me wondered how this stuff we mixed on her kitchen counter could heal people.

So I risked it, asked. Did she ever doubt what she does? These 'essential oils,' sixty bucks a pop, did she ever question the validity of this, wonder if they really worked?

On this occasion she didn't deny it—I'll give her that: 'Part of me feels like a fraud,' she said.

I tell Lynn she's a genius, she tells me I'm the one doing the work. That she couldn't do what she does—successfully—without me.

So, says the grateful, 'You're generous, too.'

I've made the trip enough times now to know my way around the cemetery like it's just another neighborhood, so find my parents' plots with no problem. Amazing, really, because the place is *big*, sprawled over 150 acres, and everything looks the same—unnaturally green grass, giant magnolia trees, and headstones. We all want to be special, will come off the cross to prove how exceptional we are (just like my dad said on that tape), yet here's where we end up: the levelest playing-field of all, nothing to distinguish us save the dates carved into the stone. We should bring kids out here on field trips, show them first-hand what it is they're up against.

Not that it matters to anyone, but when I find my folks— see the headstones looking filthy from foul weather—I take to them with a rag from the trunk of my car, digging dirt out of the letters, even. Then settle on that rich shag of green grave-hair for my visit.

I don't talk much this day. Just sit.

After a long while, though, I decide I've got something to say to them. I say I'm starting to get it, starting to understand something about their lives. Our lives. They made a hell of a mess, my parents—that's what we do, all of us. And we all have our reasons for the messes we make.

But—with a lot of luck—there's such a thing as cleanup time.

Alice has other Sadie-related strategies in mind, and blue as I am I want to hear all of them—I'll try anything. Lobotomy's looking better and better.

She shocks me first by telling me that two years ago she and Leo split up for a spell, spent about six months separated.

My god, how many lives has Alice *had*?

'It's a long story. Complicated. And I won't bore you with it because it's not the point. I was upset with Leo for what I now think are petty reasons. Couldn't see this at the time, though. Besides, those things were just a scapegoat. What it really came down to was that I sort of freaked out. We'd been living together long enough at this point, and had started talking about getting married. Maybe even having kids somewhere down the line (which is a whole *other* story, some of which you now know about). Anyway, I just kinda freaked out.'

Hard for me to imagine Alice freaking out.

'Oh Nate, I can be such a head case.'

Leo moved in with a friend of his; Alice stayed-put at their place. Over time, she says, the space—and therapy—calmed her right down, 'brought me back to center,' she says. And reassured her regarding those apprehensions about Leo.

'He's as imperfect as all of us, but Leo's a good man. Deep

down I knew it. That time apart really worked, got me to re-focus on the things about him that won me over to begin with.'

Which is why she's telling me, she says.

'One day I was in this used bookshop I liked killing time in. And there was this big display of self-help stuff. Now you know it's not the kind of thing I'd normally even bother to look at, but I just picked up this book that seemed to be about couples. Challenges in long-term relationships. And what I read dealt specifically with hurt feelings, or disappointed feelings toward your partner. (You know, I remember looking around to make sure no one I knew was there, no one to see what I was reading!)'

She chuckles at herself, we both shake our heads.

These games.

She didn't actually buy the book, but the few pages she read in the store ended up helping her. How? Seems they described a process whereby a person spends some time every day 'sending love' to their partner.

Come again?

'Sending love. You know, just sort of tapping into that part of you that loves them, and sending it out to them wherever they are. Might sound loopy but there it is. The way I did it was by focusing on the things about Leo I appreciated—his generosity with people, his kindness. Leo treats everyone the same. The same respect. Doesn't matter if it's a good friend or one of his students, or even strangers. And he'll go out of his way to help me solve a problem I'm having. To say nothing of his patience. Even his sense of humor, which is so much more important than I'd ever taken time to acknowledge. Anyway, it's just a way of moving the focus away from things about them that disappoint you. Not to *forget* them, just to keep them in perspective.'

'And you did this? You actually . . .'

'Believe it or not. A few minutes every day. You should try it, sweetie. I know you see Sadie as the woman who dumped you, but I also know how deeply you care for her.'

I shake my head, don't say anything. Skeptical, sure, but as I say I'm ready to try anything. And that's when Alice tips the scale with a favorite phrase of hers.

'What's the downside?'

'And when that warmth reached my face I opened my eyes. Like I *had* to open them—something told me to. And oh my goodness, Nate, you can't believe the *light*. I've never seen anything like it. It was *ma*gical. Every single object in Shuly's living room— all the tables, chairs, books, even the walls, I mean *every single thing*—had this glow. This aura. Oh my god it was just . . . so *yummy*. I can't even describe it. So beautiful. *Sooo* beautiful.'

Brenda's peaking, getting more excited by the minute, finally ready to spill the beans about whatever the hell all this means. Her latest epiphany. So I'm almost home, only have to get to the end of this California séance they cooked up. I'm trying to hear her, to stay focused just a little longer—this obviously means a lot to her. And hey—kooky as she may seem at times, at least Brenda never bores me to tears with inane talk of television shows.

But even in the homestretch I'm stuck on this business of Sadie never skydiving. She didn't give it the chance, like me laid-out on her table letting her cover my body with needles. She didn't understand that skydiving can be a positive place to put your energies, too. Every bit as healthy as acupuncture and aroma-therapy, massage or reflexology.

Some (me) might even say more so.

If she would've gone with me, knelt in front of the plane's

open door, she might've seen, understood the magic of that moment. You're alive. You're part of the planet, living in a body. A body that's fragile and can die if . . .

But right then? *Ifs* don't matter. Only one thing does.

It's crazy, you know. Everybody's out buying books about 'living in the moment'—between Buddhism and Sufi-ism and god knows how many other *isms*, the bookstores are spilling over with paperbacks supposedly containing the key to Ultimate Wisdom and Eternal Happiness. Look, I dig reading as much as the next guy, but if you're really looking to live in the moment, ditch the books, all those hours of sitting, like Enlightenment's going to drop into your lotus-ed lap. Give me an hour to get you suited up, and in the ten minutes it takes the plane to climb to fourteen-thousand feet I guarantee to get you well aware of the moment. You're kneeling there with your balls in your throat, holding onto a bar that's been gripped by thousands of excited, terrified hands, and it's like this current that courses through you.

At the risk of sounding like Brenda, maybe it's actually there in that bar, some of it, anyway—the energy of previous jumpers, the residual concentrated intensity from all those hands that were there holding that bar before *yours* were.

Anyway, call it what you like, but you'll find it. Looking out at nothing but endless sky, the air of it rushing over you, the Earth below just a patchwork of shapes and shades, there'll be no concern for who owes you what, who has wronged you or what mark you've made on the world. All you'll care about is *living*, the indescribable experience you're at that very moment in the midst of.

And that's Life in a nutshell, isn't it? I mean, I *know* this, and experience it multiple times every day at Psycho. So why can't I seem to stay there?

Once I leave the cemetery, there's still an hour to kill before I'm supposed to meet Margaret. Ye gods. It's been four years since I laid eyes on her, and I'm shaky, queasy, my legs all weak and quivery.

The thought of getting a quick drink to settle the nerves is tempting, but I resist it. Instead, find myself driving through the neighborhood where I grew up, almost like the car takes me there of its own volition. And what a thing to do. When I get to the house, I stop and pull up to the curb across the street in front of what was (still is?) the Petersen house. From the outside our place looks essentially the same, though there's now an American flag flapping from a pole attached to the side of the carport, where a pickup truck is parked. Right there. That's right where my dad smacked the shit out of me, blamed me for the dent in our bumper he himself put there. I try to visualize it—can't. What I see instead is me hauling off and slugging him right back.

If only.

I know nothing at all about the people who bought the house: a young couple recently married, according to what Dottie'd said. I consider knocking—take this trip down Memory Lane up a notch—but reconsider when I try to imagine what I would say to whoever answered.

Sure it's only a house—bricks, boards, glass—but just looking at it gives me all these weird sensations, a hollowed-out, welling-up feeling, and when I drive up the street to Hearst Elementary these rushes roll over me like waves. I drive around back and park the car, walk to the newfangled footbridge crossing the small creek which at one time led into that stand of woods I loved to get lost in.

ENCHANTED WOODS, reads a big brick sign.

Enchanted woods my ass—only a few token trees dot the landscape. Instead, one of those pre-fab neighborhoods with cookie-cutter houses, postage-stamp yards, each dwelling hardly distinguishable from the one next to it—probably took them a month to mow down the forest and throw up all these homes. I sit on the edge of the bridge like I used to, legs dangling down, and wonder if they found anything fun in those woods when they cut them down—the treasure-filled treefort? Bigfoot? Then scan the seepage below for the crayfish I used to gig, but there's barely enough water for a moccasin to slither through.

It's crazy, I know, but I get all sentimental sitting there. Like what happened to the haunts of my childhood?

Well, people live here now. Some of them good people who want only to help the world around them. Not their fault my memories got clear-cut.

I remember Miss Humphreys, a teacher at Hearst, once caught me smoking cigarettes beneath this bridge—I'd slipped a couple from my mother's pack. She sent me home early. And when my dad got there he pulled my pants down, pressed my face to the bedroom wall and beat the backs of my legs with a leather sandal belonging to my mom.

Memory Lane? More like the scene of the crime.

It seems silly at first, but Alice's comment about the downside coaxes me on. Trust Alice. Just trust her.

So I sit on the sofa, spend a few minutes thinking about Sadie and the way things were when we first met. And Alice was right (naturally)—it isn't easy to recall those good times without letting the end of them get the best of me. You want the truth of it? It makes me miss Sadie so much I just want to lay down and die.

I've never felt this way about a woman—now I know why.

So the first few attempts are a bust, but eventually I break through it. Sort of. I remember the day I first met her, going in to get a massage, how amazing she looked in that blue dress. And how—when I damned the torpedoes and asked her out—she'd said she wasn't looking for someone to date.

Then she went out with me anyway. *Cha-ching!*

Recalling our first breakfast together actually manages to make me smile, and the fun reflection gets even better when I think about the dinner-date that followed. How I shamed myself crying over my parents, and how Sadie had said I was beautiful.

This is when the shit hits the fan.

Before I know it the memories become punishing, unstoppable, and I wonder what's the point of putting myself through this. One minute I'm admiring Sadie's faith that we were fated to find each other—the way she'd ask where I'd come from, like I was what she'd been seeking—then the next minute I'm wondering who's the lucky bastard living my dream now? After all she'd said, all we'd been through, what other explanation was there? I know, I know—her dad died. He killed himself. But why'd that end *us*? Was it something I did, didn't do? Took her twenty lousy minutes to lower the boom on me, next thing I know a brown bag with all my stuff shows up on the Penthouse doorstep.

Some fucking healer, thinks I. More like a loaded gun, the Devil in a blue dress.

I try to shift the focus back to the woman I fell in love with, but another part of me is thinking a fraud is *exactly* what she is. Thinks, just because you've got pictures of a so-called guru all over your house, and just because you give yourself some fancy spiritual name that's supposed to reflect your 'higher self,' doesn't mean you're anything more than another lame empty book with a pretty cover on it. All that talk about the compassionate life, and opening your heart to humanity—what about *me*? Aren't I part of humanity, or don't I qualify?

Etc.

Damn, this is worse than useless. Alice is nuts. I just want to run, escape. Where are the woods of Hearst when I need them?

'The glow's part of everything—that was the sense of it. Only we rarely notice it. And now me and Shuly were seeing it. This radiance that's in everything. Coming out. Showing itself.

'And I just started talking—it was like being in a trance. I wasn't thinking about what I was saying, I was just saying it. I was so *obviously* channeling. I'm just sorry we didn't record it somehow, get it on tape. Because I have no idea what-all I was saying, except for the stuff Shuly told me. You know, I've never felt so good in my life. Never. *Ever.*'

She's probably not aware of it, but what Brenda's really doing is just reiterating the old line about the kingdom of God being spread before us, only we don't see it. I well know the sentiment, but the worst of me still wonders. Maybe that so-called Kingdom is in the eye of the beholder.

And there only.

Subsequent to that timeless Saturday when we found ourselves—and each other—in that dark wide-open space far from the dirty ground of this gaudy world, Sadie said she'd been looking for me her whole life. Not someone *like* me, she clarified, making sure I heard her. *Me.*

'I've known you before. That's why it's so easy for us. Feels so natural.'

Mind you, this kind of talk might have sent some straight for the door (me, for one, not all that long ago) but there's a catch—I *felt* what she was describing. It seemed Right. I can't claim any insight into 'past lives' or 'the soul's journey' or any of that other stuff she espoused, but the *sense* of things between us was exactly as she described it.

Did she ditch me back then, too, all those lives ago? And, if so, why didn't I see it coming this time around?

Slow learner, I guess. Next time I'm not falling for it—I'll tell her to find another sucker to stick her needles into.

Who am I kidding? One more look at Sadie the Stunner and I'll be sunk all over again.

Such is what I say to Lynn at our next session, trying to convey this maddening back-and-forth business that's making mush of my brain. But she doesn't bat an eye, just pins me down in that way she has.

'The question isn't, *When will I ever learn*, Nate. The question to ask yourself is, *Do I really* want *to learn*?'

Sure I do. But can't I use a cheat sheet?

I'm in the supermarket when I see her. Duck into the next aisle quickly, hoping she didn't spot me. Start scanning soup cans, pray she'll walk on without stopping.

She doesn't. I notice peripherally that Tyler is headed straight for me, like a missile. Tyler, damn. Memories of waking up at her place in the Projects, covered with dried blood, send an awful shiver through me. She's pushing a grocery buggy, but before she even gets to me I can see the enormous bulge of a pregnant belly.

First, an immediate panic—no way I can do the math in that moment.

But dig this:

'Don't worry,' she says first thing, smiling, like she read my mind. 'I just got married.'

My whole being relaxes, and I hope she doesn't notice. I play it off—badly perhaps—like that was the furthest thing from my mind, and congratulate her. But even being let off the hook it's still awkward as hell. I ran out on her that bloody morning, a million years ago. Hit and run.

My god, the things I did.

We swap pleasantries, then she moves to walk on, says to take care. And just as she pushes her cart past me, I summon the courage to say it.

'You know,' stumbling at first, 'I'm sorry for . . . you know . . . what happened. I mean, it wasn't you. You didn't deserve that.'

She huffs away the apology in a breath.

'Whoever said Life was about *deserving*?' she says.

Touché. Seems even the Tyler's of the world have a lesson or two to teach me.

'Now, what Shuly can confirm is that we got two distinct messages. Both important, both very clear. The first was that the consciousness of the planet is changing, lifting. Feminine energy is becoming more and more prevalent, in both obvious and not-so-obvious ways. But one thing we're going to start seeing is more and more women stepping into leadership roles. I mean, we're talking *maaajor*.'

All I can think of is The Who—meet the new boss. Same as the old boss.

'Not knocking men, but male energy's different, and it's been in charge for too long. And part of what's going to come out of this is that a lot of the energy we've been stuck with—all the violence, all the fear—that energy isn't going to command the power that it always has.

'And this isn't something that's a long way off. This is happening *right now*. The feeling was, *Okay, things have been bad. War, terrorism, lying politicians. But everything's changing.* The phrase that came out of me—Shuly actually made a point of remembering this one—was *Every Now is new.* I just *said* this. Meaning that we as a planet don't have to sit around wishing things were different, we have to raise our consciousness. We actually have to *do* it. And what the Energy was showing us was that we *are* and *have been* doing it. We're doing a good job, but we can't give up. Can't quit working.'

To hell with the planet, I want to say, I'm just trying to get through the day. We've *earned* this fucked-up world. Why shouldn't we pay a hefty price for all the damage done?

My god what a mood I'm in.

I remind myself it's not Brenda's fault. She's a kind person, truly wants the best for everyone. I don't doubt this for a second. Flaky or not, she could be onto something. Fact is, I'd love to see her have the last laugh. On *all* of us.

Besides, even if that Kingdom *is* only in the eye of pretty beholders like Brenda, maybe she's better off than those of us who see nothing of the sort. Who look at the world we live in and see one colossal mess, a mess we're all responsible for making.

And one that'll kill you, to ice the shitcake.

You may fool those new friends of yours . . .

Kimberly's note comes back to haunt me. In a blink I'll wonder if she's right, wonder if that's what I've been doing all along.

A hero-poet—a man of extreme contradictions, and with a massive ego—once confessed in an interview that the first time he read his poems in public he was petrified, and that his wife's advice was, simply, 'Just be yourself.'

His reply, however, spoke volumes: 'Which Self?'

I'm tired of the turmoil. The thought of checking out— marching through my days high as a kite and attached to no one—has lost *none* of its appeal despite all the therapy, all the well-meaning help from new friends. I mean, why is it that I have more support and encouragement than ever, yet am *lonelier* than ever, and feel lousier about myself than therapy can even begin to contend with? Maybe Max is right: I'm just like the poet, save the part about writing poems.

'But christ, Nate,' says My Lovely Man, all serious. 'Look at that poor bastard's *life*. The madness of it. It wore him out. Is that what *you* want?'

Which Me?

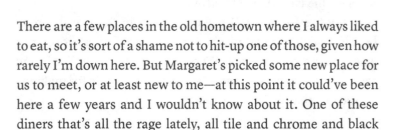

There are a few places in the old hometown where I always liked to eat, so it's sort of a shame not to hit-up one of those, given how rarely I'm down here. But Margaret's picked some new place for us to meet, or at least new to me—at this point it could've been here a few years and I wouldn't know about it. One of these diners that's all the rage lately, all tile and chrome and black booths, like everyone wants to relive the 50's or something.

No thanks—I'll stay put.

I'm too nervous for coffee, so order a chocolate shake. In honesty, I don't know that I've *ever* ordered a chocolate shake. But when the dude brings it to me he says, 'Best shake in town.' It's in this cone-shaped glass with thick ridges along the sides, and a straw. I never drink out of straws, either—why bother?—but in a case like this you kind of have to. Too thick for sipping.

Damn, I won't lie to you—that first sip is mighty fine. If I were high, it'd be the nectar of the gods.

And speaking of mighty fine, here comes Margaret, looking like a million bucks, to boot. My god, I can hardly believe it. Getting shed of me seems to have suited her.

First words out of her mouth when she sees me? 'When did you ever drink a milkshake?'

I stand, hoping for a hug, and she delivers, though admittedly it's a bit awkward. I'd forgotten how tall she is, a half-inch shy of six feet. She's wearing these tight black slacks that accentuate her great legs, even if they flare at the feet. Flats, a white blouse, auburn hair in a French braid. Blue eyes I could look at the rest of my life.

Well, I had my chance.

She orders a grilled cheese with a house salad—'I see you're not eating, but this might be the only chance I'll get this afternoon'—and water with no ice. Seems she's working, Saturday be damned. 'I'm on call,' says the Professional.

Margaret made good on her ambition, got her Master's in Speech Pathology and now works with patients at one of the big hospitals here in town. As she speaks, I'm fascinated by her every word, really riveted (why am I surprised?), as if I've never had a conversation with her before. And I don't want to talk, don't want to say a word, would rather sit back and listen to anything—and everything—she has to say. I'm experiencing a moment pulled straight from Brenda's playbook—an epiphany—and it has to do with how little I gave to Margaret all those years ago, how rarely I took the time to just sit and listen to her. Admittedly, I'm almost not listening *now*, swept-up as I am in this sudden awareness of the way we were. Or the way *I* was. But I'm watching her all the while, just drinking her in, and she's speaking with this kind of self-assured, capable ebullience I can't believe I'd never noticed.

The stab of shame—that comes next. Didn't I know how sharp she is, Margaret who made nothing but A's (an occasional B) all throughout high school and college? That, among other things, she had no intention of working for a caterer the rest of her life?

I damn the torpedoes, risk inquiring about romance. Fact is, I'd give it another go in a cold second if I got a vibe she was interested. I mean, you should *see* her. She might be just the thing to take the wind out of Sadie's heart-breaking sails.

But this full-circle fantasy gets shot down before I can fully hatch it even in my own mind. She's been seeing a guy—Paul—for just over a year now. They don't live together, though, and have no plans to. Not at this point, anyway.

'Not that we're not committed. We definitely are. Both of us.

But we like our independence, too, our own space. I'm sure we'll get married eventually, but frankly, I'm in no hurry. My life is exactly what I want it to be right now.'

I smile, a part of me sincerely happy she's satisfied. What she can't see (thank goodness) is that something inside still sinks to hear her say it.

Kooky as it may sound, Alice's crazy strategy starts to work—I won't lie to you.

After however-many-days of getting pissed every time I sit down with the notion of 'sending love' to Sadie, the thing builds some momentum and my attitude takes a turn. Before, when I'd sit down with the intention of loving her, anger came quickly, like damnit why did she say all those things if she didn't mean them? One sentimental Saturday, however, I'm stretched out on the sofa, the lethargy of yearning having sapped most of my energy, and all I can think about—*all* I can think about—is how much I loved waking up with Sadie. How I loved when she would just lie there and let me kiss her, kiss her, that beautiful head of thick black hair splashed around the prettiest face I've ever seen, the hint of a smile just perceptible enough to show she likes what I'm doing, what we're doing, just loving and loving like that's all we're here for, all that matters. She's real, I can see her, feel my lips on her face. So I send it out just like Alice said, my mouth making the shape of the words without the sound. *I love you Sadie, Sadie Ananda. Far away though you may be, I love you.*

This takes over, becomes my experience whenever I make time for Alice's suggested practice. The pissing and moaning I'd spent so much time on evaporates like a feeling, so sick as

I am of hearing it. It's a voice that only makes me miserable, and I'm tired of all it tells me. Mind you, getting dumped by my dream-girl is still the biggest drag ever, but I start to give Sadie the benefit of the doubt, like she must've had her reasons. Her dad's suicide, sure—that would throw anyone. But some of her reasons may have pertained to me: maybe all Brenda's karma talk has started to sink in, because I wonder about getting some kind of comeuppance. After all, I can't deny doing my own share of damage to people in my past. I mean, Kimberly may have been a wildcard, but it's only because she's damaged goods. The few things I learned about her history may have been mere conversation topics at the time, stations to pass through en route to the next romp, but I'm starting to see them as the things that shaped her into the woman she is. Whether it's her drug-addict parents (*both* of them) or her numerous relationships with men who mistreated her, Kimberly hasn't had an easy time of it.

I mean, this is *seriously* strange. I start out sending love to Sadie, end up feeling sorry for Kimberly. And guilty—I'm yet another guy who took advantage of the great sex she had to offer (magnificent, really) without giving a second thought to what might be going on underneath it all, what she might really want or need.

No wonder Sadie dumped me.

I take Alice to the batting cage as a *thankyou* gesture—it's a surprise. The crippling brunette who is a respected faculty member in the university's department of anthropology also happens to have a fetish for getting in a batting cage (so she once told me), smacking the shit out of machine-propelled baseballs.

Alice is endless.

Me, I've never been near one of these things, had to call all over the place just to find out whether we even had one in town. At the time she told me about this particular passion, she said she hadn't done it in ages.

I made the mental note then, now here we are.

It's fun to watch, actually, even if I feel no desire to do it. She has her hair tied into a ponytail and is wearing a batting helmet they supply, and to watch her striking that stance and swinging at those pitches is a complete turn-on. Thirty minutes later when she says she's had enough, I tell her to hit the showers.

Then add, 'Mind if I join you?'

This gets a good laugh. 'If I weren't a married woman . . . '

God I love Alice.

It's after, sharing a pot of hot tea at her place, that I tell her all about my latest little epiphany, and how her sending-love strategy is responsible. I even swallow the ego and show her the little slip of paper on which I've written a message to myself, one I now carry in my wallet and look at daily.

I want to be a thoughtful person.

'I got the idea from Brenda, who said she writes these things to herself all the time. Calls them *affirmations*.'

Alice stares at the slip a moment with a weird look, like maybe she's confused by it. Then says, 'Nate, I'd like to make a suggestion. You mind?'

I shake my head and she goes into her purse, comes out with a pen. 'It's just a suggestion,' she repeats.

She takes her pen and scratches through the words **want to be**, writes one word above the scratch-out: **am**.

Where did she come from?

'Now there's a second message we got, too. Like I said. And in a way this one was even more surprising.'

Yet another chapter. Is she kidding?

'What was made clear is that it's becoming important, really *urgent*, that *men* manifest this energy, not just women. You know, it's not like every woman is so much more evolved than the men in the world. Women are just as human as men. Now we think we know this, but even *I'm* guilty of forgetting. And that's where *you* come in.'

Uh-oh.

Brenda takes my hands on the table, grips them tightly. Stares straight into me. It's like this crazy story she's telling turns deadly serious, and all of her intensity is suddenly shifted—focused—on me. What the hell?

'I need you to listen to me, sweetie. Really *hear* what I'm about to say, okay?'

I'm frozen.

'You are one of them, Nathan. You're trying. You're doing *sooo* much good work, and I want you to know that. Really *know* it.'

Already I'm cracking—it's easier to stay outside, but hard to do so with Brenda's big browns boring into me.

'And I want to honor that. I want you to understand that I *see* all you're doing. A *lot* of us see it, and it's working. That glow, that radiance I spoke of? It's coming out of you. I sensed it the day we met—I believe that's *why* we met. Remember me telling you about the voice I heard that morning, how it told me to come to this coffeeshop? And you know, the more you started to share yourself the brighter that radiance got. This is why people are drawn to you, Nate—people like Alice and Leo, people like Stacy. Even those who aren't around anymore. Sadie or Kimberly. Your spark is *sooo* bright, so *brilliant*. And even if people aren't conscious of it, they need it. Intuitively something in them is drawn to it. Drawn to *you*.'

Slipping. Little clipped gasps I can't keep. She squeezes my hands tighter, and I'm praying she never lets go of them. It's like she's holding me together.

'Remember, Nate: what you do, what you *are*, impacts the world around you. Don't let everyone else's stuff stop you from seeing this. Or your *own* stuff. That heart of yours is big enough to hold anything. *Everything*. And the more you open it, the more you *share* it with us, the more Good we'll have in the world. Never underestimate that Good.'

But I'm a mess, I want to say. I'm *tired* of working, tired of trying to stay on top of every move I make. I'd like to burn my way through a bottle of Bushmills and a big bag of weed and spend the next seven days screwing my brains out. It's like I'm sliding right back down the pipe, and maybe people like Sadie see this, see that there's something in me hell-bent for failure.

And once they get that glimpse? They hit the ground running.

'What if it's all just a lie? Something we tell ourselves because we're afraid to face the other?'

Lynn dodges the question—probably the first thing they learn in Shrink School. 'First, let's not talk in terms of *we*. Let's talk about you.'

You ask me, I think she knows I'm onto something. Something ugly. And she wants to avoid it.

'And second, what do you mean by "*it all*?" What are you referring to specifically?'

'*Everything*! All this . . . this stuff about the so-called "work" I'm doing. How I'm making progress, as if I'm actually *getting* somewhere. Like there's some spiritual Finish Line somewhere, and once I cross it I'll live in a . . . an enlightened state of bliss or something. Never screw up again. Such horseshit.'

She considers this. I'm pretty sure I've got her on the run because she takes a long time to answer. Long even for Lynn.

'Listen, Nate. I don't disagree with what you're saying. Finish Line? As you yourself are quick to point out, we finish when we die, and up to then we work hard for our happiness—it's not guaranteed by any means. For anyone. Many people spend their entire lives unhappy, and it doesn't mean they're bad people, or less deserving of happiness.'

This is her strategy. She slows things down, enunciates every word of whatever point she means to make. It's what she does when I get going, start running off.

And the fact is it works: I can't deny it. My brain—off to the races—starts to ease up a bit, let someone else get a word in.

Starts to *listen*.

'Let me ask you, Nate: in the past, when you've said you were happy, that time you even said you were happier than you'd ever been before? Remember?'

I nod. I do remember, even if it seems like ancient history at this point. Like it must've been someone else doing the talking.

'Were you being honest, telling me the truth? In that moment.'

I don't say anything, just give her the go-ahead with a glance.

'And was what you felt, that happiness, was it as . . . did it seem as real to you as the *un*happiness you're feeling now?'

Switcheroo—she's got *me* on the run. Or *part* of me, anyway. A part I'd love to let go of.

'So,' says the Wise One, sitting back in her seat. 'What difference does it make—ultimately—even if it *is* a lie?'

Margaret pours a puddle of ketchup onto her plate from the bottle on the table—tapping the sides with her knife to get it going—then dunks her grilled cheese into it before taking a bite. I do this, too, only I'd forgotten that Margaret's the source, the one who taught me. How could I have forgotten such a thing? Hell, if I had to eat grilled cheese without dunking it in ketchup, it'd hardly be worth the time.

And don't even *consider* the shortcut of putting ketchup on the sandwich in advance—not the same at all.

'I do that, too,' says the Sentimentalist. 'With the ketchup. And I always think of you when I do.'

Hey—I know it's a lie, but I can still mean it. Because the fact is from now on I really *will* think of her.

Says Margaret: 'Glad you got something from it all.'

Damn. This statement stings so much my face must show it, because she immediately supplies the salve.

'Sorry. I didn't mean that. Just a stupid thing to say.'

I decide to try something.

'I got a lot, Meg. More than even *I* knew at the time.'

'I know,' she says. 'That's just old anger. I had a lot of anger back then. But it's done. I don't have time for it. Look, let's not get into all that. What I did want to tell you is how sorry I was to hear about your mom.'

A shock, this. Want to know why? In the moment I'd forgotten she even *knew* my mom. Crazy. Truth is, Margaret probably knows more about me than anyone on the planet. Or at least the me I was back then. And that's the rub: I want to rewrite history, show her that was the *old* me, not the new-and-improved one.

But how?

What's the point, is more like it. I'm so uncertain of all this I can't even convince myself, much less Margaret.

'I appreciate that,' I say.

'Your mom had such a time. I hope her ending was okay.'

'I think it was,' I say, lying some more. Not having been here, I can't claim to have a clue.

'How're *your* folks?'

'They're doing really well, actually.'

It strikes me that she's eating fast, going at that sandwich like gangbusters. Is she in a hurry, or am I paranoid?

Don't answer.

'Daddy's about to retire. And they're talking about traveling some. I don't believe it, but maybe they will. I kind of think he'll end up fishing every day.'

Margaret's parents have a house on the bluff, and the inlet that runs by their dock leads right to this big lake, Bryce Lake. I recall her dad used to complain a lot about not having time to fish. He's a lawyer.

I'm feeling niggled, want to steer the conversation back to the two of us, our marriage and divorce. Who knows why? Maybe Lynn's right, that I'm looking for some kind of closure (new word). But just then our waiter comes up, the bastard, and I see that her sandwich is history. Damn, she *inhaled* that food.

'Can I get you anything else?'

I'm considering a coffee, just to keep things going, but she has other ideas.

'Just the check,' she says (briskly, I'll add). And, to me, 'Sorry, but I really need to get back.'

Work, I suppose she means. The waiter pulls the pad from his waist-apron, starts figuring right there at the table. Is he eavesdropping?

'You still skydiving? I heard you were licensed and everything.'

I nod, half-smile like it's no big thing. The waiter grins, says "Sweet."

'So I guess you got over your fear of flying.'

'Not really. Put me on a commercial flight and I'm still a nervous wreck. Eating Xanax.' This reminds me of my trip to Spain, the meaningful hike on el Camino—this could clue her in.

She chuckles. 'That's so *odd*, isn't it?'

Damn, she really looks great. Were her eyes always so blue? I honestly don't remember.

The waiter puts our check down finally. Thanks us for coming. Clearly there's no time for bringing up my hike—it'd feel forced.

'Hey, will you let me get this?' says the Man-Figure, pointing at the check. 'After all I put you through it's the least I can do.'

A stupid thing to say, sure, but it's like I'm dying to show her somehow, let her know how sorry I am. Only I'm not sure how to say it. And she seems in such a hurry I'm all frazzled.

'God don't be silly. You didn't even eat. I'll take care of it.'

She pulls a wallet from her purse and parcels through the bills, eyeing the check on the table. I notice the wallet's one I've never seen.

It's been years.

She starts to say something—'I wanted to ask you . . .'—but doesn't finish since she's sidetracked by the bills and the counting.

I'm hanging by a thread, hoping. Maybe she'll bring it back to us after all. Maybe she's just as anxious as I am to clear the air between us, given all we went through together, those many lives ago. Or maybe she'll ask if I'm seeing anyone, and I can tell her about Sadie, all the efforts I made to be the perfect partner. I can tell her how I've cleaned up my act and put a bunch of bad habits behind me, and even though things didn't work out with Sadie I'm sure I'll find what I'm looking for. Someone who'll see my worth, and who's *ready*, like Alice says.

Because *I'm* ready—that'll be the unspoken message. And Margaret will hear it: she's sharp. So to spur her on I say, 'You wanted to ask me what?'

She finally finishes up with the money. 'I wanted to ask . . . what was it? Oh yeah, I wanted to ask you how was that shake? They're supposed to be real good here.'

A psychic I'm not.

I try to imagine my dad's life. Or—more accurately—*my* life were it like my dad's. What would it be like if I couldn't have sex. *Ever.* And pretty soon the question turns on me—

Forget my *life*, what would *I* be like?

Would I take it in stride, adjust myself to the sexless life in the way someone with food allergies sacrifices certain foods, or an alcoholic kicks booze? I can even entertain the notion that I might be a better person—that sex has been the source of so many mistakes and bad choices (can you say *Kimberly*?) that maybe my life would be streamlined, simplified without it.

Who am I kidding? The bottom line is I'd be a bitter son of a bitch. I'd probably dive straight into the same bottle, surfacing only long enough to slap the shit out of my wife.

Or son.

These are the kinds of questions I start asking myself more and more. And then I take them straight to Lynn, whose job (it sometimes seems) isn't to provide answers, but rather to come up with more questions.

Like I'm telling her about all the stuff Dottie said, about my dad and the stroke and the end of his sex life.

With what I saw of him, I can't imagine he *ever* had a sex life.

And this story leads me to something I'd never noticed before: history.

'History?'

'Well, this'll sound absurd. It started in Spain, walking around in these little villages—even a city like Pamplona—where everything's so *old*, you know? Started me thinking about how every place has a history. And not only every place, but all the people *in* that place. I mean, I never really thought about people having a history, a past. People were always just who they were. But lately I'm hearing so much about the other stuff. About my parents and what they went through, or how my friend Alice had all these awful things happen when she was younger. And I guess . . . that's *everybody*, right? Kimberly and her drug-addict parents, Sadie losing her mom when she was still in high school, that kind of thing. And now Sadie's father, who committed suicide—that becomes her history, *part* of her. And that kind of makes her who she is *now*. I know it should be obvious, but I never thought about this stuff.'

'Does it change the way you see them?'

'Well, maybe. At least that's the idea. What I'm shooting for.'

At this point, I'm grateful for anything new to shoot for.

'Can you give me an example?'

The hot seat. I take a minute, but damnit I'm on a roll so dredge up something that'll do. I tell her about Alice and all that sending-love-to-Sadie business. I watch Lynn's face when I say this—see if she's shocked, or maybe gives me one of those looks, like she thinks it's a ridiculous thing to do—but nothing crosses her mind that I can see.

'At some point I started thinking about her *parents*, Sadie's

222

parents. She was so into them, said her childhood was this magical time. So I'd be all mad at her, right? The breakup and everything. And then I'd imagine what it must've been like when her mom died. I mean, she was only seventeen. Like . . . damn . . . it must've really been murder for her.'

'So . . . '

'So then I can't stay mad. I just start feeling sorry for her. Even wish I could call and tell her how sorry I am . . . '

Stop here. Before it gets messy.

Lynn's quiet for a minute, digesting in that way she has. Then in this real sincere voice she says, 'That's lovely. It is. You're finding the whole Sadie, or at least a fuller picture of her. Not just the Sadie who hurt you.'

Well put. She's congratulating me, yes. So why am I sad all of a sudden?

'Let me ask you *this*, Nate. Through thinking about people's history, you're able to . . . I'd say extend your compassion to them. Would you agree?'

I nod. Good enough, I guess.

'Can you do the same thing with yourself?'

See what I mean? All these *questions*.

'But the point is to improve the way I treat people.'

'But how about *you*? Can you step back, step outside of yourself and see that even you are a person with a history? In other words, can you take what Alice had you doing for others and apply it to yourself? Send love to *you*?'

I may not say it, but I won't lie to you. What I think without a second thought is, *But that guy is such a* loser.

'Look: I don't mean to upset you. But look at me. Really: look at me.'

I do. I'm shaking, but looking back at her, Brenda's eyes lasered into mine.

'I *see* you. I see *you*. And you're beautiful. You are a beautiful man, Nate. Wounded, like all of us, but beautiful. *Know* your beauty, *own* it. It can take you anywhere you want to go. I mean it. You can have the life you want. It's inside you. You just have to make it.'

She lets go of my hands, and I use them to wipe my face, suddenly conscious of being in public. But she reaches out and puts her palms on either side of my cheeks, as if to say, *I'm not done*.

'Remember,' says my pretty teacher. 'Every Now is new.'

I want to be a believer. Is she right? Is it true? Or is every Now just another boat against the current, fighting a losing battle to stay afloat because it's loaded down with the burden of all that's come before?

Says Brenda the Beautiful: 'I gotta pee again.'

Twenty minutes: that's how long it took Sadie—roughly—to say *sayonara* to the redhead she'd been searching for her whole life. The guy she'd known, and loved—if I accept her version of events—in a previous life.

Twenty minutes.

Maybe what's amazing isn't so much the crazy notions we concoct to get along in this life, all our weird beliefs, so often based on faith rather than fact. Maybe what's amazing is how quickly we'll let go of those beliefs.

I thank Brenda for the date this morning, and for the vote of confidence I can take from it.

'No, thank *you*,' she says. 'I know things are really hard right now, so I appreciate you taking the time. Coming out. They *will* get better, hon. I promise.'

We hug, which admittedly helps, and she says she'll see me in two weeks—'If not before!'—at the birthday gathering Max and Alice have conspired to put together for me. I say that maybe by then I'll be out of my funk, but she lets me off the hook either way.

'You are where you are. I know you'll lick this thing eventually.'

'Don't say *lick this thing*,' I say, mock-serious, grinning a little.

'See what I mean? You're already on the way!'

On the way, yes, but where? I'm in the car and headed away from town before I've even figured out where it is I'm going, but in no time at all it becomes clear where my intuition is taking me. Don't ask me—something steers me south, toward Foxborough, those roads I used to race down all excited driving to Sadie's place.

It's a hell of a pretty drive, all the farms and open country along the way, but this time memory and loss has riddled old 89 with emotional potholes that make the ride a bumpy one, me wondering the whole way what the hell I'm doing headed down this haunted highway. At one point I even consider bypassing the place altogether: I could just keep driving straight into Foxborough, spend the afternoon wandering around town. But since Sadie's office is there I'd run that risk, like maybe I'm stalking her or something. Which I'm not, right? But we all know how it would look, what she'd think, and hell—I couldn't even blame her.

So instead I take that turnoff toward Majestic Oaks, then pull onto the little side-street where Sadie'd parked the time we came here together. Before I get out of the car I go into the glove-box on a whim, and sure enough there it is: the ever-present pre-loaded pipe, almost like I'd left it there on purpose. Or completely forgot about it.

Hey, I'll go either way.

What's there isn't much, and brittle-dry, but I take it just the same and actually seem to get a fine hit—it's the first time in months, and I'm sorry the second I do it, like I've committed some heinous sin that'll send me straight to Hell. What would friends think? What'll Lynn say if I fess up, all my efforts on the wagon for naught? But the second that pleasant wash starts to pour on I decide to damn the torpedoes and take the ride without guilt. *Don't spook the horse*, Kimberly would say, and she'd be right, given that I've already done the deed. Maybe I'll be sorry, but let's leave that for later, at least put it off a bit.

This is private property, but we welcome you to our place of peace. Be respectful. No alcoholic beverages, please. Closes at dusk.

The sign doesn't mention wacky tobaccky, so I'm covered. (And what does *closes at dusk* really mean? How do you 'close' an open field at the top of a hill?) The long walk up that hill winds me a little, my feet heavy with apprehension, my chest sunk from the weight of what's on it, but I know the view—if nothing else—will be worth it.

Poemhenge.

It's clear the grass has been cut recently, so someone takes care of this place. Good thing they didn't show up the day Sadie and I were here, naked on that granite table in the center of the circle. We'd have all gotten more than we bargained for.

I stop the memory in its tracks, bury it.

Approaching the first monolith (East on the compass) I read the poem engraved into its surface, one about how we should welcome trouble and travail, how they might serve a valuable purpose and open us up for *some new delight*. Does it seem directed at me specifically? Bet your ass it does: hits close enough to home to send a shiver through me. So I read the next stanza, even worse (better?), the words having the hollow stab of out-of-leftfield accuracy.

> *Open your hands if*
> *you want to be held.*
> *Quit acting like a wolf and feel*
> *the Shepard's Love filling you.*
> *Consider what you've been doing!*
> *Here's a better arrangement: Give up this life*
> *and get a hundred new lives.*

A hundred new lives? I'll take every one of them.

For no reason I'm aware of, I begin reading these stanzas aloud to the empty field, but half-way through the poem my throat thickens and it becomes hard to swallow. By the time I get to the end of the second poem it's like someone's playing a trick on me, like there's a camera hidden out here somewhere to capture my reaction to these words having been altered to fit my own feelings and circumstances.

I look around, sort of spooked, but no one's here.

The next two poems are no different: the recurring theme seems to be that suffering and loss are rampant, part of the package, but there are energies here—God, Nature—to comfort us. Like a smartass, my brain points out that these comforting forces aren't going to make love to me in the middle of Poemhenge like Sadie did, but I take to heart some of what I've been hearing from friends, 'open myself' to whatever help these powers may provide.

Moving to the center of the circle I sit cross-legged on that granite table (Indian-style, as it were, atop the Navajo prayer inscribed there), slip the cellphone from my back pocket so as not to crush it, and close my eyes for a few moments, as if readying myself for something. There's a breeze blowing, slight, and the sun's on my face only intermittently because it keeps getting covered by clouds. I breathe deeply, like a yogi meditating, hear the distant hiss of a car coming down 89. Could that be Sadie's car? I open my eyes, see a white van headed north. No dice. Still, anything's possible. What if a blue Honda materialized, took that turnoff, and Sadie climbed this hill to find me here? Magic— that would be magic neither of us could ignore. So I watch the road in the distance, almost like I can *will* her car to come down it. Her house is just a few minutes from here, so I could always just make the trip, show up and surprise her . . .

Bury it.

I re-focus on the immediate surroundings, and manage to make it work for a while. Even with all the clouds coming in, the sky is gorgeous today—its edges fringed by trees bunched up like broccoli beneath it. And I think how cool this weird little clearing is, this 'place of peace' with its upright tables of wisdom planted out here in the middle of nowhere (never mind Majestic Oaks—the buffer of trees between this spot and the community it serves is enough to render an exhilarating loneliness). Of course, every time I manage to lose myself in the moment, here comes Sadie in some stranger's car zipping up 89 to remind me what's missing.

Yogi my ass—staying 'present' is impossible.

And then the phone chimes in. My eyes are closed when it happens, startling me somewhat, and I know it's going to be her. Everything in me knows it . . . something in my bones. And when I tell her where I am, how close to her, she'll be as moved by the coincidence as I am. I let it ring a few times, savoring the restless possibility, then open my eyes and take a look at the screen.

Not Sadie. Naturally.

'I told you never to call me here,' answers the Joker, faux urgency.

'You might be able to run—*fast*,' Stacy jokes right back, 'but you can't hide. Not from me, anyway.'

God how I love this guy.

'I need to make a confession.' Cutting to the chase seems fitting.

'Oh good. Bring it!'

I tell him about getting high, my fall from grace.

'Oh good grief, I thought it was going to be something juicy. Look, remember what you're always telling me when I feel guilty about something: whatever gets you through the night. Or *day*, as the case may be.'

'Thanks for that. I feel kinda bad about it, but I only had one little hit. And I won't lie—it's nice.'

'Where are you?'

I say I'm at Poemhenge, chuckle when he doesn't get it, clarify. He's never been out here, never even knew it *was* here.

'Me, neither. Leave it to Sadie,' says I, a little sadly.

But Stacy won't have it. 'Okay, I'm calling because I've decided to take the afternoon off. Steven's hung-up with a project, though. You're not working today?'

'I'm off.'

I describe briefly my morning with Brenda, say I'm just kind of wandering and could use a distraction.

'Look no further. You're ditching Memory Lane and going to a matinee with me.'

I don't even care what it is we're seeing—in an instant I'm so grateful I want to weep.

'What time is it?'

'Two.'

'No, I mean *now*.'

'Oh. Just after twelve. The movie's at two. Let's meet at Shady's, get a slice beforehand.'

I tell him I'm going to hang here for just a little longer, but that I'll be there by noon-thirty.

'Now Nate, you planning to imbibe anymore?'

Hadn't thought about that, am just winging it.

'Because if you ask me, you should just leave it. Not that you shouldn't ever treat yourself, but let's wait until you're . . . let's say out of the woods, you know? A little less heart-sore.'

Good advice. I'll take it.

'Who knows?' he goes on. 'Any minute now the woman of your dreams might show up.'

'Oh sure,' I say, liking the game enough to play along. 'Right here at Poemhenge. And when she finds me up here I'll apologize for getting in the way, ruining her privacy. But she'll say she's actually glad to have the company.'

'Then when you both decide to leave, her car won't start.'

'Fat chance *I'd* be able to fix it!' I figure that's the end of the fantasy, my handy-man ineptitude ruining my chance at romance.

But Stacy's imagination stretches farther than mine. 'Exactly. So she'll have to ride with you. That's when you'll call me to say you can't make the movie, only I'll coax the two of you into joining me for lunch—I need to make sure she's qualified. And between the two of us, she'll have so much fun she'll be *thrilled* her car broke down.'

People.

He's right about one thing, though—not only would she win me (booby prize), she'd also score a few of the best friends she could ever hope to find, Stacy among them.

'I'll see you soon,' I say, hanging up, relieved that my next move has been decided for me. No telling where this spontaneous little trip might've landed me if Stacy hadn't stepped in.

Which is when the familiar little blue box appears in the distance, headed south on 89, a candy-colored square with one hell of a sweet center. I watch it. I watch it. I don't so much as blink, rather bore my eyes into that car like I can affect its course. Given the trajectory, it's entirely possible that Sadie is inside that blue Honda, heading to Foxborough for work. And as she nears the turnoff that would bring her (potentially) to me on my high hill, I hang on the edge of something, my hands gripping the plane's overhead bar, the Magic Moment when only one thing matters . . .

She passes the turnoff.

'Saaaaaaddiieeeeeee,' I call out, knowing she could never hear me from up here. Because it *could* be her, right? So I can't help myself, just let it rip like there's nothing left to lose.

'Sadie Ananndaaaaaa! I wanted to go on your journey with you!'

There, I said it. Something big wells up. Sitting with it, acknowledging what just came out of my mouth, I see a great opportunity to polish off my trusty old cynicism, give myself some grief. And not only me, but Sadie, too. And Brenda. Hell, the whole of humanity carrying on about 'spiritual journeys' and 'manifesting realities.' Clap on that shell that kept me stuck for so long—it's a perfect fit.

No, let's not. Let's bury that notion along with all the other not-welcomes. My brain-shovel's getting a workout today.

Instead of walking down the hill to my car, I'm struck with a childish notion. I slip off my sandals, rear back and hurl them—one at a time—down the hill in the direction of the car. They don't make it (no Olympian) but land near enough to the bottom. Taking one last look at the great view from this vantage, I move to the very spot where (it seems) the ground begins to slope downward, and I sit, hugging my knees to my chest the way we all learned when we were kids, then roll forward into a somersault that's as bitching as any ride around. In fact, it gets so fast so quickly that I can't maintain the ball: my knees break free and I'm just tumbling down this hill like I'll never stop, I'll never reach the bottom. And the only thing that keeps me breathing is the laughter—at some point along the way I start laughing like you can't believe. Who knows why? Who cares? I'm just laughing, laughing. And falling.

It's when at last I reach the bottom that the damnedest thing happens: the laughter gives way to crying. The world spinning around me, I roll over onto my stomach, bawling like the biggest baby in the world. But I'm laughing, too—it's this bizarre, both-at-the-same-time kind of thing. What the hell?

'Are you okay?'

My heart stops. I look up, and standing a few feet away from me is a woman, her still-running minivan in the road behind her with the driver's door open, a boy in the back with his face buried in a phone.

'Oh, I'm sorry,' she says, seeing that she's startled me.

'No no no,' I say, sitting up, just trying to get my bearings. I'm dizzy as a drunkard.

'That was a *terrible* fall. Do you think anything's broken or . . .?'

Her face, her whole body, has assumed a posture of concern,

and I'm putting together the picture as she must've seen it: guy trips, tumbles painfully downhill, lands sobbing at the bottom. Poor bastard.

Sloppy stoner, more like it.

'Nothing's broken,' I say, wiping my face only to find that my hands are covered with grass and dirt, which are now smeared across my cheeks, no doubt. Then I add the line meant only for myself—'Unless you count my heart'—and let the last of the laughter leak out with it.

She doesn't bat an eye. 'Did you trip?'

I shake my head purposefully, as much to clear the fog as to answer her question. 'Believe it or not I did it on purpose. Somersaulting. But I guess it just . . . it just kind of got away from me. Sort of.'

She might think I'm a nutcase, but her face doesn't show it.

'Is that your car,' she asks.

'Yes.'

'Well alright. You don't need me to take you anywhere? You're sure you're okay?'

I look up at her and what I see is a fine-looking, well-meaning soccer-mom driving a minivan, kind enough not only to stop and check on a potentially wounded stranger but also considerate enough not to laugh at the lunatic for voluntarily hurling himself down this gi-nor-mous hill. I recall the fantasy me and Stacy cooked up only moments prior, note the newish car idling behind her.

'I am A-o-kay,' says the Dreamer, enunciating each syllable, and squelching a sudden urge to start crying again. Then add, 'Aren't I?'

ACKNOWLEDGEMENTS

*Grateful acknowledgement is made for permission to
reprint the following material*:

''Rosa Mundi'' by Kenneth Rexroth, from THE COLLECTED
SHORTER POEMS, copyright ©1952 by Kenneth Rexroth.
Reprinted by permission of New Directions Publishing Corp.

Lines from "Crawling Out At Parties" by David Bottoms,
from ARMORED HEARTS: SELECTED AND NEW POEMS,
courtesy of the author and Copper Canyon Press, 1980.

Lines from "Grief" by Lou Lipsitz, from SEEKING THE
HOOK, Signal Books, 1997, courtesy of the author.

Lines from "Adultery" by James Dickey, from POEMS 1957–1967,
Wesleyan University Press, courtesy of Christopher Dickey.

Lines from "A Community of the Spirit" by Jalāl al-Dīn Rūmī,
translation by Coleman Barks, courtesy of Coleman Barks.

Lines from "The Beauty of Things" by Robinson Jeffers,
SELECTED POEMS, Vintage Books, 1965.

Lines from "Salt" by Philip Levine, POETRY magazine, 1979.

ABOUT ATMOSPHERE PRESS

Atmosphere Press is an independent, full-service publisher for excellent books in all genres and for all audiences. Learn more about what we do at atmospherepress.com.

We encourage you to check out some of Atmosphere's latest releases, which are available at Amazon.com and via order from your local bookstore:

For a Better Life, a novel by Julia Reid Galosy

Tales of Little Egypt, a historical novel by James Gilbert

The Hidden Life, a novel by Robert Castle

Big Beasts, a novel by Patrick Scott

Alvarado, a novel by John W. Horton III

Nothing to Get Nostalgic About, a novel by Eddie Brophy

GROW: A Jack and Lake Creek Book, a novel by Chris S McGee

Home is Not This Body, a novel by Karahn Washington

Whose Mary Kate, a novel by Jane Leclere Doyle

Stuck and Drunk in Shadyside, young adult fiction by M. Byerly

These Things Happen,.a novel by Chris Caldwell

Vanity: Murder in the Name of Sin, a novel by Rhiannon Garrard

Blood of the True Believer, a novel by Brandann R. Hill-Mann